EVELYN'S ENFORCER

STEPHANIE HUDSON

Evelyn's Enforcer
Lost Siren Series #6
Copyright © 2024 Stephanie Hudson
Published by Hudson Indie Ink
www.hudsonindieink.com

This book is licensed for your personal enjoyment only.
This book may not be re-sold or given away to other people. If you would like to share this book with another person, please purchase an additional copy for each recipient. If you're reading this book and did not purchase it, or it wasn't purchased for your use only, then please return to your favourite book retailer and purchase your own copy. Thank you for respecting the hard work of this author.
All rights reserved.
This is a work of fiction. Names, characters, places, brands, media, and incidents are either the product of the authors imagination or are used fictitiously. The author acknowledges the trademark status and trademark owners of various products referred to in this work of fiction, which have been used without permission. The publication/use of these trademarks is not authorised, associated with, or sponsored by the trademark owners.

Evelyn's Enforcer/Stephanie Hudson – 1st ed.
ISBN-13 - 978-1-916562-72-1

I dedicate this book to anyone that may have suffered with emotional and physical abuse, and the people out there that are kind-hearted and understanding enough to want to help others through the ever-lasting trauma.
Remember that your past does not define your future and trusting people is not a crime or a mistake… it takes strength.
Not every soul will try to dampen your own and make it a shadow, but instead they will walk beside you in the sunlight.

All my love
Stephanie x

WARNING

This book may contain triggering themes and subject matter that may be difficult for some readers.

CHAPTER I
DATING ADVICE
EVIE

"Hello, Evie... *my little runaway.*" The sound of his voice was echoed by the sound of the locks turning. Yet despite this, I couldn't help my gut reaction kicking into gear as I turned around and started fighting with the doors, tugging frantically on the handle. In fact, I was doing this to such degree, that I didn't hear the chair moving behind me. Nor did I hear the footsteps of the predator approaching at my back.

"Easy now." His voice hummed at the same time I felt gentle fingertips caressing my neck. Which was when I hit my limit and my anger exploded. I spun around to face him, my face full of thunder and every curse word on the tip of my tongue ready to release a verbal lashing. When suddenly, his hand entangled in my hair, and my face was being tipped up to meet his lips that descended on my own before I had a chance to utter a single word.

It was a kiss that I was powerless to stop.

Not because I was being held against my will or being

forced in any way. But because I physically couldn't bring myself to stop it. I was a prisoner to my own desires.

They all started and ended with him.

I couldn't help but want him. Couldn't help but crave his touch, his taste, and every hard line of his body I could feel pressed against my own. Which was why I instantly opened up to him, inviting his tongue to explore the taste of me, while I, in turn, did the same.

Of course, this only managed to turn that intensity dial up a few notches and I couldn't help but moan in pleasure. A sound he consumed and quickly returned. Then I felt my back hit the door, after first being tugged to the side to avoid the handle from hurting me. His fingers threaded in the high ponytail of my hair before they were gripped in a dominating hold. As if he feared me breaking free of him.

As for my own hands, it was like I didn't know what to do with them, as if he were some mythical being I was forbidden to touch. He must have realized this too, because it gave him cause enough to pull back and whisper down at me,

"Put your hands on me, little bird."

"I… we…" I started with my excuses, now having some shred of clarity… enough to realize that kissing in this situation wasn't the most practical reaction to potentially getting kidnapped.

But then he casually unbuttoned his suit jacket in one of those one-handed super-sexy ways. Once again, he took the choice away from me by slowly slipping my jacket from my shoulders and letting the worn material find its place on the floor. Free of this offending item, he then took my hands in his own and guided them around his waist, under his suit jacket. At the same time, he stepped into me so my hands would reach, despite there being no way they'd make it all the way around.

Jesus, this guy was huge!

I swallowed hard, my hands shaking as they felt solid, nothing-but-intimidating, boundless muscle. Yet it wasn't enough. My hands wanted more. And if his knowing grin was anything to go by, then he knew it too.

"Look at me, Evelyn," he ordered, and as if he had just flipped the switch on my impulses, my eyes snapped up to his. A pair of intense, dark-blue eyes stared down at me. And this time, his gaze came with the clear intent for what he wanted to do next; something that started with him dipping his head once more. But when he claimed my lips, I couldn't help my fingertips tensing in response, gripping onto his shirt like I needed something to hold on to, just so the memory of us never faded away.

As if it ever could.

Because the reality was that I had tried so hard. Tried to let go. To just move on and forget the memory of what it had been like to have his lips on mine. The feeling of being in his arms as if I was the most precious thing in the world to him. In fact, I didn't know that kisses could do that. Could be that powerful. Could create one of those perfect memories that you know would be forever imprinted on your soul. That you would be more likely to forget your own name before letting go of that memory.

That was the power of his kiss.

And that was what made it dangerous.

Which was a thought strong enough to snap me out of this lustful spell he had cast on me. Starting with using my hands for something other than gripping on to him for dear life. No, now I started using them to push him away, and it was enough to get him to stop kissing me for long enough that I could slip by him and put space between us. Although I had to say, the growl of frustration coming from him was a bit much... I mean, who the hell growled these days? What was he, a damn Viking fan or Pirate enthusiast?

I took a deep breath, using both hands to smooth back my hair, and at the same time trying to calm my pounding heart. I still couldn't believe I was here and what had just happened, prompting me to say,

"I can't believe... how... how did you find me this time?" I stammered out before turning to face him and finding his fist to the door, his back slightly arched as if he was trying to control himself. It was an intense reaction, and one I feared enough to look away from him to take in the room. And what I found was exactly what I would have expected being an office belonging to Ryker Wyeth.

It was stylishly modern space, with a wall of windows that showcased the view of the city. A large rosewood desk by those windows was the focal point in the room, with tall-backed, black leather chair now left unoccupied. Its owner clearly had something more important on his mind than running what was no doubt a multimillion-dollar business.

Over to the right was a wall of frosted glass shelving, holding what looked like very little in the way of books. The hints of rosewood continued to be a theme throughout the room, with the wooden floor holding the same high shine as his curved desk. This also continued with the seating area on the left-hand side, with the three-piece sofa and armchairs made from a rosewood frame and soft looking black leather.

By the time my eyes returned to the double doors, he was back to being in control, standing straight and removing his jacket. Damn, even in a suit he looked big. It seemed the streamlines of a fine cut suit did nothing to hide the muscular bulk of the man.

"Your resourcefulness is impressive, Evelyn, but in the end, it means nothing."

I twisted my features at this, frustration and shock merging into one as I presented him with a hard look. So, I folded my arms across my chest, feeling my small shirt tighten across my breasts. Thankfully, the gaping holes between buttons were hidden by the burgundy sweater I wore, or I doubted he would have taken me seriously right now.

That is, if he even was.

"So, what then? You think I should just throw my hands up and give in? Let you kidnap me and be thankful? And why, because you're hot and a good kisser?" At this his eyes widened before narrowing to what I could only class as some 'movie star smolder' before he stormed over to me, framed my face with his large hands, and growled down at me,

"I am more than just a fucking good kisser!" Then before I could respond, he proved his point beyond any reasonable doubt and kissed me like it could be his last. I swear, my damn toes curled like that green chick from *Wizard of Oz* to the point I was close to panting by the time he finished, pulling back enough to tell me,

"And yes, you can class this as being kidnapped." Then he winked at me, as if being charming and handsome in this picture would help. Okay, so yes, it totally did help in one of those totally irrational, my lady bits wanted me to throw myself at him, kind of way.

"Are you serious?!" I screeched.

"Deadly," he replied in a body shuddering tone that screamed for me to take caution. Which was why instead of throwing the mother of all shit fits, I released a deep sigh and sat down on the sofa I was standing next to. Then I asked in a deflated tone,

"Why are you doing this to me?" It was a question I emphasized in frustration by tossing my hands up, but even that lacked the luster of the fight because I was clearly getting tired of it all.

"Doing this to you?" he asked. However, his tone was definitely displaying the more angry side of frustration than mine was.

"I don't understand, why do you keep going to all of these lengths in trying to find me? Why do you want to kidnap me when you know I won't tell anyone about what happened? Why do you…?"

He quickly cut me off and in the most astonishing way.

"Because I am trying to keep the woman I love, safe!" he shouted, making me gasp.

"The… the… woman you love?" I asked in what was clearly an astonished tone, one he ignored as he continued to steamroll right over my shock.

"Everything I have done, every lead followed, every man-hour spent, every single second I have ensured that you were kept safe, and yet my biggest obstacle has constantly been you." I swear I was dreaming at this point.

"I… I…" I stammered, unable to form actual words. But Ryker obviously didn't have this problem.

"You continue to run from me and then ask me why I have gone to the lengths I have. You ask me why, when you are the one forcing my hand to kidnap you," he argued and, again, I barely knew how to respond to this.

"Erm… okay," I replied in confusion but again, he seemed to be on a roll here.

"I tell you that men are after you, the fact is then proven and even as I fight to keep you safe, you run from me. How much more can I do to prove myself to care for you? I honestly ask you, Evelyn, what else would you have had me do? What more could I have done to prove myself to…" At this it was my turn to interrupt him.

"Ever thought about just asking me out?" At this he frowned, pausing his rant as if I had just sucked the air right out of his argument.

"Excuse me?" he asked with deadly calm.

"You know, like a date," I offered because, clearly, he needed me to elaborate here.

"A date?" he repeated, and it seemed the shock of my suggestion hadn't left him yet.

"Yeah, a date. You know, drinks, dinner, maybe a movie… if it goes well, a kiss at the door."

"Yes, I am aware of the concept," he replied, despite his dry comment telling me otherwise.

"The concept? You have dated before, right?" At this he looked even more confused, going so far as to shake his head a little.

"You wanted me to ask you out?" he asked incredulously, as if this was some solely foreign 'concept' to him.

"Well yeah, that's usually how this works when someone

likes the other person," I pointed out but, again, his perplexed face said it all.

"And when exactly was I given the chance to ask you out?" he asked, as if I were being unreasonably crazy.

"Well, maybe after I saved your life outside the office building," I offered.

"You ran from me!" he shouted back and, well, yeah, I guess he had a point with that one. Although before admitting to the fact, I argued my own point.

"Yes, and did you ever ask yourself why that was?"

"Because you were afraid the cops would be called?" At this I stood up and yelled,

"No, because I woke up to hear about how you planned to kidnap me, you big doofus!" I nearly flinched the second I said this, thinking this was quite possibly the worst comeback in history. I mean, who the hell used words like doofus anymore, unless they were some Saturday morning cartoon character?

"Did you just call me a… *a doofus?*"

I naturally ignored this complaint, trying not to focus on that slip up and instead continued with my own complaints.

"Why oh why couldn't the hot guy interested in me just be normal?! I mean, I could have woken up, found your handsome face right there and then we get chatting, maybe your hand touches mine, we have a moment, I laugh nervously and then…"

"And then what, we both realize we are not in some cheesy romance movie?" he snapped, interrupting me and making me flinch, despite pushing through, continuing with my, 'movie'.

"No, and then you ask me out, you big…"

"Do not say it," he warned but it was too late, that ship, train, and car had set sail, left the station and was barreling its way down the highway.

"DOOFUS!" I shouted, making him narrow his eyes at me.

He moved and suddenly I found myself being walked backward until my ass had only one place to be, and that was parked back on the couch. Then with his towering frame closing in around me, he rested his arms at both the back of the seat and the arm rest before claiming my space.

"First of all, beautiful, call me a doofus again and I will have you bent over my desk, baring your delicious ass to my palm before you know it..." I swallowed hard at the mental picture he sexually painted. But then I also couldn't help but look nervously to his big desk. I swear, I was close to popping at least two buttons with how hot and heavy my breathing suddenly became.

"And the... erm... second" I asked breathlessly.

"Have dinner with me," he replied, making my eyes widen so much I thought they would be the next thing to pop.

"Excuse me?" This shrill sounding question made him grin in such a way, it could only be described as bad. Very very bad.

"You heard, Evie, have dinner with me."

"You're asking me out?!" I asked like it was now a totally foreign concept to me.

"That's usually what have dinner with me means, Little Dove," he replied, making my mouth drop, his smirk deepening as he focused on it.

"Let me get this straight, you chase me from state to

state, stalk me, kidnap me, hunt me down after my escape and now, only minutes after admitting to me that I am being kidnapped again, you are asking me out on a date!?" I asked, less for clarification because I hadn't missed that crazy memo, but more so to get across how fucked up and insane this was!

"That's about the sum of it," he admitted unapologetically.

"But that's... that's..." I naturally struggled to find the right words.

"Smooth?" he asked cockily, shocking me.

"Bonkers!" At this he laughed, took my chin in his hand, shook it, and told me,

"You're fucking adorable." Then he backed off a little and gave me space enough to stand.

"No, I am not. What I am is pissed off," I told him as I followed him toward his desk.

"Yes, and well, if this is the extent of it, then it too is adorable," he informed me, making my eyes widen in response.

"Ryker, be serious." As soon as I said this his head turned, with his heated gaze now intent on mine.

"Say it again," he asked. With that one predatory look I found myself backing up. However, when he started to circle around me, I changed direction.

"Be serious," I all but squeaked. I then felt my ass cheek bump against the top of his desk, and I foolishly looked down for half a second to make sure I wasn't about to knock anything off it. However, the second I looked back up, he was directly in front of me, making me gasp in shock. Damn he was fast... *and too fucking tall!*

"Say. It. Again," he ordered in a dark tone this time, and I swear my pussy was damn near fanning itself, whereas my nipples had turned into cheerleaders and were frantically trying to burst free and show themselves. But seeing as I now understood what he wanted, I couldn't help myself, being far too curious to see what would happened once I did.

"Ryker." I said his name and, damn it, making it come out like some sexual purr wasn't helping matters. Not when it clearly had an effect, one strong enough that he even closed his eyes as he demanded,

"Again." I swallowed hard before whispering it this time, and damn, even *I* wondered if my next job shouldn't be as a phone sex worker.

"Ryker."

At this he stepped fully into me, wrapping his arms around me before lifting me onto the desk and planting my ass where he wanted it once more. My natural instinct was to instantly open my legs and invite him to step right on in there. However, the stupid dumb skirt wouldn't allow it, making me question, why did I buy a fucking pencil skirt... or what now seemed more like some cloth-made chastity belt?!

"Erm, my skirt, it's erh..." I said embarrassingly as I tried swaying my legs in one direction and then the other with my knees together. He smirked down at my lap and current dilemma before he suddenly took matters into his own hands.

"Eyes on me, beautiful," he said, and the second my gaze snapped to his, I heard the tearing of material and the freeing movement as my legs were forced wide open. I yelped in shock, which was soon overwhelmed by the man who had me in his grasp.

"Now this time when you say my name, I want to feel it being said over my lips." Well, I didn't know about his lips but as for mine, they dropped a little in shock.

"I can't," I told him, making him smirk and tease in a knowing tone,

"No?"

So, I told him, "I mean, we aren't even dating."

At this his lips rose to a full smile, and I swear it was near blinding he was that handsome.

"Then let's change that, should we?" he whispered after first dipping his head down to my neck where his words became a promised caress.

"So, what… what would that make me? Your girlfriend or…" At this his smile and his answer was spoken over my lips.

Oh, and it wasn't his name that was spoken like he wanted but instead,

My new title…

"My sweet little prisoner."

CHAPTER 2
THIS MURDEROUS SIDE OF CRAZY

After he declared me to be his prisoner, I should have been horrified and done something to prevent the kiss that felt more like it was sealing my fate. But no, unfortunately not. Because once again, I got completely lost in all that was him, like a trap I had willingly stepped into. Because the truth of it all was, that despite knowing what was good for me, in this... *I was powerless.* And all because of one word...

Addicted.

I was addicted to him. To all the dreams, to the few fleeting memories of reality I had. To those blissful moments we touched. I had played it all out in my mind like some persistent loop, even finding myself going to bed early just so I would have another dream. Dreams that felt so physical, I could half convince myself that they had really happened.

They had felt real.

Too real in fact.

And it was with this thought that I froze in his hold, and

he instantly felt it, now pulling back after ending the kiss abruptly.

"Evie?" he questioned.

"My dreams..." The second I said this, I watched his features harden with realization, which in return, told me everything I needed to know. The truth. The facts. The reality.

They weren't dreams at all.

"Let me explain," he said quickly as he saw that same realization take shape on my face.

"Get off me!" I shouted when he tried to take me in his arms again, making him take pause. However, when he didn't take an even bigger hint and step away, I gritted my teeth before demanding,

"Back away." The seriousness in my tone must have had its desired effect as he sighed before stepping away, now lifting his hands up as if I was holding a weapon pointed his way. Which was when I shimmed off the desk, now holding my torn skirt together and twisting it so as the spilt was to my leg and not showing my, admittedly, wet panties.

"I want to leave," I demanded, trying to keep my voice as steady as I could get it. Especially when every damn dream I ever had of him replayed in my mind, and let's just say that the embarrassment was building.

"In that case, I think you need a firmer definition of what the word prisoner means," he told me, now folding his arms across his chest, and damn him for looking hot while doing it!

"How about crazy, psycho, stalker... do you have a clear definition of what those things are?!" I snapped, actually making the crazed bastard shrug his large shoulders and smirk.

"Oh my god, you're bat shit!" I groaned, throwing up my arms dramatically.

"The truth is that I could stand here and lie. I could tell you all the things you want to hear, like how I am sorry for invading your privacy. That I never wanted to take it any further than simply watching you while you slept," he told me. I gasped, his words only managing to drive home the gravity of what he had done.

"Oh, so I should appreciate your psycho stalker honesty, is that it?!"

"I am not seeking your appreciation, Evelyn, just you're understanding," he told me.

"And what is it that I am supposed to understand exactly? Other than you're obviously mentally unstable!" At this he gave me a pointed look in return and told me,

"Something I will explain should you be willing to listen without hurling further abuse at me."

"Further abuse... Jesus Christ, Ryker, you deserve far worse and should count yourself lucky I'm not attacking your gorgeous head with a damn stapler!" I snapped, making him focus on entirely the wrong thing.

"Well, I will take gorgeous over psycho."

"Yes, well even crazy people can be hot, Ryker, so I wouldn't focus too much on that part if I were you," I retorted with a roll of my eyes.

"I will take them where I can get them, sweetheart," was his smooth reply. Despite how nice as the endearment was, I still acted as if it wasn't appreciated.

"Less of the sweetheart and more of the explaining," I demanded, making him release a sigh before informing me,

"I didn't trust anyone else to keep you safe."

Okay, so this sounded more like a confession and less like the actions of a guilty man. It also managed to take some of the anger from me. Some, not all of it.

"Ryker, I can look after…"

"No, Evelyn, you can't. Because unlike you, I can see what is lurking in the dark," he interrupted, and I swear his eyes started to change at this. But it must have been a trick of light.

"Yes, and after today, I realize that it was you."

He growled at this before snapping,

"No, I was the one there ensuring they never got a single chance to take you. Of course, that would be a damn sight easier to do if you didn't continue to run from me," he countered irritably.

"Excuse me for wanting to get myself away from crazy people who want to kidnap me!" I shouted.

"And look where that got you, or have you forgotten the man with a gun to your head? If my men and I hadn't been there, then they would have taken you and what then, Evie?!" he asked, making me try and think of what to say. Which, in the end, made my own voice sound unsure as I tried to argue,

"I… I would have…"

"What? Risked your life trying to escape and no doubt ended up being shot. So yes, I kidnapped you, and clearly, have done so again. But at least you're safe. At least you're still breathing."

"So, what, that's it? I just spend the rest of my life with you and…"

"Have I hurt you?" he asked, interrupting me.

I thought back to what I said to him the last time he asked me that, and decided not to throw the fact that I was forced to throw up the drugs he had given me out of my system again. However, the look on my face must have said it all, because he quickly added,

"I regret giving you the drugs, but I am afraid you forced my hand." I narrowed my eyes at him when he said this.

"Oh right, I forced you to drug me… sure, sure."

"I needed you compliant, something I knew I would not get when your first thought was to start screaming for help. I needed to get you somewhere safe, in an environment that I could control so as we could talk." I looked around the office and spread my arms wide, telling him in a sarcastic tone,

"Well, here it is, Ryker, your safe, control environment… so have fucking at it!" I shouted, losing my cool once again.

"Have at it? Are you welcoming more than my kiss, Little Dove?" I gritted my teeth, ignored the fact that I had indeed kissed him back, and instead let my anger fuel my words.

"Tell me what the fuck is going on!"

"Fine, you want to know? Then here it is. I never should have walked away from you that night. I should have picked you up and put you in the fucking van and stole you away right there and then. But I didn't. I fucked up and as a result of that, you got hurt. So, I made myself a promise, Evie…" He said this last part while moving closer to me, making me back up to try and maintain my distance from him. Something that created this intensity to grow between us.

"…I promised myself that I would do everything and anything in my power to stop that from happening ever again. I would not allow anyone to hurt you or try and take you from me," he said like some dark vow.

"Take me from you?" I asked this time in a guarded tone.

"You want to take this slow…? You want to let caution take the lead…? Then fine, but don't you dare try and tell me that this between us is nothing. That you don't feel it too," he pushed, backing me into both the proverbial corner as well as an actual one, making me stammer,

"I…I…"

"You know as well as I do that there is a connection…" He finally reached me just as my back hit the wall of windows. Then he raised his fingertip to my cheek and traced the line of my lips.

"This burning need and desire only grows in its intensity," he hummed, making me swallow hard at what both his words and the deep husk in which he said them did to me.

"Well, I think we have established that I think you're hot," I replied to try and ease the tension, something his smile told me I had managed to accomplish.

"I'm pleased you think so. However, simple attraction is not what I mean," he replied in that smooth, knowing tone of his.

"Then what do you mean?" I dared to ask.

"I want you. I have wanted you like no other. But not just your body…" At this he paused and started running the back of his crooked finger down my neck and over the center of my chest.

"I want it all, everything you have to give. But most of all..." I held my breath at this, waiting for what I knew would be the words that could impact me the most and... *he didn't disappoint.*

"I want your heart." I sucked in a startled breath at this, barely believing this moment was even happening.

"But... but you don't even know me," I told him in a small, unsure voice, one that caused a small smile to play at the corners of his lips.

"I know enough," he told me, and just because my own mind and heart needed reminding, I said,

"Because you stalked me."

"Yes, I stalked you," he admitted shamelessly.

"You know how messed up that is, right?" He simply shrugged at this, like he just didn't fucking care that it was.

"I have never lived a conventional life, Evie, so it stands to reason that when I fall in love, this too would be unconventional."

Again, the sound of that word was filled with enough power to snatch my breath from me, something he didn't miss. He even tilted his head a little, as if trying to take in my scent and making me question for what felt like the millionth time...

Who the hell was this guy?

"Fall in love... Ryker, you don't even..." At this he hushed me by placing two fingers over my lips.

"I know everything I need to, to know that I want to know more," he said with a grin, making me ask,

"Why are you smiling?"

"Why wouldn't I, when I know that I will have more than a lifetime to learn it all?" I swallowed hard at that, shocked by the easy way he wanted to commit himself to our forever.

"But I know nothing about you!" I argued back, because it was far too true.

"Then you, too, will also have a lifetime to learn it all," was his easy answer to this, like that was all it took to get me to agree.

"And if I don't like what I learn, what then?" I tested, and he actually seemed to take pause at this, as if suddenly pained by the idea. Then he eased my fears slightly by telling me,

"I will never force you, Evelyn, no matter what you may think of me, I am not a monster."

I couldn't help but feel a slither of guilt at that, as it may have been foolish, considering all he had confessed to, but I knew deep down that he was right… *he wasn't a monster.* Which was why I couldn't let him believe I thought this way.

"I don't think you're a monster, but you have kidnapped me and admit to that freely enough."

"Everything I do is to keep you safe. Now, once the threat is over and has been eliminated, then I…"

I almost choked on that one word…

"Eliminated?!"

"Yes, eliminated. As that is what I do, Little Bird. I eliminate my enemies or people that threaten to harm all I care about." I was once again swallowing hard.

"Are you like… in the mafia or something?" At this his lips quirked up in a flash of a smirk, and it was answer enough, without him needing to say,

"Of a sort, yes."

"Well, you did tell me you were dangerous," I said as if

talking to myself.

"And I didn't lie, but that being said, like I told you once before, I would never be a danger to you."

"All but a danger to my heart," I confessed again, and at hearing this he seemed pleased that I had remembered.

"And yet even in that, you still have a choice. For don't forget when I told you that you could choose to gift it freely, and therefore it cannot be stolen."

"Well, that wouldn't make you much of a thief now, would it?" I teased despite the circumstances of our conversation, making him smile.

"Perhaps it is you that is the master thief in this scenario, for you clearly have stolen mine," he replied, and I couldn't help but be affected by his words enough to blush. Because he was once again declaring how he felt about me, even if I wasn't yet able to do the same in return. So, in order to protect my heart, or being foolish enough to trust him with the knowledge that it was already his, I tried to steer the conversation back to where it needed to be.

"I think we are getting off track here."

"Oh, I think we are precisely on the track I want to be on," he hummed, making me laugh nervously, playing with the tattoo on my wrist with my hands held in front of me.

"Like I said, I know nothing about you." At this he brushed the backs of his fingers along the apple of my cheek, watching his movements with a kind of tenderness I didn't think a man like him would be possible of giving.

"Then why not take the time to find out?" he offered, making me close my eyes for what felt like long seconds. But the moment they snapped open again, I was quick to point out,

"And be your prisoner at the same time…? That's a little too Stockholm syndrome for me." At this he sighed and told me,

"If I could be assured of you staying of your own free will, then we would have no need for such a distasteful label."

"I think that trusting ship may have sailed there, buddy," I snorted, making him smirk.

"Then I suggest we spend this time learning how to earn such trust in one and other, for it goes both ways… or so I am told." I laughed at this tease.

"And how do you suggest we do that? Because, no offence, but I'm getting the impression you're pretty new to the whole dating scene and I hate to break it to you, Ryker, *but you don't normally kidnap the girl before asking her out,*" I whispered this last part behind my hand as if I was letting him in on a big secret.

"Ah, so this is where I have been going wrong all these years," he teased again, making me giggle.

"Drugging them is also a big no no." At this he granted me a wry look before admitting dryly,

"Duly noted."

"Okay, so in all seriousness, how can we possibly…" I started shaking my head when he framed my face with his big hands and told me,

"We start by not over-thinking things, let us not focus on the past that was, but concentrate more on the future that could be."

Damn him for his softly spoken words of wisdom. However, I wasn't yet willing to give in so easily.

"Easy for you to say when you're the one in the wrong," I argued.

"Yes, I think we have established that I may have acted too hastily in certain factors, but at the end of the day, you are still breathing, unharmed, and will remain so under my protection. This is what matters the most to me, now and always."

I felt like gulping, and would have done so had he not been so close, being merely inches away.

"Your protection?" I questioned, picking this one word out of what seemed like a solid vow.

"Why not think of this more like a witness protection program?" he suggested, making me look doubtful.

"As in, when *I* witnessed *you* commit a crime?" I pointed out.

"I do believe I am not the only one who has committed a crime here."

I gave him a guilty face and pulled out of his gentle hold, needing the space before accusing,

"So that's what this is... this is blackmail?" At this he narrowed his eyes and suddenly looked angry.

"No, Evelyn, this isn't fucking blackmail. This is me reminding you that only the innocent gets to cast judgement over others."

I flinched at this because it was true. In more ways than I ever wanted him finding out. What right did I have to judge him stealing when, in the eyes of the law, I had done far worse?

"You're right, I have no right to judge you," I agreed. making him release a soft, yet frustrated sigh before he told me,

"As I do not judge you, for I am glad you were brave enough to protect yourself. Something I am trying to ensure never has to happen ever again."

"So, the day of the shoot-out, I really was their main target?" I found myself asking.

"Yes, and unfortunately, this was proven further when they tried to take you at the station."

I shuddered as the memory came back to me, and had to force myself not to think about it so I could ask further questions,

"And you think this has something to do with my asshole ex-boss, Bill?"

"I do," he replied sternly, his dark blue eyes narrowing slightly at the mention of him.

"But why though? I just don't understand it."

"I am not sure, but if I were to hazard a guess, I would say that they believe you have information they want," he told me, making me think back to what that thug had threatened that day in my apartment when this nightmare began.

"Well, they did believe we were dating," I told him, and clearly granting him a piece of information he didn't know.

"They did?"

"The guy they sent, they told me to 'tell my boyfriend' that they want back what you had stolen," I said, making air quotation marks in the air.

"So, you think they are still trying to use you to get to me?" he asked, making me shrug.

"I honestly don't know," I told him truthfully.

"I suppose if they believe us to be an item, then it stands to reason they might think to use you as bait or a bargaining chip to get me to give them the piece of the scepter if they have you as a hostage."

"Scepter... wait, hostage... you think that's what they want with me?" I asked, changing my question to one I thought was more important right now.

"Yes, for I cannot see any other reason, can you?"

"But if they have been watching me, then wouldn't they have wondered why we were apart? Wouldn't they think we had broken up or something?" I asked. The only time we were really seen together was when I was jumping on him outside his office and the short time we spent dancing in the club.

"Not necessarily. They might have thought after the heist that we were keeping a distance from each other for your safety, especially after the attack on you," he offered, making me think about it this way.

"I suppose," I mused quietly before muttering, *"I bet it seems like a lot of trouble from just a kiss, eh?"*

"Hey..." he said softly, and I felt his bent finger lift my chin before he told me, "The only thing I regret is you getting hurt from it and nothing more."

I nodded a little, again feeling the blush rise from his words. But then I reminded him on a quite breath,

"I killed a man." Which was when he completely shocked me when he lowered his head and told me,

"No, you didn't..." I gasped before he quickly stole the last of my held breaths when he added...

"But I did."

CHAPTER 3
CHAPS AND CHAINS

The moment he said this, everything in my body just froze. In fact, I had to spend the next few moments trying to convince myself that I had actually heard him correctly. Hence why I started stammering out,

"Ex-excuse me?"

"I think we should sit down," he suggested, nodding to the seating area.

"Okay, so now you sound like a doctor about to tell me some bad news."

At this his lips quirked as he took my hand and led me to his sofa, one this time he joined me on. Of course, with the great big tear in my skirt, it became a lot more obvious when stretched tight over my legs and, therefore, ended up showing most of my thigh, if not all of it.

Meaning, I got a bad boy smirk when he didn't miss the way I was now tugging down on it. Well, at least I wasn't flashing him anything more than leg, because spinning my skirt had been my only option after he had nearly ripped it from me in that heated, hot as fuck kiss of his.

Jesus, how did it just keep getting better and better?

"Well, doctorate or not, it is news I would have liked to have had the chance to tell you, that is, if you hadn't been…"

"Running every five minutes, yeah, yeah, I get it," I said, beating him to it with a roll of my hand in the air for emphasis.

"After the phone call, I went to your apartment," he told me, making me gasp as my hands flew to my mouth. Shame was what came next, knowing he had seen what I had done. His gaze instantly softened, and he grabbed my hands to pull them from my lips.

"No, Evelyn, you don't need to react this way, I was extremely proud of you for defending yourself the way you did." I swallowed the thick lump of emotions down and nodded.

"I hit him with a TV… well, that was after first hitting him with a DVD player." At this Ryker didn't seem quite as horrified as any sane person would. But then I was soon to find out why.

"Yes, well it was a shame you didn't have the whole fucking electrical store at your disposal. He deserved far worse for hitting you," he practically growled, clenching his fists, and because the sight of him struggling with the knowledge of this affected me, I reached out and covered his fisted hand with my own.

"Well, I was tempted to grab an old boom box radio I had lying around to hit him with next, if that helps," I joked, making him scoff a laugh and relax his hand in mine instantly.

"Then you also must know that the asshole who hurt you wasn't quite as dead as you thought," he told me, stunning me enough that my hand tightened over his before flinching off it.

"He… he wasn't!?" I hesitated to ask.

"No, of course, after I discovered what he had done to you… let's just say he wasn't breathing for long after that." My shock at hearing this was understandable, considering he was talking about murder like it was some mundane thing he did as often as brushing his perfectly straight white teeth or his thick, perfectly styled black hair.

"But why… why take that risk? Why commit such a crime for me?" At this he released a heavy, weighted sigh before whispering my name,

"Evelyn." This was said almost like the answer was obvious. "I know this might be hard to understand right now, what with everything that has transpired between us so far and the turbulent start to our relationship…"

"Relationship?" I questioned in a slightly high-pitched tone, something I should mention, he chose to ignore.

"…But I would never allow anyone to harm you and live another day to speak of it."

At this I tensed all over, and he saw it before he heard the panic in my tone,

"Oh my god, so you're a killer?!"

"No, I'm an Enforcer," he stated, making me tense because that didn't exactly sound much better.

"An Enforcer? What is that, like being some mob boss's henchman or something?" At this he smirked, and I didn't know if it was because of the name I used or the fact I was well off the mark. Clearly, I hoped for the latter.

"No, Little Bird, it's not like a mob boss's henchman."

"Then what is it?" I asked, feeling like this was most definitely an important factor here.

"My position among my people is complicated to explain. All you need to know for now, is that I keep the peace."

"You keep the peace?" I repeated, making him grin as if he found me endearing with my constant echoing of everything he said.

"Yes, and with it comes certain aspects of the job that allow me to punish those that wish to… um…" He took pause, clearly trying to work out how best to say it.

"Disrupt the peace?" I offered, and again his grin didn't exactly put me at ease.

"Exactly," he agreed.

"So, you're a vigilante… like Bruce Wayne… oh my god, you're like a real-life Batman, aren't you?!" I shouted, making him jerk back a little.

"Excuse me?"

"Well, Bruce Wayne is rich, and he keeps the peace in Gotham city, and clearly has no problems about killing bad people, so I just thought…" I let this fantastical thought trail off the moment I saw his face, one that was obviously amused and trying not to laugh at me. Jesus, he even looked close to biting his damn lip.

"Fuck me, you're cute," he commented, and it was said in a more, 'I find you endearing' kind of way, than the 'yes I am clearly mocking you' kind.

"Okay, so you're not Batman." At this he smirked and told me,

"No, but given how much the idea seems to excite you,

then I have never before wanted to go out and buy a cape so much in my life."

I couldn't help but burst out laughing, something again he seemed to find cute and endearing.

"Not sure we are ready for role play yet, Ryker." At this he grinned big and warned,

"Mmm, I see… so what you're saying is, give it a day or two before I bring out the leather and chains?"

I choked on another laugh and issued what I thought was a witty comeback.

"Oh, don't hold back on my account, if you are into wearing leather chaps and nipple chains, then each to their own. I won't stop you… ridicule you, yes, but I won't stop you."

It was then his turn to burst out laughing before he hooked a hand behind my neck and pulled me in close enough for him to whisper over my lips,

"Behave, funny girl." Then he kissed me and effectively, stole my breath, even if it was only for a minute. Once he had finished, he pulled back to look down at me, and I started to squirm under his hot and heavy gaze. So naturally, I pressed on with our earlier conversation before chaps and chains got involved.

"Okay, so I think we have established that you're not Batman but I have to say, you're not really explaining what you do or why it is you need to be a thief. No offence, Ryker, but you don't exactly look like you can't afford to buy golden birds," I said, looking around the expanse of his impressive office, knowing in all likelihood he owned the damn building.

At this he laughed, picking up my hand and laying it in

his lap, before then stroking his fingertip down the length of my palm. Something that admittedly gave me shivers, especially when he started to trace the lines of my tattoo.

"This artifact is different and was long ago once stolen from me." I frowned at this before questioning the obvious,

"So, you stole it back?"

"I did, and with a little help from some sexy assistant that happened to have a photographic memory." I blushed at the compliment.

"And now I'm guessing some bad people want it back?"

"They do indeed," he replied, still seemingly happy to answer my questions all the while playing with my hand and wrist.

"Damn, I didn't know there was such a demand for golden birds. Seems like serving greasy burgers and refilling bitter coffee was the wrong job choice," I joked, making him laugh softly.

"A job you will not have to do ever again." I frowned at this.

"Not that I love the job or anything, hence why I applied for this bogus job, but that doesn't mean that I will be happy to just give up working at all because you want to keep me safe," I said wryly, but then he bumped my shoulder, at the same time reminding me,

"Prisoner, remember?"

"Seriously?"

His reply first came in the form of taking a deep breath, and I didn't exactly think it meant good things for me.

"I admit, it is not the ideal situation I had in mind and had our circumstances been different, then perhaps you would have trusted me enough to choose to stay."

"Ryker..." I said his name in a soft reprimand because talking about me being his prisoner and explaining the reasons why came far too easy for him. However, he promptly ignored my softly spoken protest and continued regardless.

"...But the reality remains and therefore so does the outcome. You are to remain by my side, Little Bird, and that also means that you are my responsibility to care for..."

At this I quickly interrupted him, despite what good it did me.

"But..."

"No, there are no buts, Evie," he stated firmly as he got to his feet.

"You can't possibly believe that I would..."

Once more he didn't let me finish. "Now I will, of course, allow you your personal space."

"Oh jee, thanks," I muttered sarcastically, something he promptly ignored.

"And we can date, as you suggested." My mouth dropped again.

"Okay, but I was..."

"But in doing so, you will not work, you will be cared for, and you will be guarded all twenty-four hours of the day."

I gasped at the audacity of it all. Which was why I was now the one to stomp to my feet and fold my arms to stop myself from strangling his handsome neck!

Jesus, how can a neck even be handsome? I didn't know the answer, I just knew that his was.

"And what's next? Someone going to be there while I wipe my ass?!" I shouted, hitting my limit.

"Don't be ridiculous!" he snapped.

"Good, great, fabulous… in that case, you won't mind me just taking myself off to the ladies room now then, would you?" I retorted before storming to the door and waiting there with my hands on my hips. I was also taking this time to hold my breath and silently pray he would make a decision quickly before I was made to continue to stand here and look like a fool. Of course, this time when I heard the sigh of defeat, I hoped it was in my favor.

"Alright, Little One, I will yield."

Yield… just who was this guy? I mean, who even said that this side of the 21st century. Strangely, I heard the door unlock despite feeling him at my back, making me wonder if he had remote for it or something else pointlessly high-tech and fancy. I reached for the handle, one that was quickly covered by Ryker's hand as his arm came around me. I naturally shifted to the side a little, only to have his other hand rest at my hip, holding me still so I couldn't put space between us.

Just the feel of his fingers applying slight pressure there on my flesh made me wish it was naked skin to naked skin, with nothing between us. However, the moment he opened the door, I quickly bent down to retrieve my jacket that was still on the floor and ended up putting my ass into his crotch. That was when both hands held firm on my hips, and I didn't know if this was to steady me or to ensure I didn't move away too quickly.

Although by the feel of things, I would say it was the second. The considerable hard length I could feel prodding into the crack of my cheeks was unmistakable.

"Gods, have mercy on me, Little Bird," he growled,

making me blush before quickly straightening and stepping away from him, leaving his hands now empty of my flesh and fisting at his sides because of it.

I decided it was definitely for the best if I put my jacket back on, especially with the way his eyes were roaming down my body. It was enough to make me worry that I was going to have to start fanning myself. That or just outright turning into some black and white movie star, placing the back of my hand to my forehead before fainting gracefully. Oh, who was I kidding? If I were to faint, I would most likely land like a sack of potatoes, tear the rest of my skirt, and pop some skirt buttons that become projectiles powerful enough to take his eyes out.

Well, at least I was still wearing the sweater. But what turned out to be even more of a Godsend was that the jacket was long enough that it hid the indecent exposure of my thigh, thanks to the split in my cheap secondhand skirt.

"After you," he said, holding out his arm like a gentleman and letting me lead the way.

Of course, the impulse to sprint down the hallway like an Olympic runner was, admittedly, hard to resist. But it was as if he knew what I was thinking, because after about three of my brisk steps, he got closer into me and while maintaining a steady walk, he leaned in and told me,

"I am very fast, Little Bird… and…"

"You wouldn't get far."

CHAPTER 4
BEHIND THE MASK

" I am very fast, Little Bird... and...*You wouldn't get far.*"

The moment he said this I tried not to visibly gulp, wondering if this would soon become a habit while being around Ryker.

So, deciding not to let him see how breathless that comment just made me or how affected I was, I replied in a cocky tone,

"Perhaps. I think you need the workout." At this he scoffed a laugh before informing me,

"Trust me, sweetheart, with you around, my preference of workout wouldn't be running." I tried not to grin at that.

"Funny, I never took you for a spin class, kinda guy." At this he laughed again, only this time it wasn't mocking or smug, it was just one full of easy humor and a rolling, deep timber I knew I would never tire of hearing.

We walked through the fancy office space and when he held the door to the ladies room open for me, I couldn't help but gently slap a hand to his chest and say,

"I think I got it from here." However, he must have thought otherwise because he jerked his head for me to go ahead before following me inside.

"Seriously, Ryker, we are on the top floor, I know I'm good at escaping, but I am not that good," I said with huff, one he ignored as he continued to check the cubicles.

Unsurprisingly, they were all empty because, other than Faron, the guy who had walked me into this trap, I hadn't seen anyone else up here. Making me now wonder if he had sent all his staff home for the day before implementing his second kidnapping attempt? Or was this his third? I didn't suppose the hospital counted as one because he hadn't even had the chance to act before I had disappeared.

"It's all clear," he told me, making me give him a wry look.

"Thank you, deputy Ryker... Wow, you really are taking this protection gig seriously," I commented in a teasing tone, one that gave him cause him to raise a brow at me.

"If you expected anything less, then I would say I need to work on your low opinion of me... *with my cuffs in hand,*" he added, and holy hell, I really didn't need that visual right now. Especially not after our role play conversation. However, I couldn't seem to help myself when I replied with,

"Coming from the guy who calls me his prisoner... Forget about deputy, I should have said Prison Warden Ryker." At this he grinned and although it was a sexy one, it was also labeled in the 'not in a good way that meant happy things for me' category. Although when he snagged my hip and yanked me into him, I was rethinking the category pretty quickly. Especially when he dealt with our obvious height difference by tipping my head back so I could maintain eye contract with him.

My heart once again played that knowing beat within my chest as my treacherous mind wondered if he would kiss me again and, of course, secretly hoping that he would.

"A title I am hoping to change very soon... *my pretty little prisoner,*" he whispered down at me as his lips lowered to hover over mine. It was a teasing action that automatically made me close my eyes and tip forward slightly to meet him halfway.

However, with his hold still on my chin, he gave my head a playful little shake and told me on that same self-assured whisper,

"Time to pee, Little Bird."

Of course, this was enough to break the spell, making my eyes snap open and narrow at him. Something that, of course, made him laugh. I then stepped away without trying to let him know how much he affected me, having no idea if I had achieved it or not. Because I was pretty sure that ship hadn't just sailed, it was currently lying on the bottom of the ocean floor and was as far away from sailing back to the dock as you could get.

I waited for him to leave, something he did when I glared at the door, forcing him to take the hint. Then once he had taken his annoyingly handsome, smirking face from the room, I finally sighed out all my tension and practically deflated onto the toilet seat, one I had no intention of using. Because I had only said this as a test to see what he would do. Of course, had I really expected him to give me the opportunity to run again... no, not really. But what I had wanted was to see if he would get one of his lackeys to take me or if he would, in fact, do it himself. Well, now I had my answer because, clearly, he wasn't leaving anything to chance. Nor was he letting me out of his sight other than to use the facilities.

But as I sat on the toilet seat, I couldn't help but wonder what my future held for me. I was his prisoner, yes, but considering the way I felt about him, I was now asking myself if that was actually a bad thing? Because he was right, other than slipping drugs into my drink in hopes of making me sleep, he hadn't actually hurt me. He saved me and every time we met, he always spoke about keeping me safe and protecting me. And, clearly, bad men were after me. So, the question remained, was I better off with the devil I knew and clearly had an attraction to, or the devils I didn't know who had already tried to hurt me?

Was it really time to stop running?

Just the knowledge that I hadn't been the one to kill the man that had attacked me in my apartment, did manage to lift the burden that had admittedly weighed heavy against my soul. Of course, if it ever happened again and I had to defend myself in such a way, I knew I would.

But at the very least, I knew now that the police would not be after me for murder. Ryker had admitted to killing the man and he had done so without guilt or remorse. He showed nothing but confidence in his reasoning, which I had to confess, worried me. Along with worrying about the type of life he was involved in. But more than that, it was the type of life he would involve me in should I continue to give in to attraction. Of course, deep down, I knew it was more than just desirability keeping me on his hook. Especially considering I had been obsessively dreaming of him since that very first kiss. Dreams that apparently, were not all fantasies bred from my subconscious.

I think that was the part about all of this that shocked me the most. To find out that he had actually broken into my room at night and watched me sleep. That he had sometimes touched me, going as far as to kiss me, happily making me believe it had all just been a dream centered around him. I didn't know whether to be outraged or just allow myself to continue to be strangely turned on. It was crazy, to want that type of attention from a guy. But then, when that man was Ryker, I knew that given half the opportunity, I might have been tempted to do the same.

Christ, now I was fantasizing about what it would have been like stalking him. It was all kinds of messed up but, right now, it was a reality I had no choice to face because I was currently living it.

But I didn't know how I could trust him. Trust that he felt the way he said he did. He'd used the word love like he was so sure. And if I were being honest with myself, it also made me question and, admittedly, be a little self-conscious, wondering how many other women before me he had said that to. How many more damsels in distress had he saved and thrown around the L word with before realizing it wasn't true. Perhaps this was how the insanely rich spent their free time?

I also knew that, in all likelihood, I was just trying to create excuses when there weren't any… and all because I was scared. Scared of letting someone get close. Scared of trusting that they wouldn't just make me fall in love before then casting me out to deal with the cruel world all alone. Of course, I also knew that I had hang ups, likely more than most.

But then it was like he had said, trust was earned and the only way of doing that would be to stop running long enough to let it grow. To let it be found through the gift of time. The fantasy was that he really did care about me. That he had kissed me that night and felt exactly what I had. As if fate had brought us together and that first kiss had bound us in such a way that both of us knew we should not ever be apart.

Because hadn't fate also intervened that day of the shootout? He had obviously been as surprised with my presence, as much as I had been surprised with his. And since then, he had stopped at nothing in trying to protect me. Okay, okay, so it did come with the title of stalking and, like he said, it wasn't exactly the most conventional way to fall in love. But then it hadn't been conventional the way that we had met either.

I knew that I couldn't throw all blame his way for my current circumstances. I'd had a choice that night, I could have screamed the second I saw them walk in the office. I could have fought them. But most of all, I could have let them get captured. But I had chosen to help them and, even now, I didn't find myself regretting it.

Which begged the question…

Would I regret running once more?

I released a sigh and knew that I had spent far too much time in this bathroom contemplating all that had happened as it was. I had to make a decision. I had to choose to go forward acting willingly, or once again fight against his ideal of what was best for me. Which meant there was only one last question I needed to ask myself…

Could I learn to trust him? Or should I say…

Could I trust him with my heart?

I closed my eyes and let my head fall back, moaning aloud at my current predicament in trying to make sense of it all. But then a sound above me like metal grating being shifted made my eyes snap open. And the second I did, what I saw horrified me.

Because now, for the second time in my life, a Demonic face was looking down at me.

And this time, I knew for certain…

It wasn't a mask.

CHAPTER 5
THE HEART OF A DEMON

The second I saw the Demonic face staring back at me, looming from the moveable panel in the ceiling, my natural reflexes kicked in. Meaning I scrambled out of the bathroom stall like my life depended on it. I slammed against the sinks just as I heard the body drop from the ceiling and with my back to the basin, my hands gripping onto it for dear life, I watched as it rose up to standing.

I kept trying to tell myself it must have been a latex mask or something, but the closer it came, the more my eyes wanted to deceive me by telling me it was real. Because whatever this thing was, the guy started to change shape. One look up at the ceiling and I soon knew why. The square panel he had dropped from was only big enough for a slim body. But as he started to rise to his full height, his skin started reacting, like something living was beneath it, trying to fight its way free.

His face was all teeth and tiny scales, like some lizard man with a constant creepy grin on his face. His slanted eyes glowed red and were made even more murderous with the harsh diagonal slashes of his brows and deep set of his eyes. Eyes that were framed with greenish scales that dusted the dirty-grey leather skin that covered most of his bald head.

"Oh... My... God..." I uttered, my fingers aching when my grip on the sink turned desperate, and my nails practically bending against the porcelain bowl. Because the moment his skin started to split and reveal another body beneath, he quickly became the stuff of nightmares.

Like a lizard bursting from its scales, the body beneath became too big for its own skin, it now preceded to shred off massive flakes and bits so big, they looked like discarded pieces of a map. Veins and marks from his old body were still imprinted on the paper-like skin that he walked away from, leaving pieces of the timeworn body in a trail on the floor.

Of course, what was left was like a giant lizard man pumped up on steroids! His body was every inch of bulging muscles, and I forced myself not to look down too far because it was clear shedding his skin left him naked. And well, my eyes had already noted something dangling between his legs of a substantial size. The guy terrified me enough without adding that new horror to the situation.

The skin on his body was similar to that on his face, smooth in parts with sections of it scaled. Like the top part of his chest near his neck and the sides of his torso. Only instead of these scaled segments being only green, there were also patches of dark red mixed in, especially down the sides of his body. One that thankfully he covered up, magically bringing forth his clothes.

I knew I should have been screaming for help at this

point, but my chest was heaving like I was close to passing out from fear. I felt locked within myself and was trying desperately to pull myself together enough to fucking act!

His towering height would have meant even looking down at Ryker, because this monster of a man looked to be closer to seven feet tall! Which meant that even if Ryker did hear me screaming, I didn't know what he could do about it to save me, unless he carried a gun on him!

His legs were now covered in a leather type material that looked more Demonic in nature. This along with his jacket that looked armored in places, with spiked plates at his shoulders and back. His bare chest was left exposed, with only straps across his muscles that's only purpose seemed to be for holding weaponry.

I knew the only thing I could do was run and hope that I made it in time. But if not, I needed to make sure Ryker got out of there before this beast could get him as well as me. But then suddenly the memory of how he had fought the men back in the train station came flooding back to me, and I only hoped that if he couldn't get away that he would be strong enough to fight him.

So, with my mind now finally kicking into gear, I screamed,

"RYKER, RUN!" Then I bolted for the door, only to feel myself being grabbed from behind and dragged backward. This was before I was quickly put into a choke hold as he fumbled for something in his jacket, like he needed a weapon or something. I struggled against him, gripping onto his meaty arm and trying to rip it from my neck where I was now struggling to breathe. This was at the same time as Ryker suddenly burst through the door, ripping it open with enough force the whole door went backward and flew off behind where he now stood.

His eyes burned so bright, I thought they had been replaced with flames, like he was staring into the mouth of an inferno. I would have gasped had I the extra breath to lose.

"You're too late, Greed!" the man snarled at my back when suddenly, I heard a loud whirling sound echoing behind me, as if some kind of machine was firing up and gaining speed. I could almost feel the pulse of it pounding against the air.

"Let. Her. Go!" Ryker said in a voice that surely wasn't his own! Jesus, it was utterly terrifying, like he had suddenly been possessed or something. Because humans couldn't produce such a sound… *it… it wasn't possible.* But then again, neither was the Demon currently trying to choke me… but that's where we were.

"The last Scepter piece, Greed, that will be the price, remember that," he said, pulling me backward and toward the pulsating sound behind. The feel of the waves of air flowing around me were getting stronger and, naturally, it wasn't a feeling I could fully understand. Almost as if I was suddenly outside and standing with my back to a tree as the wind whipped around me from behind.

Well, whether I could see it or not, it didn't change the fact that this maniac wanted to kidnap me, and I doubted very much it would be like when Ryker did it. No, I couldn't see it coming with a hot sexy guy whose main power over me was his toe-curling kisses.

So, I could decide, let myself be taken or fight and, well…

Arthur didn't raise a coward.

So, this time I gripped him by the wrist, hoping Demon bones broke just the same, and then I bit down hard enough I heard him grunt. It was also enough to allow for his hold to drop so that I could force his arm to bend in a way it had to go unless he wanted me to snap his wrist. Then the second there was a space, I dropped to my knees and rolled out of the way, closer to Ryker, and ignoring the pain. At this Ryker saw his opportunity and launched himself at the massive beast, shouting an order at me to leave,

"EVIE, RUN!" He then ducked and avoided the blow, before delivering one of his own and then kicking him so hard, he fell back into the cubical, quickly followed by a loud ceramic smash. Jesus, how hard did he kick him to cause such damage and how...? The guy was freaking huge!

Water spilled over the floor, gushing out along the tile from the broken toilet. Meanwhile, Ryker was standing there, breathing heavily and looking to where he still expected his enemy to get back up, even after that bone cracking kick to the upper body. Christ, he looked so powerful right now, his white shirt stretched tight around his muscles... a material that was getting stretched tighter with each heavy breath taken. His fists curled tight and ready for more. He looked born to fight. But despite this remarkable sight, it was one made supernatural with the spinning light framing the silhouette of his body with an ominous red glow.

Fuck me, it looked like some kind of magical portal or something. Light swirled around like the monster had opened up a small black hole and on the other side, was a sun glowing like a beacon trying to draw me closer to it.

"Evelyn!" Ryker's voice snapped me out of my daze. It

was enough to get me to tear my wide eyes from the impossible sight.

"Run!" he ordered, but then I saw the flash of silver coming from the stall as magic flew at Ryker and hit him dead square in the chest. The force made him fly back and land in the mirrors over the sinks, shattering them instantly.

I put my arms up as those natural instincts kicked in once more, protecting myself from the shower of glass. Then I watched as the beast walked from the stall, rolling his big shoulder and snarling at Ryker. There was a flash of metal in his hand and I soon realized that this fight just got even more deadly. He was holding a long, wickedly curled blade that looked almost Demonic in nature, with its black handle made from what looked like cooled lava.

I gasped in fright, but it was a sound lizard man ignored as he had set his whole focus on Ryker, who was lying on the ground. As for Ryker, he shook his head and started to get his hands under his body to push himself back up. Suddenly, the monster lifted up his other hand, holding his palm out and tipped it so something could fall before stopping on the chain he had hooked around his thick, scaled fingers. A glowing gem hung there, spinning around and looking as if it was a shard that had been chipped off a much bigger piece of red stone. Ryker's eyes grew wide in horrified shock before he gasped,

"Impossible!" The monster laughed before he started whispering down at the stone he raised higher to his lips.

"I evoke thee, the lipiš šà, of Empusa!" Then, the second he finished, I sucked in a quick breath as streams of red smoke snaked from the stone, curling around his hand and arm before reaching out like tenacles moving in the air like

oil under water. They reached for Ryker, making him scream in pain just as they wrapped around him and held him immobile.

I silently cried out into my palm, pained by the sight of him caught in such a thing. His eyes, however, went straight to me, and he mouthed a single word once more, looking like it took all his strength to do so.

"Run."

I looked back to the door and then back to him, knowing I had a choice to make, just like I had that night. Just like I had outside of his office when I wanted to save his life, putting my own on the line. Because I knew that, deep down in my heart and soul, I would do it again. I would do it over and over until there was nothing left of myself to give. So, I whispered, somehow knowing he would hear me,

"It's time to stop running."

I also knew that I had to do something to give him the time to get back to his feet. So as the Demon got closer and now had his back to me, I slipped off my jacket. Then as he crouched down over him, I knew it was now or never.

I walked slowly over to him, creeping and stepping through the water on the floor, trying not to make too much nose. The monster then raised his dagger hand and told Ryker,

"I have waited a long time for the chance to kill you, Son of Greed." His dark, Demonic voice spoke of the hatred in his heart, and I steeled myself against the power of it, trying not to give into my fear and just run. I couldn't just abandon him, not when I loved him. Not when I knew that he wouldn't do the same. That he wouldn't have left me.

That he would stay and fight for me.

So, with the monster kneeling closer to him, it put him at just the right height for me to make my move. Which meant the second I was close enough, I quickly threw my jacket over his face and yanked hard at his head, taking him off guard but, more importantly, off balance. He fell backward and both the jewel and blade slipped from his hand, breaking whatever spell it had on Ryker. The red serpents made of smoke evaporated instantly and, with it, their hold on him.

Ryker then wasted no time, as he was on his feet in a second and just as the Demon ripped my jacket from his head, he was now facing who he had called the Son of Greed. Naturally, I didn't know what that meant, but I think considering who he was about to fight, I could gather as much that it meant that Ryker wasn't entirely human either.

And speaking of Ryker, he quickly grabbed the Demon by his jacket, yanked him hard into his knee and burst open his face with the impact. The creature groaned in pain, but didn't have chance for much else as Ryker got him in a head lock. Then he reached out behind him, and I yelped when the fallen blade shot to his hand by magic. I was utterly shocked to see he had this ability, but not as shocked as when seeing what it was he did with it.

"Send my regards to your executioner!" Ryker snarled before stabbing the blade into the monster's eye, making him howl with pain. Then Ryker used his impressive strength to drag the huge body over to what I assumed was a portal of some kind, looking as if this took him no effort at all.

He then ripped the blade from his eye and while keeping a hold on him from behind, he told him,

"Oh, and say hello to my father!" Then he plunged the knife into his back before pushing him through the portal,

where he quickly disappeared screaming. However, the second he did, the strange red jewel exploded with light all around us, a deafening pulse emitting from its core. The power of which seemed to have a far more dangerous effect on Ryker, as he suddenly dropped to the floor after gripping his head in what looked like pure agony.

I looked to the stone and then to Ryker, seeing what it was doing to him and knowing what I had to do. So, I quickly grabbed it by the chain, not trusting what may happen if I touched the stone, and then quickly tossed it in the portal that I could see was now closing.

Then the second it did, and the sound vanished, I rushed over to Ryker when he keeled over onto his side.

"Ryker!"

"Eve... lyn... my... Siren," he stammered out before he suddenly...

Lost consciousness.

CHAPTER 6
PIECE OF A MISSING HEART
RYKER

The moment I opened my eyes, the very last thing I expected to see was the place of my birth.

The Realm of Greed.

Any other time and it would have been a welcome sight, despite such a place no doubt striking fear into the heart of any mortal man. But as for me, I had spent more centuries surrounded by this rocky landscape with its warm, amber-colored quartz and its river of fire flowing in the distance.

The entrance to my father's Kingdom was as grand as any that you would find in Hell that signified the wealth of a king. But there was no wealth like that of my father's. For he was the treasurer of Hell and, therefore, was tasked by Hell's King of Kings, Lucifer himself, to be the guardian of the Devil's treasure. And there was nothing that the Devil treasured more than that of souls.

My father's payment in return was to rule a realm rich with gold. So, it was not surprising where I stood, facing the gleaming gateway ahead of me that shone like a beacon drawing someone like me closer. I was my father's son after all.

A true Demon of Greed.

Which was why the sight of such wealth should have been more of a welcoming one. But it was in that moment that I knew I had truly started to change, for the only sight I wanted to see now was that of my Siren. Not the veins of gold I could see glistening from the flaming torches that lined the entrance way. Gold that was embedded in the rock wall that rose up like jagged battlements framing each side of the clear pathway.

These flaming torches danced and licked at the air from their golden bowls, held in place by gilded hands. Gripped in Demonic claws, they were fixed in place atop of tall poles and had been positioned by cooled magma at their bases. This fiery glow reflected off the copper-colored glass I now stood on. I often wondered how a pathway like this had been forged, for it looked created in a more natural way seeing as it flowed around the rocks as though it had once been a river. Even the steps that led to the gateway were rounded and looked more naturally formed. Like waves settled after first hitting the rocky shore and being pulled back to the sea.

As for the entrance itself, this acted as a contrast to its more rugged surroundings. What with its sleek, smooth lines and graceful architecture. A doorway as big as any castle tower you would find in England. Its mechanism to this had been buried underground for it was as large as the doors themselves. Gold and gleaming, the light from the fire that surrounded the arch made them look more like the portal the Demon Azhdar had tried to take my Siren into.

In fact, it was almost like looking at a mirage in the

distance, everything shimmering and almost distorting the air around it like heat was pulsating from the doors themselves. A great domed arch rose above the doorway, its gold so highly polished it looked like glass, for you would have surely been able to see your reflection in it. There were a series of elaborately carved pillars that were staggered toward the door. This making it look as if the distance from the top of the steps was one that was far greater, when it was merely an illusion.

As for the rest, battlements built on either side of these pillars where what framed the entrance and they continued along the Great Golden Wall, one that signified the start of my father's realm. I could see from here the lines of soldiers all standing guard and ready to slay any intruder that should think to steal from the King of Greed, the mighty Mammon.

Any other time and I would not have hesitated in my steps when taking me toward the entrance to my home. But right now, all I could think about was what I had left behind, questioning how I had come to be here?

Had I been dragged through the portal as well? I remembered snippets of a fight that ensued and the desperate cries of my Siren making me quickly act. But it was like pieces of the puzzle were missing and without them, I couldn't yet see the full picture of what had occurred.

Either way, my concern for Evie grew by the minute. Because despite knowing I had sent the Demon Azhdar back through the portal, to deal with his own torturous fate, it still left my Siren alone. Which meant one of two things, the first being that the threat had managed to infiltrate my building and therefore could again and the second…

She could take this as another opportunity to run.

Both thoughts plagued my mind and made me grit my teeth. I was ready to lash out at whoever had brought me here. But with my memory of events severely lacking, I had to confess to being confused as to what had actually happened. More specifically, after I had tossed that reptilian asshole back into Hell.

Until today, I knew him by reputation only, as it was believed in Persian mythology that Azhdar wass a creature of great strength, something I could account for, although if I had taken my Demonic form, the fight would have been over a lot quicker. However, I had been reluctant to do so for fear of what Evelyn's reaction would have been. So, in my naive confidence, I had believed myself more than capable of taking him on in my mortal form. Confidence that would have been rewarded with victory, had he not possessed something I never thought possible.

Speaking of which, I felt her presence seconds before she made herself known.

"You are restless, Prince of Greed," she said, and as soon as I heard the voice speak from behind me, I didn't need to look to know what I would find.

My father's sorcerer was dressed all in black with a long, hooded robe hiding her Hellish features, casting her entire face in shadow under the veil of the thick, heavy material. The long lengths of her dark attire covered only her head and half her torso, the rest hung open, exposing a body made for sin. Her pale skin was left bare for a purpose when showing off the lower part of her stomach, the soft looking curves of her hips and the tops of one of her creamy white thighs.

As for the other leg, this was made of copper, and attached to her body in such a way it looked as if it had been fused on to her hip. The join looked forever painful as the skin around it was burnt and puckered. The metal that did show became a stark contrast to the rest of her flawless skin. Both legs, real and not, were covered in thigh-high dark boots made from the skin of a Vipera. They were known as a Demonic grass snake that usually lived underground in the soul fields, and were often hunted for their skin and succulent meat.

These boots were also wrapped with long lengths of thin straps made from the same material. As for her the junction between her thighs, this too was covered by the same straps of dark Vipera skin. Being wrapped across her hips, and in between her legs in a V shape, covering only some of her hairless feminine mound.

"Annika Empusa." I uttered her full name and title, doing so with a grit of my teeth.

"My Lord Greed," she replied softly, tossing back one side of her robe and folding her real leg back so as she was free to gracefully bow.

"Is my father aware that I'm here?" I questioned sternly. I wanted whatever this was to be done with and fucking quickly!

"No, my Lord, for you are not really here, as it is merely your connection to this place that I sought out, doing so subconsciously," she admitted in that gentle, unnerving voice of hers.

"You brought me here... but why?" I practically growled the question, knowing what this time unconscious could cost me.

"Drastic measures are cause enough for drastic actions to take place," she replied, giving me nothing!

"Why? What has happened? My father, is he…" I pressed, to which she held up her hand and stopped me before my concern could grow further.

"Fear not, for the King is well… however, I do not know for how long the peace will be maintained, for we are on the cusp of war." I scowled at this.

"What?! How? And why was I not informed?!"

"Because the fate of that war lies solely in your hands and the hands of your Siren." I gritted my teeth again. I didn't like hearing my father's sorcerer speak of her.

"What do you know of my Siren?" I demanded, yet she didn't answer me the way I hoped.

"I brought you here, my Lord, despite the risk."

"And just how did you bring me here, Annika?" I asked suspiciously.

"The crystal that was used as a weapon against you not long ago is the very one that runs through my veins and beats at my core," she told me, making a red glow emit from beneath her hood as if coming from where her eyes would be.

"But how is this possible?" I asked, shocked to hear such a thing could happen. But then she surprised me further.

"A piece of my heart was stolen and now I fear it is to be forged as a weapon against the very gateways of Hell," she said before unclasping her robe and revealing her chest, now showing me the large angry scar that ran between her small breasts. One that had marred the skin surrounding it with branches of angry red veins.

"You speak of the Veil?" I asked, as this was what we called it when an old, deactivated portal was so close to the veil of Hell. She bowed her head at this, indicating that yes, she did, now adding to the long fucking list of things that had cause for great concern.

"You must recover the scepter before it is used as a weapon against us all and before the mortal world is lost to whoever wields it."

"What is it you think I have been trying to do all this time, Annika?!" I couldn't help but snap.

"Ah but, my Lord, you were missing a piece, and I do not speak of the gold you can hold in your hand but the treasure you will now hold in your heart. For your Greed has now shifted in nature." I thought instantly to my Siren and knew she spoke the truth, for I could feel the change myself.

"Again, you speak of my Siren," I said, stating the obvious.

"She will be the key." I narrowed my eyes at this and felt my hands fist at my sides.

"No! I will have her nowhere near this danger, if and when it may arise" I snarled angrily. Just the thought of that dark part of my world touching her any more than it already had, enraged me. When I think back to what had happened in that bathroom, or more like what could have happened had I not heard her cries for help... *it made my Demonic blood boil.*

"Her path is already being walked upon, and it is paved by the stones the Fated God lay themselves... but you know this, for they led her to you and as your father's son, you also know that nothing can fight against destiny."

"You will no longer speak of this!" I snapped, slicing a frustrated hand down through the air, one that was getting hotter with my anger and crackled like thunder. But she shook her head slightly, re-covering her breasts as she told me,

"My silence will not stop what is near, as Baal Zabu *is* coming for his revenge."

I growled at the name, for it was true, he had been an enemy of my father's for over a thousand years. But then he did blame the House of Greed for the part we played in getting him banished from Lucifer's good graces.

Baal Zabu, better known to the mortal realm as Beelzebub has had his sights set on Lucifer's throne from the very beginning. And although the fucker was cunning, in the end, he just didn't have the same kind of power that Lucifer held. This despite having a fucking big army at his disposal. Which meant that, now, it seemed his aspirations of ruling had shifted and become focused on the mortal realm. Hence why, even from his imprisonment in Tartarus within the very depths of Hell, he had somehow possessed the man I had been hunting for years…

Hector Foley.

He had merged with the mortal, feeding from his evil essence and feeding it until the two became one. Only, unfortunately for me, killing Hector only rid me of one dark soul, not two. Meaning that Baal Zabu would still be living, despite rotting away in the very worst prison Hell had on offer. But if Hector actually managed to get hold of the complete scepter and opened one of these deactivated portals, then not only would he have the power to release Hell on Earth… but even worse, he would have the means of freeing his counterpart…

Baal Zabu.

After that, there would be no chance at stopping the end

of humanity. The mortal world would simply become the Hell that Baal Zabu had always envisioned himself ruling.

"Then he shall come and when he does, he will find himself facing me and my army on the battlefield," I told her, despite hoping it didn't come to this. Because as much as I would relish the chance at killing the fucker and ending him for good, I also knew of the chaos that would ensue. For if such a battle was to take place, it was unlikely to happen in Hell but instead in the mortal realm. And I was not the only one thinking along these lines.

"But at what price? For the battle he brings to you will not be one fought on Hellish ground but in the land of mortals, something they would never be ready for."

"I will tell the King of Kings, he will..." She held up a hand at this, one barely seen from the long sleeves of her robe.

"He has his own Chosen One to protect, for the great prophecy is upon us and therefore he will soon find his own battles to fight in."

"What are you saying?" I asked, now shaking my head.

"That you and you alone must choose what comes next, and to trust the last option when it is gifted to you." Gods, I felt like fucking roaring an inch from her face when she spoke like this!

"You speak in riddles, sorcerer!"

"As you speak with anger," she countered calmly, making me wish I was permitted to shake her! But instead, there was little for me to do or say at this point, for I had heard all there was for me to hear.

"I am done with this! Release your hold on my essence and send me back to my vessel!" I ordered firmly.

"Very well, my Lord… May you chose the right path to follow, Prince of Greed." After this ambiguous farewell, I suddenly came back to my vessel with an impacting force, making me bolt up right now with my eyes wide open. Unfortunately for me, the first face I saw was Van's. Any other time it would have been a welcoming sight, but right now, the very first face I wanted to see was the only thought on my mind.

"She has run again!" I barked out like some snarling dog, quickly getting to my feet. I had been on the sofa my second had obviously put me on, seeing for myself that I was in my office once again. Faron was there too, along with Hades standing guard by the door.

"Ryker, she…"

"She is in danger! The foolish girl! We must find her immediately, for I will not be able to live with myself should anything happen to her, and I will not rest until she is…"

"Still alive and well for a foolish girl?" The second I heard her voice, the one I would know anywhere and the one that would blissfully haunt my dreams, I froze in my movements. Then I turned at the same time Van stepped out of the way, revealing behind him the blessed sight of…

My beautiful Siren.

CHAPTER 7
EXPLAINING THE UNEXPLAINABLE

"Evelyn!" I shouted her name before cutting the distance between us so I could take her fully in my arms.

"Whoa." She laughed as I lifted her from her feet, a sound of surprise I was determined to add to with a kiss. Then the moment I'd had my taste, knowing I wanted far more, I stopped long enough to turn my head and snarl out my order,

"Everyone, out!" I felt Evie jump in my arms slightly and, no doubt, at the sound of anger in my tone. Which was why I allowed my fingers to trail gently up and down her back in hopes of soothing her, silently communicating that I wasn't angry at her.

No, this was utter relief I felt and astounding gratitude that she hadn't taken the opportunity to run. But to explain this, I first wanted to be alone with her.

Van smirked at me before bowing his head in respect and nodding to the others who were rightfully looking concerned. Something like this had never happened before, as let's just say that taking down an Enforcer was not an easy thing to accomplish. Especially not for one as old and powerful as I was.

But now I knew how it had been done, it made sense. As Annika's essence was embedded within that stolen piece of her heart, so it was not surprising the effect it had on me. Any longer with the heart stone held at my body and I would have been forced to leave my vessel permanently. Then I would have been cast back to my father's realm with nothing more than my soul in tack and locked to my Demon like the day I was born. Only now I would have been roaring in rage before licking my wounds and howling in pain at being torn from my Siren.

But then I also had to wonder if it even had the power to destroy my soul as well, for during the time I writhed in agony on the floor, it had felt as if a darkness was creeping around the edges of my soul. Did it have the power to do more damage than I first thought?

The actual power to kill an Enforcer?

I must have been deep and lost in my thoughts for I felt a slender hand touch my cheek, its softness there jarring me back to the moment, only to realize that my wish to be alone had been granted.

"Hey, are you okay?" she asked, making me want to laugh at the irony of it all. Was I okay? The answer to that was no. I was not fucking okay. I was losing my damn gluttonous mind and was ready to lay all I owned at the feet of this woman. Just so as I may experience an eternity of her touch. Of her softly spoken words and her caring expression. Ready to give her everything and take all I wanted in return was as simple as it wasn't.

The highest price to pay.

I wanted her heart.

For with it, all would follow. Her body, her mind, her spirit, and her soul would all become mine to treasure above all else. Which was why I answered her.

"No. But I soon will be." Then I kissed her and, this time, it was far more heated than the one I had given her upon waking. Because now we were alone, I wanted to take my time to savor her.

My hands explored more of her beautiful body, as if I needed to reassure myself that she hadn't been harmed during the fight. Because the second I burst through that door, too many fucking emotions had hit me all at once.

Of course, the first was fearing for her safety. But then came others, like concern for what she may have seen. I didn't know whether the Demon Azhdar had masked his true self or not. Fuck, but I didn't even know what had happened after I passed out. Most of the details leading up to that were hazy at best. I was putting this down to the heart stone's control over me, stealing my memories seconds after it had all taken place.

Which was why I needed to know...

"What happened?"

"I think I should be asking you that, all things considered," she replied, making me tense.

"You don't remember?" she then asked, no doubt guessing as much based on what she saw from my features. Of course, I remembered enough, but I decided to see what she would say first. This was so I could assess whether I needed to add more or ideally to see if I could get away with saying very little for now.

"I think that stone did something to my memory of it," I told her, not exactly lying about this part but also not exactly divulging the entirety of it either.

"And the monster, do you remember fighting that?" she asked with her hands on her hips, as if she didn't believe me. Of course, the use of the word monster I couldn't help but find endearing.

Granted, the terminology used wasn't far off the mark, no matter how juvenile it sounded. But obviously the word Demon hadn't even entered her head, which had me dodging that particular bullet for now.

Although I knew that I had to tell her something, and I doubt trying to convince her it had just been some fucked up crazy guy in a rubber suit, taking cosplay way too far, would pass as a workable explanation. So, I told her,

"His name was Azhdar."

"Jesus, it had a name," she muttered on a breath and, again, this didn't exactly go in my favor.

"What was he and why was he here after me?"

"What he was is more complicated to explain but the reason, I believe, was to use you as ransom to the bird I stole back," I said, hoping this was enough. However, when she asked her next question, I knew I was about to head further into dangerous territory.

"And that portal thing, where did that lead?" This was where I had to get creative so as not to lie.

"I am not sure exactly but most likely to where they were planning on keeping you until an exchange could be made," I said, holding back on some vital information.

"Christ, do you know how crazy this all is? I mean, did you see that thing?! I never knew shit like that existed but, clearly, you did," she said, now putting more space between us and running a hand down her face.

In truth, it pained me to see her struggling, but then I guess this was the inevitable I faced. I knew, at some point, I was going to have to tell her what I was.

"I did, sweetheart."

"Of course, you did, you fought the bloody thing!" she shouted, and I could see her getting more worked up by the minute. So, I walked over to her, took her by the shoulders, and told her,

"Calm for me, Little Bird."

"Calm, how can I stay calm? I..." I quickly cut her off by reaching up from her shoulder to the ponytail of hair and gripped it, enticing a shocked little gasp from her. A sound I had quickly become addicted to extracting out of her. Then as I pulled her head back, I told her,

"Because right now, he does not deserve your attention or your thoughts." At this she swallowed hard and gave me what I desired, starting with her brave little thoughts forming her next sassy question,

"And you do?" she asked softly and without malice.

"I do," I replied confidently.

"Well, I guess you did save me... *again,*" she said, making me smirk down at her when she muttered the word 'again' in a begrudging tone.

It was fucking adorable.

But I had hit my limit on being in this office building, knowing now the danger it could present. No, I needed to get her to somewhere more secure and to do that, I first needed to get her on a plane.

So, I took her hand in my own and started to walk from my office, with her trailing behind slightly in my haste.

"Wait… where are we going?" I ignored this question, too focused on what I wanted to happen next. Which meant, when I found my men waiting for me in the main office space like I knew they would be, I started barking out my orders.

"Van, Faron, you are with us. Hades, I want you to gather your men, I want a convoy to escort us." Each of my council members bowed a head and replied with 'My Lord.'

Evie's reaction to this was to tense next to me and squeeze my hand tighter as if on instinct. In return, I gave her hand a gentle, reassuring one in return before walking to the bank of elevators and pressing the button. Then once the doors opened, I pulled Evie inside with Van and Faron following us.

However, it was only once the doors were closing did Evie hit her limit on waiting for an answer as she asked once more,

"Ryker, please… where are you taking me?"

I finally told her in an unyielding way…

"I'm taking my little bird home with me."

CHAPTER 8
OUT OF THIS WORLD
EVIE

As soon as he said this, I pulled my hand from his and took a quick step back, making him growl like some wild beast denied of his dinner. Even his dashingly handsome, blonde friend looked shocked enough to warn,

"Easy, Ryker."

However, to this, he reached out and pressed the button for the next floor, making the doors open seconds later.

"Both of you, take the stairs," Ryker ordered in a way as if he was also grinding glass between his teeth.

Van released a knowing sigh, now leaning closer toward his friend and whispering something in Ryker's ear before stepping back. I didn't know what was said, as it was too quiet for me to hear. But whatever it was, it made Ryker take a much-needed breath before nodding his head in some kind of acceptance. Faron had already stepped away from the elevator, clearly ready to obey with his boss's request, getting out only one floor down.

As for me, the second the elevator doors closed in front

of them, I couldn't help but feel like a cornered animal. Especially when Ryker turned around and faced me. As if I was the newest conquest to battle and win. I knew this for certain when he then hit the stop button without taking his eyes off me, making the elevator jerk to an abrupt stop. But then, this was nothing compared to the predatory way he stepped toward me, making my back hit the wall before my hand rose in front of me, trying to get him to stop in his pursuit.

However, he didn't even look at my hand, let alone take it as a sign to stop. No, he simply took it in his own before rising it above me. Of course, my reaction to this was to try and twist out of his grip, making him take my other one in hand and then raise that one too. Doing so until both of my hands met above my head. Then he took the last step until he was against me, breathing hard and making me afraid to look up at him. Because despite how much I wanted to deny what I had seen in that bathroom, I knew now that there was so much more to this world than I knew. So much more than what most people would be able to comprehend without seeing it with their own two eyes. It was the unbelievable made believable as there was no other explanation.

Monsters existed.

And I was pretty sure that now, I was faced with one of them.

But then even as I thought it, something within me told me I was wrong. For how could a monster want to risk his life to protect that of another, if he was evil at his core? Unless everything I knew, which, granted, was more based on fairytales and folklore, was wrong? That it wasn't clear cut and monsters weren't all bad? For starters, Ryker had never hurt me and seemed like he was extending a lot of effort on his part just to keep me alive.

So, what was I so afraid of? Was it more to do with my heart and knowing now that I hadn't simply fallen for a dangerous man, but more like a dangerous other worldly being? But that was the problem, as now I didn't know what to think. Because just when I thought I didn't know this man before, now, I felt like I knew him even less.

Of course, none of this seemed to matter to him because, clearly, he was trying to lay claim over me, and the power he wielded against me was nothing other than *intimidation*.

Something that wasn't hard to do considering he towered above me, was built to kill, and obviously had no issue with doing so. But most of all, my fear now stemmed from not knowing what or who he truly was. Which was why I was now close to panting, admittedly in both fear and arousal shamefully combined. I couldn't seem to get my body in gear with what my mind was screaming at it to do.

"You pull away from me, Little Dove?" he asked in a dangerous way, one I knew to be cautious around.

"I... you..."

"Speak freely," he told me when he saw me obviously struggling.

"I... I don't even know you," I braved to say for what felt like the millionth time, making him smile before he dipped his head and reminded me,

"Your lips know me."

"Thinking you're hot and a good kisser isn't enough for me to just..."

"Ssshh... *you think too much,*" he whispered this part over my lips, a pair that foolishly opened for him like he had spoken words of a spell, not a simple observation. Because this was a statement made that ended with his lips on mine and like I said, my treacherous body responded like he had just flipped a switch. I melted into him and, in turn, his hands stroked down my wrists before placing them around his neck and holding them there long enough for me to get the hint.

After this, he granted himself the freedom to lightly caress his way down my spine, before enveloping me in his arms at the same time deepening the kiss.

I practically sighed against his mouth, a pleasured moan escaping me the second his tongue started to duel with mine more firmly. It was a kiss that escalated quickly, and his arms suddenly tightened around my waist before I was picked up to an easier height. I was then left with my feet dangling off the ground, sandwiched between the brick wall at my back and the wall of muscle in front of me.

"Gods, woman, you taste fucking incredible, and I can't wait to fucking eat you!" At this I froze and started struggling, at the same time, screeching,

"Eat me!?"

He suddenly burst out laughing before telling me,

"Easy, little morsel, I speak of devouring your pleasure, not that of your flesh."

I shuddered at the thought and most definitely not in a bad way. Christ, just thinking about what it would be like for this man to 'claim me' like he said he would... I had never given much thought into having that type of relationship with a man before, but then again, I had never met anyone like Ryker before.

"Although, make no mistake, for I will be soon tasting...

every... inch... of... you," he said while kissing his way up my neck, pausing between each word to nip playfully at my skin. Skin that was half on fire for the man as I squirmed against him, making him tighten his arms.

"I don't know you," I half moaned again in a weak attempt at fighting this. At this he pulled back from my neck and gave me an intense look, before warning,

"Soon, Little Bird, soon you will know everything."

"But?" I asked, because his statement definitely came with one, I could hear it in his tone.

"But now is not the time for this and I am eager to get you on my plane and back to the safety of my own territory."

"Territory?" I questioned, pushing for more. Unsurprisingly, he gave me none.

"My home, sweetheart," he reiterated.

"And your home is in Canada?" I asked, remembering something he had said in the hospital about getting their assess back on a plane to there.

"Yes, Toronto, more specifically," he offered, making me quickly wonder what his life was like there.

"Can you put me down?" I asked, making him smirk.

"I can but I won't."

"It feels kinda weird having this conversation with my feet off the ground," I told him, and his reply was simple, making me cry out in surprise when he suddenly swept my feet up into his arms. Meaning now he was carrying me like something off the front cover of an eighties cheesy romance novel. What was next, a bellowing half button white shirt, and long dark hair with the picture of a pirate ship in the background?

"And now I feel weirder," I commented dryly, making

him laugh. Then without even touching the button, the elevator started up once more and I couldn't help but yelp in surprise. I wasn't expecting it.

"How did you…?"

"All in good time, my little bird," he told me in a satisfied and pleased tone because, clearly, he seemed happy about something. Was it because he felt free to be his natural self with me? Whatever that natural self was…

I didn't know, only that he seemed as through some weighted secret had just been lifted from him. And speaking of weight, just how was he strong enough to continue to hold me like this without even breaking a sweat? Even after the elevator doors had opened and he was now walking inside an underground garage with me grasped tightly in his arms, he wasn't breathing heavily.

Duh, Evie, because he wasn't human, that was why. Which was when it suddenly occurred to me to ask,

"Are you an alien?" At this he stopped dead before actually throwing his head back and howling laughing.

"Well, nice to see someone can tame your foul moods, Ryk," the blonde man said, now exiting through a metal door and what had no doubt a shit load of stairs behind it. However, it was Ryker's reply to this that had me near squirming again, because it was undoubtably one of the sweetest things anyone had ever said about me.

"Like no other treasure before her."

I must have blushed scarlet at this. I even dipped my head down to try and hide my reaction, which he, of course, didn't miss.

"I am Vander, by the way, I would shake your hand, but boss man here might rip it off and my sewing is shit… also, I have no inclination to look like Frankenstein any time soon," Vander replied, making me cough a laugh before informing him for no good reason,

"Frankenstein wasn't the monster, he was the mad scientist."

"Huh, I guess you're right," he replied, making Ryker smirk down at me in amusement, no doubt aimed at my randomness. Then he walked us over to a line of four, super sleek black SUV's that looked brand new, straight off the forecourt. Three of which were already full of men in dark combat style gear, and the empty one in the middle had the doors open and ready for us.

This was when Ryker finally put me on my feet, but even after doing so, he still didn't step away or let go of me. It was as if he feared that if he did, I would run away or someone would try and steal me away from him again. And well, I would have called him paranoid before the bathroom incident.

Which also told me that even after I had taken away the confusion and the uncertainty about staying with Ryker, I knew now that I had no choice. If I wanted to stay alive, which I very much did, I knew that I had a better chance at doing so with Ryker than on my own.

Because the hard fact was that I was no longer just dealing with gangsters or whichever bad men I had thought they were. No, I was dealing with something not of this world.

Now if that be of the Supernatural variety or creatures from another planet, I was still yet to find out. Although with the way he had laughed at the Alien question, I was starting to lean more toward things that go bump in the night.

Perhaps he was a Vampire? Or a shifter? There were plenty of TV programs about those to tell me the basics. But then I had seen him walking around in the daylight and I was pretty sure that was a big no, no, because he didn't exactly look like Mr. Crispy in the natural light of day.

"Still wondering if I am an Alien, Miss Parker?" Ryker mused after hooking a finger under my chin and raising my head up to find his eyes glistening with mirth.

"Why? You gonna take me to a place that's out of this world?" I asked before I could stop myself, and our surprise mirrored each other's. Because whereas I covered my lips with my mouth, he slowly grinned down at me in a solely predatory way.

Then he leaned down and told me in a whispered vow…

"It's a fucking promise."

CHAPTER 9
THE WORLD

I had to admit that the more time I spent with Ryker, the harder it was getting to think of him as anything other than a man I was seriously falling for. My mind would wander back to what I had seen of him in the bathroom but then one glance at him sitting next to me in the back of the car, and any fear I should have felt, simply disappeared. Especially with my hand held firmly in his.

It was like being locked in some kind of dark fairytale but instead of being rescued by a dashing white knight, I had, in fact, been saved by the sexy villain. One that wouldn't let me go, and in all honesty, I wasn't sure at this point I would have wanted him to.

I then had to question whether I was in my right mind or not because I knew I should have feared him. However, the truth was that I didn't. But then, how could I fear someone who treated me with such care, such love and affection. He handled me like I was the most precious thing in the world to him. And admittedly, that feeling was addictive.

But then my experience with men had been limited at

best. I had always found it hard to trust anyone other than Arthur. He was the only true father figure I had ever known, because I had seen the other side of what bad men could do. I had grown up witnessing the hurt, both physical and mental. I had seen the control men could wield with the hand of fear and it sickened me.

Which was why I had always guarded my heart. Because that was the key to keeping myself safe. The key to not gifting anyone with that kind of power to hold over me. But then I had to question, where was that fear now? Because I had no guarantee that Ryker wouldn't just suck me in and hold me prisoner in another way. And once there, I knew he had the power to destroy me, just like my mom. I shivered at the haunting memory. One I had tried so hard to bury that day.

"Turn up the heating, Van, my little bird is cold." The sound of Ryker's voice was strength enough to shake me from the memory and free me from the clutches of the past.

"I'm okay," I said in what sounded like a weak voice, even to my own ears. However, he just gave me a pointed look and told me,

"I will be the judge of that." Then he raised my hand up to his lips and kissed the back of my hand, this time making me shiver for a whole different reason. He was so domineering but, strangely, I didn't find it off-putting where I thought I would. Perhaps it was because it was only ever done with my best interests at heart. I could most definitely say that it turned me on, and that part was the most surprising of all.

Of course, the moment the private jet came into view I

knew that the surprises would just keep on coming. Which prompted me to say,

"I probably should have mentioned this before, but I don't have a passport." At this he scoffed a laugh and told me,

"And thank the Gods for it, or I would have had a much bigger job on my hands if chasing you from country to country."

I gave him a wry look in return, making him laugh again.

"There is no need to worry, Little Dove, you won't need one."

He said no more about this as we pulled up alongside the plane. Both Vander and Faron were in the two front seats, with the big blonde heart-throb driving. They had barely spoken during the journey, making me wonder if this was at Ryker's request. But then again, I had been quiet and, clearly, was given this silent time to try and make sense of the next crazy turn my life had been forced to take. Something that Ryker had seemingly wanted to give me because he must have known I had a lot on my mind.

Which meant that the second Vander and Faron exited the car, I found myself nervous to be alone with the handsome Devil next to me.

"Holy shit, you're not the Devil, are you?!" I suddenly blurted out the second it came to me. At this his eyes widened slightly before they crinkled at the sides when granting me a soft look.

"No, sweetheart, I am not the Devil."

"Well, that's a relief," I said after letting out a whoosh of air.

However, the moment I said this I felt him tense beside me before strangely asking,

"Is it?"

In fact, the question took me by surprise. So much so that I faulted with my response,

"I… er… well, it's just that…"

"Now is not the time for such conversations," he said abruptly before getting out of the car and leaving me feeling shocked.

"Okaaay," I muttered, jumping when I heard the door beside me being opened seconds later.

"Allow me," Ryker said, holding out his hand for me and helping me down from the large SUV. I tried not to take his response to my comment to heart, but it was hard, especially when I felt like I had offended him. But then I also had to question why that was.

Did he have something to do with the Devil?

Oh my God… was he…

A Demon?

Of course, having this thought didn't help when being faced with his hand held out for me to take. A hand that had done nothing but protect me and fought to keep me safe.

I raised my eyes to his and, there, I found only tenderness looking back down at me. It was a look that said so many things. Like windows to the soul, they drew me in and kept me feeling safe and secure. I may have taken a few unsure moments before putting my hand in his but the second I did, his smile was all the comfort I needed.

It was like he knew I was letting my trust in him grow, and that terrified me more than anything I had seen in the bathroom. Which was why I didn't even flinch when I felt his hand rest on the base of my spine as he led me toward the plane, and what was to be a new experience for me. But then I also knew that as soon as I got on that plane, I was making myself totally vulnerable and in his hands. Because I didn't really believe that I was his prisoner, despite doubting that he would let me go without a fight. And well, I knew he had long ago started fighting for my heart.

Now the question remained...

Would he win?

He held out an arm when we reached the steps of the plane, telling me silently to go first. I wondered if this was the gentleman in him, or more to do with the fact that he didn't trust that I wouldn't try running from him the moment his back was turned? I guess, in that regard, I wasn't the only one struggling with trust.

I entered the plane and couldn't help but gasp at the sight of such luxury. Of course, we weren't alone; Vander and Faron were already in their seats ready for takeoff.

Both were so very different from one another. Faron was already set up and looked ready to work, with his laptop open in front of him. As for Vander, he already had a drink in hand and was spread out on the sofa, eyeing up the air stewardess like a hungry wolf. But then my eyes landed on two faces that I recognized and, once again, I realized just how deep Ryker's deception and planning to kidnap me had lay.

"Evelyn, let me introduce you to the other members on my council."

"Your council?" I questioned, but with a slight shake of his head it was enough to tell me this was yet another thing that would have to wait for an explanation.

"As you already know, this is Katra and her brother Kenzo." I nodded in acknowledgement, but that was as much as I would give them because it seemed most people, at one time or another, had worked with Ryker to deceive me.

The one called Kenzo, he had been the limo driver that had taken me to the club. And Katra, she had been the one to dangle the carrot in front of me when first sitting down in a booth at the shitty diner I had worked in. A carrot that had led me to this point. Of course, I knew they had only been doing their jobs and what Ryker had ordered them to do. So just how much I could hold it against them, I didn't know. I guess orders were orders in Ryker's world, and he seemed like the type that was used to being obeyed.

The third extra person on this flight included another man I instantly recognized as he turned to face us. He had, admittedly, fucking terrified me on the night of the heist. The bald head alone was enough in identifying him as being the asshole who was rough with me.

"And this is Hadrian, also known as Hades. He is head of my security and now yours as well." I visibly took a step back and landed against Ryker, who was standing behind me. His hands instantly came to my shoulders to steady me.

"Looks like she remembers you, dickhead," Van said mockingly, only chuckling when the big brute, Hades, gave him a dark look in return. However, Ryker must not have liked my reaction to him and my obvious fear of the huge, beast of a man, because he tucked me in by his side and told his security guy,

"And of course, he is more than willing to apologize for his treatment of you that night, *aren't you, Hades?*" Ryker said, as if knowing exactly why I had reacted this way and, clearly, he was making a point to make it right by the tone in his politely spoken demand. Hades bristled slightly at this, but he eventually released his obvious frustration with a sigh before stepping forward and telling me,

"I am sorry for my mistreatment of you, my untrust was proven to be unfounded. It will not happen again, milady."

"Milady... I am just... er, I mean, thank you," I said after Ryker coughed behind me, squeezing my shoulders enough to tell me to just accept the apology and not correct this old fashion title. He nodded his head before returning to his seat without saying another word. After this, Ryker led me to four seats that faced each other and had a gleaming polished walnut table in the middle. I sat next to the window in a seat that looked more like a plush armchair in a cream soft buttery leather. It was so comfy, in fact, that I couldn't help but shift around a little as if trying to smush my ass as far into the seat as it would go. I must have looked like a cat trying to find the best spot.

"Comfy?" Ryker asked in amusement after taking the seat next to me, surprising me because I would have thought the obvious choice would have been the seat opposite and next to the window.

"Erm, don't you want the window seat?" I asked, and he raised his brow up in question.

"You know, to get the best view?" I said, jerking my head slightly toward the window.

"I have the only view I am interested in right here," he said, taking my hand once more and, like in the car, he raised it to his lips and kissed the back of my palm. Again, I blushed at the compliment and tried to hide the fact by looking out the window to find that we had started to move.

"Champagne?" Ryker asked, and I turned to find the stewardess standing there holding out a tray filled with glass flutes. He picked one off for me and held it out for me to take, at the same time telling me,

"I believe it is one you will enjoy." I frowned in confusion before taking a slip, catching Kenzo's eye to find him winking at me.

Clearly, he had heard this and was reminding me of my limo ride. I knew this for certain when the taste triggered the memory, realizing it was the same champagne I'd had during that journey. Kenzo smirked at me before raising his own glass, telling me this piece of knowledge was down to him informing Ryker. Hence why I said,

"You don't miss a thing, do you?" I placed the glass down on the table in front of me, as he told me,

"I make it my business to know all there is to discover about the treasure I gain and, like I said, there is none more precious than you to me." I tried to contain my blush and hold back from sighing like some love sick teenager.

"So, what's next then? A gilded cage of gold and a perch for me to sit on?" I commented wryly, only sort of teasing. But his response surprised me as he dipped his head lower at the same time his arm snaked across my lap.

"Mmm, now getting you in a cage of gold does sound appealing but as for the perch, well I think we can forgo that part for I would need you within reach for what I have planned."

I swallowed hard at the sexual image he created and ended up jumping a little when I heard the click of the seat belt. Something that was followed by a little gasp of breath when I felt him tighten it, using his fist on the strap to do so.

The whites of his knuckles told me he was as sexually frustrated as I was, and out of the both of us, there was only one of us that had first-hand experience in sating it.

"Wouldn't want you flying off now, would we, Little Bird?" he said with a grin, winking at me and brushing the back of his fingers down my heated cheek.

"You're not making this easy for me," I told him softly, an admission that only deepened his handsome smile.

"I never said I would, sweetheart," he admitted with ease, while caressing his fingertip down my cheek before brushing it across my lips. Then the plane suddenly started going faster, shocking me enough that I quickly gripped his hand.

"Whoa... we are taking off!" I shouted, half excited and half nervous, making him chuckle.

"Am I to assume this is your first time flying?" he asked as I turned my head to the window, glued to the sight of us taking off. I sucked in a deep breath as the plane lifted and the world beneath us started to get smaller and smaller.

"Oh my god... *look at the world,*" I whispered, making him hum next to me before telling me softly,

"I am looking."

I then turned to see that just like before...

He only had eyes...

For me.

CHAPTER 10
KNOWING YOU

It soon became clear that the window full of worldly wonder held no interest for him. But *I* did. His eyes didn't wander from the sight of me, and I would be lying if I didn't admit how much it affected me. How much it warmed my heart and made me wish I knew how to gift it freely in return, just like he wanted me to.

"It looks so small from up here," I commented, needing something to say to mask my pounding heart. But then the world disappeared and was quickly replaced by a white mist.

"Oh my god, we are going through the clouds!" I shouted excitedly, ending with a gasp as we broke through and the fluffy white blanket was as far as the eye could see.

"Oh wow... *beautiful,*" I said as my emotions rose at the sight, straining my voice.

"No more than your reaction to it."

I grinned at the window before turning back to look at him, feeling overcome by the moment. So, I decided to shock him, by hooking my hand behind his neck and telling him,

"Then let's make the memory of it really count." Then I pulled his lips to mine and kissed him, making this moment as perfect as it could ever get. His surprise didn't last long and he soon took control of the kiss, cupping my face and holding me to him. The kiss ended with his forehead to mine, so he could tell me tenderly,

"Perfection."

"Oh, I don't know about that…" I paused when he raised a brow, and I giggled before whispering in his ear,

"The plane could be empty." At this he laughed and told me,

"Don't give me murderous ideas, Dove… or Van will be first out the door." He added this part when he saw his friend walk up the aisle toward us before taking a seat opposite.

"Did I hear my handsome name being mentioned?" he said with a wink, making Ryker growl.

Then to add humor to the moment, I lifted my hand up and made a motion of falling. Something that started with a whistling sound before ending with a splat on my knee and a 'pew' exploding noise. At this Ryker burst out laughing, a reaction that made me feel like I had won the lottery. His whole face changed, turning that usual stern handsomeness into something even more striking. The wide smile, the crinkles at the corner of his eyes… gorgeous eyes that glittered with humor, it softened his features to the point that I couldn't help but give him a tender look. If witnessed by anyone looking, they would have used the word for such a gaze as 'lovingly'. Something that Van seemed to be doing right now, because he wasn't looking at Ryker like I was.

No… *He was looking at me.*

He was assessing my reaction to his friend, whereas the

man in question was too busy laughing. Meanwhile, everyone else was looking at Ryker like they were seeing someone new, as if this side of Ryker had never been witnessed before. I couldn't help but blush at the realization that I could do that to him. That I could bring out something new, something so unexpected. A side to him undiscovered by others.

It was the stuff of dreams.

But the second I saw the raised brow his friend aimed my way, I ducked my head to avoid his assessing gaze. Because I knew these feelings I was experiencing were of the dangerous kind. I was getting myself in too deep.

It seemed like running was all I had ever known, and it was easy compared to this. It felt safe. Secure. Despite, in reality, it being anything but.

Now as for falling in love, well, that terrified me more than anything else I had ever faced. Because I knew what it was like to allow another to have power over me. The power to crush me and break me in a way that was difficult to heal from. Leaving the type of scars that burned and fused to my very soul.

The unfixable kind.

And speaking of that exact type of danger…

"That's my funny girl," Ryker said, pulling me closer and kissing my forehead before lifting my face up with a gentle grip on my chin. Jesus, the sight of him smiling down at me like that nearly robbed me of my breath.

"Wow, Ryk, for a minute there I thought you would start snorting," Van teased, and it was enough to get his eyes to shift from mine back to his friend.

"I know better than to give my best friend any

ammunition he may use against me," was Ryker's reply, making Van smirk. It was also confirmation that Van and Ryker's relationship went far deeper than just boss and employee.

"Oh, something tells me that with Girl Scout here in your life, soon enough, there will be lots more to add to that particular vault," he said, tapping a finger at the side of his head while looking at me.

"Ironic that, especially considering you couldn't find the real one that night," I replied, making Ryker smirk this time, to which Van tipped his glass of champagne my way and said,

"Well played, Evie… or is it Grace? I forget?"

I frowned at this, just as Ryker warned,

"That's enough, Van."

Van held up his hands at this, the glass tucked against his large palm with his thumb in feign surrender.

"Hey, it's all good and Evie it is… that is unless you're planning on adding any other names to the list any time soon?"

"She is not," Ryker stated firmly, giving his friend a warning look to go with his tone.

"Then I can shut my big mouth and enjoy seeing my friend happy, rather than like some crazed asshole worried out of his mind about some little thief," he replied, raising his glass to salute us both, even as I narrowed my eyes at him. This was just as Ryker closed his eyes as if he was getting even more pissed off.

"I am not a thief," I told him as he rose from the seat. However, he paused long enough to tell me,

"Yeah, Girl Scout… *you are.*" Then he gave a pointed

look to his friend before walking away and downing his drink as he did. However, when Ryker made a move to get up and go after him, I stopped him by putting my hand on his arm.

"Don't."

"He shouldn't have said that," he said with a hard tick in his jawline.

"Maybe not, or maybe it was his right to do so, seeing as it came from a good place," I told him, making him sigh.

"I have known him a long time," he offered like a confession.

"He cares about you," I said, stating the obvious and making him say,

"We have been through a lot together."

"Including hunting me," I added, knowing the reason for Van's not-so-subtle warning. Because he had seen what my running had done to his friend. As well, Ryker wasn't exactly holding back when it came to his feelings for me. Which meant his friend must have witnessed first-hand what my actions had caused. Of course, in my defense, I knew I had my reasons. But those reasons would mean nothing to someone like Van, whose only loyalty was to the man sitting next to me.

"Vander has never seen me like this," he replied, confirming my suspicions. At the same time, he took my hand in his and kissed the back of my palm while entwining our fingers.

"You're lucky to have such a good friend," I told him honestly.

"And what about you, do you have such a friend?" he asked, making me hold myself still for a moment as I thought on that question. Because despite it being an innocent one asked, it came with a whole host of others that would follow. Questions I wasn't ready to answer.

"So how long is the flight?" I asked instead, looking out the window and still trying to get used to the sight of being above the clouds.

"Alright, Little Dove, I will take the hint but be warned…" He paused as he stretched an arm across me so he could hook a finger under my chin. And once more using it to turn my head back to face him.

Which was when he warned…

"I will soon know you."

CHAPTER II
SINS AND THE WORLD
RYKER

I couldn't help but clench my fist by my side the moment I felt her pulling away from me. I may not have been able to read her mind, but I wasn't foolish enough to miss the way she struggled with her feelings for me. It was as if she battled against what she wanted and what she feared. And right now that fear was based on me centered at its core.

I also knew there was more to her past than she was willing to admit to, which was why the seemingly innocent question about friendship had been met with a wall of insecurity. She had been so used to running, and not only in the physical sense. I knew this was more like a natural response kicking in for her.

She didn't yet trust me.

But she would.

I just needed to have patience. Something I would admit to being a failing of mine. A fact that was unsurprising seeing as I was a man that was used to being obeyed and getting his own way. But Evelyn wasn't just some object that could be bought, nor was she someone I could order to do as I wished. She was a heart I wanted to win, so I could feel the gift of such a treasure being given freely to me.

I just couldn't make demands of her when it came to her feelings, ones I wanted her to trust me with. But I knew in order to gain such, then the only weapon in my arsenal was that of time. Time spent trying to gain her trust freely, so when I was finally gifted her heart, she would do so with the unbreakable knowledge that I would keep it safe. That I would keep it cherished for the rest of eternity. That I would spend the rest of my many lifetimes being worthy of the beauty that was her... *inside and out.*

So as much as it went against the grain, I allowed her the veil of secrets and untold stories, issuing her only a hint of the future to come. I would soon know her, something she seemed to worry about for the rest of the flight. The problem was, I didn't know why. What was so bad about her past that she feared me discovering?

The problem with this was that I had no way of finding out. I didn't even have the name she had been born with. I even questioned the name Evelyn as being her own. Not that it mattered to me what she had called herself, despite Vander's snipe earlier. One I knew came from a place of concern for me and not from malicious intent. For he worried for me, and it was unsurprising. Especially seeing as he had borne the brunt of my foul and murderous mood these past weeks. But as for Evie, his warning had been loud and clear. She had been the only one in my life to hold such power over me. A fact that worried Vander.

I was worried also.

My Demon was already addicted, just as I was. However,

the more time we spent around her, the deeper that spiral of addiction sucked us under. Which meant that battling my Demon was not a fight I was certain I would win again, should she try to run once more. The power of the other unearthly side would be too great.

And speaking of power, a few hours later and the moment we started to descend, she reached out and suddenly grabbed my hand, doing so as if acting on impulse.

"We are going down."

I couldn't help but smile at the innocence and wonder in her voice, trying to put myself in her shoes and recalling back to my first flight. A man named Tony Jannus flew the first scheduled commercial airline flight on January 1, 1914. I remember reading how it had only been a twenty-minute flight between St. Petersburg, Florida, and Tampa, Florida. After discovering that, I knew I had to be one of first to experience it for myself. As unlike many other Demons I knew, I wasn't born with wings, so I would not miss out on the opportunity the moment it arose. The Airboat line, as it was named at the time, remained in operation for close to four months and, within that time, carried over a thousand passengers at the cost of only five dollars each.

Naturally, after this, as soon as private jets were being made, I had purchased one, now having a number of them in my fleet. But then witnessing this fresh new experience through the eyes of someone I loved... well, it took something I had spent decades taking for granted, and turned it into something special once more.

But I didn't share this, instead responding to her obvious observation that we were, in fact, going down.

"That usually happens when you reach your destination,"

I couldn't help but tease softly, making her give me a pointed look in return. I couldn't help my smirk because of it.

Gods but what fun I could have with her. For the first time in my life, I had a future to look forward to. I could share my past life experiences with her, doing them all over again and enjoying them through the eyes of another.

Only, she would be the one I would be looking at with each new place I showed her. Her reaction would be the only experience I would ever want. Just the sight of her wide eyes of wonder, and the slight parting of her lips were all I needed to fill my heart with pleasure. And that look of wonder was one I was witnessing now as the world once more came into view, awarding me with that beauty within as she smiled at the window.

"Tell me your thoughts," I whispered, finding myself unable to hold back any longer. But when her only reply was a sigh, I didn't think she would tell me. However, she surprised me yet again as she granted me the pleasure of her thoughts…

"It all seems so insignificant from up here."

"In what way exactly?" I asked, surprised by the trail of her thoughts.

"All my fear, all my worries… from up here I am so far away from them… like they could never reach me here above the world below." I felt my tensed muscles soften before I lifted her hand and offered what I hoped was the comfort she needed.

"Remain by my side and they never will, for you have to trust me when I tell you that I will protect you from whatever it is you fear."

"I have to trust you?" she replied with a pointed look, making me grin and rephrase.

"I would *like* you to trust me."

"Well, that's a start but, honestly, how can you promise something like that when you don't even know what it is that…" At this I cupped her cheek and interrupted her.

"Because there is nothing capable of coming between us."

"What if it's me, what if *I* am what comes between us?" she asked in a quiet voice as she lowered her eyes to her lap.

"I have never lost a battle, Little Dove, and I have certainly never surrendered to one," I told her, knowing the battle of her heart would be the most important victory to date.

"You make it sound as if you're ancient," she said, making me inwardly wince.

"My age is of little matter, other than offering me the edge of experience," I said, skirting around my age.

"Oh, and you have much experience in kidnapping and trying to get captive women to fall in love with you, do you?" she replied wryly, and it seemed to fall from her lips before she could stop herself. I knew this for certain when she blushed and looked awkward.

"You're right, in that I happily admit that I have no experience, but time has awarded me with the abilities needed to often get me what I want, and even if I must battle for it, I am confident of winning."

"Wow, cocky much?" she commented dryly, making me grin and shrug my shoulders unapologetically.

"I am what I am," I told her, making no excuses for my greedy nature.

"And what is that exactly?" she asked.

"You will find out soon enough but, for now, just know that I will not give up so easily in winning your affection." Again, her beautiful, light-brown eyes widened slightly at this, telling me that my words had affected her in a positive way. This was the beauty of being awarded a Siren with an expressive face.

"And what then?" she continued to ask, as if still allowing doubt to cloud my words.

"What do you mean?" I asked because her question confused me.

"What then? What happens when you have conquered me, won the war on my heart? What then?"

"I am afraid I am not following," I admitted with a frown.

"And I am afraid that a happy ever after isn't on the cards for me, Ryker." I could feel my gaze narrowing further at this.

"And what makes you say that?" I almost snapped the question, not liking that she believed this. That she believed she did not deserve such happiness. At this she looked back out to the world as it got closer to us before she answered and, with it, I found myself speechless at her reply...

"Because no sin goes unpunished, even if the world is cruel enough to those who often deserve better." I sucked back a quick breath before I could act on my annoyance and shock. But then, she grabbed my hand and squeezed it as we got closer to the world she feared would catch up to her, giving me pause to be angry.

After this, I heard her gasp and hold her next breath captive as the wheels hit the runway and sped down it before coming to a stop. I wanted so badly to understand her and discover where this deep-rooted fear stemmed from. But most of all, I wanted to eliminate it altogether.

However, for the first time in my life, I found myself fighting against an enemy I knew nothing about and, worst of all, one I couldn't see. But, in the end, I would fight it regardless and I would never stop. Which was why I told her,

"Then my advice..." I paused long enough to draw her attention back to me, turning her face away from the world she feared and told her, *"...Give into sin and fuck the world."*

Then I kissed her, hoping she would, at the very least, take the first part of my advice. Something I achieved when I felt her moan against my lips before she opened up to me like I owned hers. Gods but the taste of her, it was the very meaning of the word addiction, and all from a fucking kiss. The Devil only knew just what it would be like once I had finally had her, for my thirst for her would never be sated. Though I got the impression she feared that it would.

Of course, she hadn't said this, but I could very well imagine this being one of her fears. I had heard as much in her tone when questioning me about conquering her. The question of what would happen once I got bored or tired of her was just there, unspoken words upon her lips.

But then she didn't know what I knew. That she had been gifted to me by the Gods. She was my perfect little Siren and forever mine to keep. For how could I ever tire of such sweet temptation, even after it had been consumed? I wanted every piece of her, and I was not only speaking of her mouth-watering body, but I wanted her mind, her soul, and yes, her heart. And once I got all of those things, I would never let her go. Nor would I ever take any ounce of her for granted.

I wanted no other but her, and I knew deep down in my corrupt soul that I never would. But she knew none of this and most likely thought of me as just some Billionaire playboy. She believed herself to be a conquest to win before I moved on to the next challenge.

Oh, but how wrong she was.

Something she would soon find out.

The moment the plane doors opened was when I finally managed to tear my lips away from hers, doing so reluctantly to the sound of me unbuckling her seatbelt.

"You really should stop kissing me like that," she complained in a dreamy tone. One I had promised myself to hear again, and soon.

"And why is that?" I asked in a hard manner she shivered against.

"Because I forgot I was even on a plane."

I had to allow myself to chuckle at that, happy that it was for no other reason. Now telling her,

"Good, then I have achieved my new goal."

"New goal?" she asked as I rose from my seat.

"To get you to give into sin and forget the world around us exists," I answered before offering her my hand, something that, in that moment, felt far more symbolic due to my words. I got the impression she knew it too, her expressive eyes told me of what she dare not speak. But regardless of these fears, she placed her hand in mine and let me help her to her feet, making my heart lift at the unspoken gesture of trust.

"So, this is Canada, huh?" she commented, as if she had

the sudden need for something mundane to say in the shadow of her nervousness.

Like most things she did, I couldn't help but smirk along with squeezing her hand as I led her over to the convoy of vehicles waiting for us. But then as I opened the car door for her, after first jerking my head for my driver to allow me to do this for my girl in his place, I placed a hand on her belly. This was so as to pull her back against me. The sound of her little gasp once again was a sound that went straight to my cock. Which had been fucking hard most of the day. And well, having her tucked against my much larger frame wasn't easing the pressure building in my suit trousers any time soon.

"Welcome to my territory, *little bird of mine.*"

Her shiver was one I even had to close my eyes against as I looked up to the sky and forced myself not to growl in approval. I did, however, flex my fingers over her belly, telling her all she needed to know in that moment.

I wanted her.

However, the sound of my men approaching the vehicles behind us was enough for me to let her go so as I could get her alone quicker. So, I released her and took her hand to guide her into the car. Something she did, but not without me catching sight of that delightful, mouthwatering blush painted across her skin. Then I turned to Van as he approached and, because I was still pissed at him, told him,

"You can ride with Faron in the car in front." He frowned at me but when he opened his mouth to say more, I jerked my head toward the vehicle in front and ordered sternly,

"Now, Vander."

He shook his head a little before submitting to my demand, knowing now how he had fucked up.

"Alright boss," he replied in a defeated tone before walking away and nodding for Faron to follow.

I watched him walk away with a tensed jaw, feeling conflicted by my decision. Because I knew he only had my best interest at heart, but he had to know that speaking to my Siren, and my Chosen, in that way would not be allowed.

So, after shaking my own head in frustration, I followed Evie inside the car, soon joining her on the back seat. Then I told my driver,

"To the estate, Anthony."

As for the drive from Toronto Pearson International Airport to Bayview Ridge, where my home was, it was mostly done in silence. It seemed I wasn't the only one with a lot on my mind. Which meant had I not had her hand entwined with mine, it would have been a completely uneventful journey home.

However, when it became clear that we were nearing our destination, thanks to the large, gated entrance the car was pulling up to, I felt her tense next to me. She also tried to slip her hand from mine. But this wasn't something I would allow. Instead, I gripped it tighter and used my hold on her to pull her closer into me. Then I cupped her cheek and told her,

"Don't be nervous about being in my home."

She swallowed hard, but this was my only reply as she didn't speak. But then, she didn't need to. Her expression once again told me all I needed to know. I nodded for the car to pull to the front of the house, instead of following the rest of the convoy into the garages we kept at the back of the property.

It was a French style chateau, sitting on a sprawling ten acres, and was the biggest lot on the prestigious enclave of Bayview Ridge. It was a pale stone building with curved turrets at the corners and a grand entrance framed by its two-story pillars.

"Wow, this place is incredible, I can't believe you actually live here," she commented in awe the moment she was out of the car, now standing back and looking at the grand structure in front of her.

This was when I thought it well to remind her of the gravity of her new situation. Doing so first by wrapping my arms around her from behind so as she couldn't escape the truth of my words.

"I do and while you're at it, you can also believe that you live here too, for may I be the first to welcome you to your…"

"…New home."

CHAPTER 12
MY ROOM

I had to admit, once I finally got her inside my home, I felt myself relax more than I had done in months. It was as if having her here was the first major hurdle to overcome. The first big step had been taken, and now that I knew her safety was ensured, I could then spend the time trying to get her to fall in love with me. To hopefully get her to the point that she would want to remain here of her own free will and not as the prisoner I had been forced to claim her to be.

But that was not all. I also wanted her to feel comfortable in my home, one that I hoped she would willingly claim as being her own very soon. Hence why her impression of it was important to me. It was also why I didn't take my eyes off her when leading her through the different rooms. Those wide eyes of hers looked on in wonder, which I was a good sign. But it was when leading her to my bedroom I was most intrigued, for in truth it was one sacred place I hoped to spend a lot of time in.

Of course, the moment I opened my door and led her

inside, I found her reaction both adorable as well as amusing. She looked like some nervous fawn making its way out into the meadow and beyond the tree line of safety. Out in the open and stripped bare of her defenses, as if stepping into the wolf's lair.

"Is this…"

"My room, yes," I replied, again trying not to laugh at her trepidation. Especially with the way her eyes scanned the room, lingering on the large bed. One that was set against a curtained wall of black velvet, draped to the sides and fixed to the elaborate wrought-iron headboard. These matched the gray and black Egyptian cotton sheets, with a velvet comforter draped at the bottom of the bed. These dark tones matched other elements in the room, with the scattered rugs on the light-gray marble floor.

I watched as she purposely avoided going too close to the bed and instead made her way around the space, and I found myself leaning back against the door frame watching her.

She took tentative steps further inside and away from the main feature of the room. Black lacquer furniture with gold accents in an oriental style were dotted throughout the suite, that followed through into the sitting area. The pale walls showcased black and white abstract paintings, with bold gold brush strokes highlighting the swirls of paint.

"This is your room?" she asked again, and I swear I had to stop myself from putting a fist to my mouth to prevent even more laughter that wanted to erupt. Which was why I had to take a minute before replying.

"As I said, it is." At this, she made a slight 'hmm' sound

before moving toward the sitting area and running her fingers over the back of the dark-gray sofa.

After this she walked toward a large black dresser that held an ornate mirror above it, and therefore offered me her reflection. One that held a delightful mix of confusion, surprise, and curiosity. Then she picked up a rare black and gold Thomas Tompion clock, being one of only three clocks ever produced at the turn of the 18th century by England's most acclaimed watchmaker. I thought it best not to tell her that I had paid nearly two million Euros for it back in 1999. She placed it back and once more wanted confirmation.

"Your room?" I allowed myself to laugh this time before answering once again,

"It is."

"Hmm," she replied again before stepping away, and this time over to the large bay window that held the beautiful acreage beyond it. The manicured estate was like a blanket of green laid out in front of her, surrounded by woodland. The tamed surrounded by the untamed. A sentiment that was mirrored inside this room as I stepped closer, no longer content at the distance between us.

"It's a beautiful view," she said, and I could tell with her breathlessness that she was nervous. I grinned to myself and agreed.

"That it is."

Of course, I wasn't speaking of the view that met me most mornings, but the one I hoped would soon replace it. Because there was only one beauty in my life my eyes wanted to feast on daily, and it was the sight of my Siren now standing in my life.

So, with this in mind, I moved with silent steps and was

awarded with her gasp of breath when she felt my hands come to rest at her shoulders.

"So, if this is your room…" she said in a quiet voice, one that I found utterly endearing and I couldn't help it when my lips found the graceful line of her neck.

"Mmm?" My reply became a contented sigh against her skin, and my reward for such was the slight tip of her head, allowing me more access.

"…Where will I be staying?" she asked on a barely heard whisper. This made me grin, which I knew she could feel against her neck, before she heard my reply hummed at the shell of her ear,

"My room."

Then before she could fight me on the decision, I spun her around and pressed her up against the wall of glass, before taking her face in my hands and tipping her head back. With her mouth still open in shock, I took advantage of the fact by tasting the surprise for myself.

Just like she always did, she relaxed into my kiss as if unable to hold back the urge to do so. As if Fate wouldn't allow it. Because she may have tried to resist what was building between us. Deny her feelings. Run from her fear. But like this, there was nowhere to run to. Nowhere to hide. Because her kiss didn't lie. Just like mine didn't.

And our love would be the same.

For there was no hiding from it in the end.

Not when I now had time on my side. So, with that in mind and eager to get certain things out of the way so as I could concentrate all my time on my nervous little Siren, I pulled back. Despite being near pained to do so. For I swore that when I finally had her, I would be locking the door and shackling us together in chains in fear of spending even a minute without her being within arm's reach.

Fuck! But what was becoming of me?

Falling in love, was what.

But as for now, I had to ensure we had our time, and it was spent unhindered by business or rule. So, I ran the back of my finger across her wet lips and grinned down at her.

"Beautiful," I hummed, making her blush. Before I could get even more lost in the sight, I told her,

"I have to go, but I will be back shortly."

"Oh... oh, of course, well I can just..." I stopped her nervous yet adorable rambling and told her exactly what she could do.

"You will relax, have a shower or a bath perhaps. Whatever you prefer. There are new clothes in the closet for you and you should find everything you will need in the bathroom."

"But this is your room," she told me softly.

I grinned and, this time, it was one that might have been classed as Demonic, for I gripped the sides of her waist and yanked her harder to me before growling down at her,

"My room no longer, *for it is now ours.*" Then before she could utter a word of protest, I kissed her once more. This time wrapping a fist around her hair and tugging her head down so as I had full access to her lips. She would deny me nothing. Her sigh of pleasure all the acceptance to this I would ever need. The scent of her arousal filled my senses and made it a heady experience to get addicted to.

An addiction I could feed my Greed on soon enough but first...

"I will be back soon."

"You said that already," she hummed, making me smile.

"Then it must be doubly true," I teased, making her giggle. A delightful sound that only added to the million reasons I wanted to stay. But I knew that if I didn't deal with responsibilities first, then it would only be harder to leave once I had her naked in my bed.

"I won't be long, Little Dove," I told her, making her nod as if still caught in my trance. One that, if I had my way, I would keep her in so as to cast her uncertainties into the abyss along with the shadows of doubt that she wore like a veil.

But that time would come, so I walked away and closed the door, knowing there was no need for locks this time. Not when I had enough guards on the estate that would have been considered a small army. She wouldn't have even made it a single step out the front door.

Yet despite this knowledge, it still wasn't enough for me to take my time as I made my way to my office on the ground floor and found Faron there, waiting for me.

"Oblivion?"

"He is awaiting your call," Faron replied.

"Good… and Van?" I asked after glancing around and not finding my second in sight.

"Licking his wounds with a bottle and boxing gloves." I rolled my eyes at this and told him,

"Find his ass and tell him to get it inside my office by the time my call is finished."

Faron sighed but nodded, despite his inner feelings on the matter. Then I left him to his chore, knowing that with his gift of air manipulation, he would have no issues dodging whatever came in his direction in the way of a fist. Then I sat down behind my desk, at the same time making the call I knew was overdue.

"Ryker Wyeth, I would ask to what I owe the pleasure, but considering you have only just left my territory, I would say this call is long overdue, wouldn't you?" the smooth, assured voice of West Coast's Enforcer said in way of answering my call.

"My people informed you of the situation, Wye," I said, shortening his first name of Wyedari.

"Ah yes, your people, how kind of you," he replied dryly, making me groan in frustration.

"Don't be a prick, Wye, you knew what I was dealing with," I said, cutting through the territory bullshit knowing that I was, in essence, speaking with a friend. Something that caused the famed sorcerer to laugh.

Wyedari Oblivion was a Demon half-breed, with the Fae side of making him one of the most powerful sorcerers known in our world. But this wasn't surprising, given his origins being very similar to my own. His father was King Minos, ruler of the Oblivion realm, but better known to the mortal realm as being the circle of Limbo.

He was the Judge of the Damned, declared so by Lucifer himself. A position that determines where a soul is condemned to spend the rest of their eternity. Hence why his son's supremacy made for a powerful edition to the King of Kings' Enforcers.

"Yes, and would you believe since the day of the shootout, I am also dealing with a similar situation." Now this was a surprise, and had enough of a hit that I sat up straighter, feeling myself tense.

"Explain."

"It seems as though you are not the only one to be gifted with that of a Siren, my friend."

I sucked air between my teeth.

"Timing cannot be a coincidence," I stated firmly.

"Only a fool would believe so," he replied in return in his usual collected way. Yet I was able to cut straight through it, hearing the undertone of something else he knew but was not yet saying. Hence why I stated,

"You know more."

"And you know me well… yes, I know more," he agreed, and I would have grinned at this had the situation leant itself for me to do so.

"Tell me," I almost growled.

"The King of Kings has found his Electus." This time my shock was heard from both sides.

"Gods, then the Fates' prophecy begins."

"For all of us, it would seem," Wye said, making me look to the door as if my own Fated was standing behind it, prompting me to admit,

"And what of you? Please tell me that you are having as much trouble with your Siren as I am with mine."

He laughed at this and it wasn't a malicious sound, but more one of understanding, despite what he said next.

"Ha, but would I ever be the one to offer such comfort, my friend?"

"Bastard," I scathed without malice.

"And known such by many. But alas, I will at the very least tell you this…" He paused long enough for me to hear the rattling of metal before telling me, "I do find chains come in handy."

I laughed, already having had the thought pass me by many times.

"I am happy for you, old friend," I offered, thinking of all the Enforcers around the world that I knew and there were, in all honesty, only a dozen names I could think of to be deserving of such a gift.

"Eucharistō," he replied, thanking me in ancient Greek.

"I take it no more was discovered on why the men I fought couldn't be controlled?" I asked. My men had already been working with Lord Oblivion on this, seeing as he was the authority on magic and sorcery.

"Magic for sale, I am afraid, but have no fear, they will not hide from me for long. As you know, it is an offence I take seriously. Naturally, I will inform you as soon as there is someone to kill, have no fear of that."

I grinned. "I appreciate it."

"Of course, you do, Son of Greed," he said with amusement, which I cut through with the next question.

"So, what of the other Enforcers? Do we know if there is any other who has found their Siren?"

"Ah, well, we may be friends, Ryk, but it's not like we are in a fucking club, we are, after all, the rarity." I laughed, knowing this was true, as most of us kept things very close to our chests for a reason.

"So, you don't know?"

"Now I didn't say that, only that we are so inclined to do what I image the others are, by keeping such knowledge a safe-guarded secret for fear of our new weakness being exploited and used against us." I scoffed at that, knowing firsthand the truth of it.

"Well, if the Lost Siren prophecy is following the guide of the Fates, then eventually they will all come together, which in turn means…" Wye finished this sentence off for me,

"The Enforcers will be forced to do the same. Then perhaps in sight of such, it is worth reaching out and establishing as many allies as we can gain." I released a sigh and agreed, even if doing so reluctantly.

"I will reach out to those I trust."

"And I will do the same." I nodded, despite not facing him, although this ended up being seen by Van, who now entered my office just as I was about to end the call.

"Then I will wish you luck with your Siren, for if it is anything like my own situation, then I would say we will need all the luck we can get," I said, making him chuckle before mirroring my inner feelings.

"Yes, but what a fucking good battle it is to fight for."

"To the death, my friend, to the death."

He laughed once more and bid me farewell before hanging up, leaving me with the annoyance of dealing with my second's poorly-timed insolence. Of course, with the casual 'I couldn't give a fuck' relaxed state of him, I knew it wasn't going to go well.

"And how is the cocky Lord of all manner of magic fuckery these days?" he asked, making me grit my teeth.

"Well, that depends on whether or not he has an asshole best friend whose ass he wants to kick?" I replied, making him scoff.

"Lighten up, Ryk, it was nothing but a friendly warning."

"Friendly?" I seethed, to which he just shrugged his shoulders.

"I saw her face, Ryk, she will fucking run the first chance she gets, and you know it."

I swear I thought my teeth were going shatter along with my bones for how hard I clenched my jaw and fist.

"Oh, and you think your 'friendly' warning is going to help with that, do you?!" At this he finally got it, now looking from my anger and finding the floor, having no response to that.

"Besides, she didn't run from the bathroom, like she had the chance to," I reminded him.

"That's not what she is terrified of, Ryker," he said, causing a bitter taste in my mouth, as I didn't like the way he thought he knew her.

"You know nothing!" I snapped.

"I know that she is hiding something big enough to give me reason enough for concern," he replied, making me feel like snarling an inch from his face.

"Whatever it is, it matters little to me," I told him, seething inside.

"No, but it matters to her and that's the point." I narrowed my gaze at my second and had to force myself to stop from growling.

"Look, I get it, she could have been the cause of a fucking massacre and it would matter little to a bunch of Demons like us, but she doesn't know that and, therefore, won't trust you with that information like she should."

I took a much-needed breath, trying to take in his words, ones I knew that, despite being hard to hear, I needed to heed regardless.

"It's true, she doesn't trust me yet, but she will," I stated firmly.

"And you're sure about that, are you?" he questioned, going too fucking far!

"I am still your fucking lord, don't forget that!" This time I did fucking growl.

"Yeah, but you're also my friend first, and don't you forget it. So, fuck the consequences, as here it is, Ryk… The girl won't allow herself to have you when she doesn't feel like she deserves you." I gritted my teeth at this.

"What the fuck are you talking about!?"

"She may have found the old man, but that doesn't mean she ever stopped running." I went to pass him, knowing that if I was in his presence any longer and I would end up strangling him.

"I don't have to listen to…" He grabbed my arm and stopped me in both my tracks and my words.

"Let me find out what she was running from before it happens again." Now this time I did snarl, inches from his face, knowing now what he wanted to do, *something I would never allow.* He wanted inside her memories, to invade her mind and take hold of it. To make her sleep and control her through that vulnerability.

He wanted what no man deserved.

A piece of her.

Which was why I soon had his throat in my hand and his body pinned against the wall, the panels splintering around his frame from the pressure.

"Never!" I snarled, making him swallow hard, which I felt travel the length of my palm as it was forced down his throat.

"Now you listen to me, Vander, you may be my friend, you may be my second, but Evie belongs to no man but

ME... every... fucking... piece of her! Now do I make myself fucking clear!?" I gritted out in my anger, making him nod the once, despite my hold. However, before I could say anything more, the reason I ended up dropping him wasn't because I was finished in my threat.

No, it was because I wasn't the only one making threats in my home. I knew that when I heard the worst fucking sound in my entire life. The one that chilled my already stone-cold bones to the fucking core.

My Siren's scream.
  Evie

CHAPTER 13
THE EX IN LIES
EVIE

To say I wasn't nervous now being here in his room, I would be lying because I couldn't even fake normalcy. Because Ryker had known… of course he had! The man missed nothing and why would he? Seeing as he had barely kept his eyes off me for long enough for me to hide anything. If anything, he seemed to enjoy my nervousness.

Of course, I wasn't a fool and knew what being here could mean for my immediate future. He had made as much clear when declaring this now my room as well. But then I also knew that if I said no and pushed him, wanting my own room, he would have given it to me. Making me now question why I hadn't.

"Because every time he kisses you, all you can think about is him ripping your clothes off and throwing you on the bed, that's why," I answered myself in the bathroom mirror, ending this truth with a shake of my head before turning away from my own worried expression. I decided to have a shower, despite the bath being a sight I nearly wept at. It was incredible.

The room was huge for a bathroom, and most definitely not a luxury I was used to. Especially when I could have fitted my old bathroom in the space where just the bath sat. The tiles were super stylish slate that had an almost burnt copper tinge and covered half of the walls. Including the huge shower that had enough room to fit so many people you could have classed it as a party.

"Don't go there, Evie, don't go there," I told myself, not wanting to even think about Ryker's past escapades. Or should I call them Sexapades?

"Nope... stop it," I told myself, trying to get out of my second hand, now-*ripped* clothes. As for the bath, it was a large oval that thankfully wasn't big enough to fit a party in, but it most definitely had plenty of room for two.

But seeing as I knew he was coming back soon, I decided to forgo the dream bath, opting for a quick shower instead. Because I knew if I ever got in that tub, then I wouldn't be out again until my digits were that of a ninety-year-old. So, I turned on the fancy shower after stripping out of my mismatched fitting clothes, a skirt that was now bordering along being obscene, thanks to Ryker's hot and heavy hands.

Then I spent a few seconds under the powerful spray of the hot water, wishing I had longer. But then considering I didn't know how long Ryker would be until he was back, I grabbed the expensive looking shampoo and got to work on my hair.

Ten minutes later and I was walking back into his room in a white fluffy robe, scrubbing a towel over my wet hair.

Although the sight that met me made me almost stumble to an abrupt stop. I even dropped the towel in my shock because there was now an unwelcome edition to the bedroom that hadn't been there before. And well, it soon became clear I wasn't the only one shocked by the other.

Because, there, on the bed, was now a beautiful, stunning woman lying seductively upon the sheets, clearly in the middle of pleasuring herself! Something that looked easy to do too, considering she wasn't wearing any underwear under her short, shimmering gold dress. One that was strappy at the exposed sides, and the single piece of gold string tied around her neck like a bikini top.

She pulled it off too, what with her lithe body shape, legs that went on for days, and the golden tan that she wore like a badge of honor. Even her long black hair was like a glossy mane, one she had pulled back tight to her head in one long ponytail that almost looked wet, it was that tight. Jesus, she looked like she was one some pornographic photoshoot!

I gasped and her eyes snapped open before narrowing dangerously at me.

"Who the fuck are you?!" She bit out angrily, making me instantly take a step back.

"I... I'm Evie," I stuttered.

"You're fucking human!" she snarled, and again the sound was so hostile that I would have been stupid not to see it as the obvious threat it was.

"Er..."

At this she practically slithered from the bed like some golden snake. Then, she strutted over to me, her legs crossing slightly like she was walking on a runway. I couldn't help but tense, rooted to the spot as she scanned her assessing eyes down me and back up again, the look of disgust clear on her face.

"Why, by the Gods would he bring something like you home?" she snapped venomously.

"Home?"

At this she sneered, "Well, it is as good as being mine." I frowned at that, and she grinned because of it, telling me,

"I don't know who the fuck you are, Evie... but I know who I am."

"Y-y-yeah... and who... who is that?" I stammered again, trying to get my words to sound braver than I felt. Especially when she uncurled her fingers and allowed me to see her painted gold nails beginning to grow to impossible lengths. Like, fucking Wolverine had nothing on this chick!

"I am his fiancé and as for Greed..." At this she got in my face and snarled against my cheek,

"He is mine!"

Then she drew her arm back and swiped out, aiming for my head and making me duck out the way before she could rid me of my head and maim me. Then I did the only thing I could think to do, and that was to run to the door, open it, and scream as loud as I could.

"HELP ME AHHH!" This ended with having my wet hair pulled, the force of it yanking me backward as I was then tossed behind the crazed bitch. I skidded on the floor until coming to a stop at one of the chairs in his living space. So, I did the only thing I could think of and got to my feet, and picked up the smaller arm chair, now holding it out in front of me like a weapon.

"Oh please... now just what do you think you can do with that!?" she said, laughing before charging at me, and at the same time I swung it to the side, hoping to knock her to the floor before she reached me. However, she just ducked like a professional athlete and grabbed my ankle, tugging it hard enough that I fell to the ground. I quickly managed to turn onto my belly as I tried to scramble away, crawling toward the window. The night beyond showed me the deadly sight behind me as my attacker started to walk over me, and I felt her heeled foot dig into my lower back, pressing me down just as I was trying to reach out to hold onto anything.

Yet the desperate sight of me trying to survive would soon take the place of another trying to cling onto life. Because what I witnessed next was the most terrifying sight yet, one that started when I saw a dark entity begin to move along the floor at speed. It alternated between disappearing under the floor and erupting from it in deadly black spikes. Like crude oil had been given an ever-changing form. One moment being a fluid moving liquid, and the next an unbreakable solid rock. It traveled straight toward me in two parallel lines either side of the crazy bitch standing over me. But for now, she was too focused on killing me to notice the hellish danger coming up behind her.

Because in the second it took her to raise her arm and the weapon that was her hand, the black entity did the same. It was like the extension of some phantom of death looming behind her. The reflection of which was terrifying as the ends formed deadly spears that quickly stabbed into her hands before she could do any damage to me.

The sound of her howling in pain was one that seemed to almost whistle in the air as she was dragged away from me with such speed, her movements became a reflective blur of gold. After this and hearing her screams, I could do nothing but cover my head with my arms and cower in fear that I would be next.

"Ryker, enough!" I heard a stern voice say, and it received nothing but a hellish growl back.

"Fuck, Ryker! Leave the bitch to me and go to your woman!" Vander said again, and I instantly started shaking at that, not wanting to believe that the man I was falling for had anything to do with what just happened. No, it couldn't be possible! I mean, I had seen him fight that monster in the bathroom, but I didn't think it possible for him to be one far scarier!

Just what in the world had I fucking stumbled into? But most of all...

What the hell was he?!

"Fine, but the bitch will pay for her crimes!" he growled, and this time it sounded a little less Demonic, at the very least. But then I heard something being spoken quietly to him, and it sounded very much like whispered words of advice. So, I cracked an eye open and looked through the gap in my arms long enough to see the reflection of them both looking at me. Vander, with a now passed out, limp, and bleeding woman in his unforgiving grasp. I watched as Ryker nodded before jerking his head to the door, silently telling his friend to leave. Even the sound of the door closing made me flinch, but nothing like the feel of Ryker's touch when he reached me.

"Easy now... I won't ever hurt you, Little Dove."

The sound of his gentle words battled in my mind, because as fearful as I was, a part of me still trusted in his words. That he wouldn't hurt me. But how could I still believe this after what I had seen? I didn't know. So, I thought back to all of the times where our paths crossed, right up to the very first meeting. All those gentle touches, when surely, if such a monster existed within him, he wouldn't have extended such kindness toward me. So, what if all I had seen was his brutal reaction toward someone who wanted to hurt me, possibly kill me?

After all, hadn't he just saved me?

Wasn't he the hero in my story and not the enemy?

"Come on now, there is no need to hide from me," he said gently, before lifting my arms up from my cowering head. When I allowed him to do so, he took this as his sign to do more. Something that came in the form of him shifting me to my back before sliding his arms under me. This was so he could lift me up into his arms, and I couldn't help but admire his strength in doing so.

His eyes lowered to the sight of me now shivering in his hold as he walked me toward the bed. However, instead of just putting me down, he sat with me in his lap and wrapped his arms around me. Then he pulled the comforter from the end of the bed and draped it across me, tucking it close and allowing me this moment of quiet to calm myself. His hand rubbed gentle, soothing circles on my back and along my arm.

I don't know how long we stayed this way, but it must have been until he felt me relaxing enough into him that he trusted himself to speak.

"Please, Gods, tell me she didn't hurt you?" I swallowed hard, trying to get past my fear enough to speak. But then I felt my chin being raised so he could look into my eyes when he asked,

"Tell me I wasn't too late?"

I shook my head, telling him no, she hadn't, and the relief was easy to see. But then shame filled my veins as I admitted,

"I didn't fight back." At this his gaze grew even more tender as he whispered my name,

"Evie."

"I usually fight back… I've always fought back, Ryker," I told him, making him sigh.

"To fight back against such a being might have been the difference in getting to you in time," he told me, making me shiver once at the thought of the crazed bitch. A reaction he clearly didn't like, because his features hardened as if the thought of what could have happened crossed his mind, making him hold me tighter.

"I don't understand your world," I admitted quietly, making him sigh again before agreeing softly,

"I know, sweetheart." Then I felt him kiss me on top of my head before I remembered something.

"She told me you were hers, that she was your fiancé." At this he scoffed and told me,

"Not fucking likely."

"But why would she say that? Is she… is she a girlfriend?"

I felt the deep inhale of frustration instead of hearing the sigh that no doubt followed.

"Oh god, that's it, isn't it?!" I said when he didn't answer me, pulling back away from him and letting the blanket slip to the floor. To which he stood, so he could put me back on the bed off his lap. This allowed me the freedom to shift myself up the bed before tucking my legs up against me. I also realized I was still only wearing a robe, so I purposely held the collar together with a fisted hand held at my heart. One that felt like it would break depending on what he told me next.

Of course, it didn't look good when he rose from the bed and started pacing the floor, as if struggling to find the right words.

"That's it, isn't it?" I repeated, to which he stopped walking and turned towards me to say,

"Fuck no... not anymore, not for a while have I..." He trailed off, clearly not knowing how to explain, and I tried to find comfort in this. But then just the thought of him with that crazy bitch must have been written across my face like an open book to read.

"I know what you're thinking."

"Yeah, and what am I thinking, Ryker?" I pressed.

"That I must have been out of my fucking mind to be with someone like that." Okay, so yeah, he knew what I was thinking.

"It doesn't exactly say much for your taste in women," I admitted.

"My taste in women..." he muttered, mimicking my words.

"Gods, Evie, if only you knew," he added in sight of my frown.

"If only I knew what?" I forced myself to ask.

"I don't date, Evelyn." Needless to say, this statement didn't do anything to dispel my frown.

"I don't understand, then what did you intend for me?"

"Not to fucking date you, that's for damn sure." I had to say, this was a fucking blow I wasn't expecting, and I swear,

I jerked back from his words as if he had been the one to strike me.

"Right… *right,"* I stated at the same time I straightened my whole body. This before launching myself off the bed, making him look shocked because he clearly wasn't expecting it.

"Well, I think you have made yourself perfectly clear," I told him as I stormed toward the door, hoping that when I opened it, the crazed bitch was long gone. However, not surprisingly, I didn't get far.

"Just where do you think you're going?!" he snapped, grabbing my arm and turning me back to face him. However, my anger burst from me enough that with the forced movement came retaliation, and I used both hands to push him back.

"Getting the fuck away from you, that's what!" I shouted before turning back to the door and trying once again to get through it. In truth, I didn't know where this bravery had come from, considering what I had seen him capable of doing. Clearly, he wasn't fucking human! It was like I'd been keeping it in reserve or something, because I could have done with it about ten minutes ago when faced with the raging psycho.

But then I felt the door ripped from my hold just as I managed to open it, making me jump when it was slammed back shut.

"You're not going anywhere!" he demanded at my back, both of his hands moving to the frame, caging me from behind.

"Let me go," I demanded in a strangely calm voice, one he snarled back at a single word,

"No."

"I said, Let. Me. Go!" I forced out through gritted teeth, this time fucking all the calm I had in me. To which I felt him leaning closer into me and snarl in my ear,

"And I said no."

I swallowed hard, seeing the way his grip on the door caused the wood to crack, making me test just how far he would go in his anger.

"You won't hurt me," I stated as if this was a fact I knew deep down to my very breakable bones.

"Never," he growled, making me shiver at the power of the word.

"But that doesn't mean I will let you go either," he warned, making me sigh in defeat.

"Ryker, please," I pleaded, making him finally relax his splintering hold on the door frame. Then I felt him dip his head so he was now resting it against my shoulder.

"Gods, what it is you do to me, Little Dove?" he admitted, making me suck back a breath when I felt one of his hands snake across my belly and hold me to the wall of muscle at my back.

"But not enough to date me, huh?" I snapped, reminding him of his hurtful words, making him scoff.

"So that is what caused you to take flight?" he hummed, making me tense against him.

"I am not just something to warm your bed and fuck whenever you need an itch to scratch!" I bit back, making him tense against me before growling against my neck.

"Be careful, Little Bird, you tread on thin ice with that one," he warned in a dangerous tone. One I knew to take seriously. Then he yanked me back hard against him enough to feel the very large and obvious bulge there, before he asked me in a dark tone,

"Does this feel like just some scratch I need itching to you?" Something he followed by dipping his hand inside my robe so his fingertips met my quivering flesh. I swear, my belly trembled at the first touch. I didn't know whether to try and bat his hand away or to try and guide it lower from my stomach.

"Oh, Little Bird, if only you knew of all the plans I am making for you." I stiffened at that, but then he told me in my ear,

"Not a fucking one of them starts with dating, but every single one ends with you remaining in my bed for the rest of my days."

A startled breath left me, making me stammer,

"I-I don't understand."

"I know, sweetheart, but you soon will, this I promise you." And with that I ended up calling out in fright as my legs were suddenly swept out from under me. Then I was up in his arms, and I foolishly asked,

"Where are you taking me?" My panicked tone was one he seemed to revel in as he replied with a confident,

"To end the night with a promise made."

And from the looks of things, it was a promise made in only one place…

His bed.

CHAPTER 14
PUTTING THE V IN VERY NERVOUS

"Tell me, sweet girl, why do you shake so?" he asked as he lay me down, and this time following me there, now with his large, intimidating presence looming over me.

"Am... I?" I asked, hearing for myself the shake in my voice.

"You are... and if I didn't know any better, then I would say this is your first time with a... Evelyn?" he paused when something in my face must have given it away, but then again, it could have been feeling me wince beneath him. And it was when I saw the realization dawn on him that I managed to slip from beneath him in state of his shock. I then got to my feet, pulling my rope tighter together as if this was enough to protect my dignity, one that felt as if it was being stripped from me against my will.

"So, this is your room," I said stupidly, feeling myself spiraling out of control and not knowing how to cope with it.

"Evelyn, look at me?" he asked softly, only I couldn't. Because I knew what I would find there.

Pity.

And I couldn't stand that. I couldn't stand the judgement. Not from him. Not from the one man I had dreamed of being my first. The man I was so close to trusting it with it. Which was why, even without doing as he asked, I told him,

"I don't trust people." Again, I didn't look at him, even after I said this, knowing it was easier if I didn't. And when he didn't respond to me, I knew it was because he was giving me the time to continue and get out what I clearly needed to.

"You spoke to Arthur?" I asked, focusing on the window and purposely avoiding the reflection of him sitting at the edge of the bed, a glimpse I had allowed myself.

"I did."

"Then you know more of my past than most people," I admitted.

"He told me how he found you," he admitted, and I could almost picture it. Arthur there, signing away and standing looking proudly at all the artwork he had filled his little cabin with. The smell of the fire burning, mixed with the wildness beyond the wooden walls of what felt like the only true home I had ever known.

"Did he tell you how long it took me to trust him enough to stay?" I asked, not shocked when he told me,

"He did." At this I finally looked back at him and said,

"Then maybe you can understand why." At this he stood up, putting his hands to his thighs, and I didn't know why but I found the sight such a breathtaking one. It was as if he did it in the wake of coming to some unspoken decision.

"I understand why your trust and fear go hand in hand." I

closed my eyes at this, knowing he had hit the nail on the head.

"I have a past, Ryker." At this he made his way over to me and lifted my gaze from the floor I had felt it safer to look at. He did this by cupping a hand to my cheek, and what he found was my watery gaze looking back up at him.

"You're not the only one with a past, sweetheart, but the question you need to ask yourself, is what you want to do with it?" I frowned a little before asking,

"What do you mean?"

"Everyone has a choice in life, Evelyn, and with it you can chose whether to let the past define your future, or you can shape it to the one you want to live. No one wants to live the lie we tell ourselves is living, when in fact it's simply going through the motions." I released a held breath at this, being forced to admit,

"You're right, I know what I have been living is just a lie but I…" I paused, needing to take a breath.

"What… *what is it, Little Dove?*" he asked me softly, running the back of his fingers down my cheek, one I could feel turn wet as I blinked away the first of my tears. So, I let my forehead fall to his chest as I told him quietly,

"*…I don't know how to stop running from the lie.*" At this he cupped the back of my head, holding me to him as he whispered down at the top of my head,

"*Then trust me to free you of it.*" I felt more tears fall before telling him,

"I can't." At which he sighed before kissing my forehead, and just as he was about to give me the space he thought I would need, I did something I had never done.

I gave him a piece of me no one had ever received

before. Something that started by laying my hand on his arm, stopping him from stepping away from me. He looked down at my hand resting there on his forearm, as if the sight meant a great deal to him. Well, if that was the case then I really hoped my next actions meant even more, because I braved to tell him,

"But I can trust you with a different part of me." Then before I chickened out, I reached down and untied my robe, slowly pulling the knot free and letting the sides fall open, baring more than I ever had to a man before.

A moment of shock rolled through his features before his eyes made the slow and sensual journey down my body. Eyes that heated quickly and even started to glow slightly, making me fight the impulse to take a step back at the sight.

He won't hurt you, Evie.

He doesn't want to hurt you.

I told myself this, adding to the voice in my head that the hungry look in his eyes was nothing more than of a sexual nature. And to have such a man look at me in such a way, it was almost like taking a sexual drug for the effect it had over me.

"It's dangerous to tempt me with such a sight if this isn't what you want... *if you're not yet ready to be mine,*" he warned, which was why I decided to be braver still, and I answered him by slipping the rest of my robe from my shoulders. And this time, giving him everything I could in that moment. Something he drank in and consumed as his eyes glowed an even deeper shade of dark blue, a glowing hue in the centers.

Then before I could take another unsure breath, he had me in his hold. One hand embedding itself in my damp hair, and the other arm he used to wrap around me before his lips claimed my own. It was a kiss that doused all my fears into the cage he was slowly building around them. A kiss that I wanted to drown in and grin knowing the last breath I took was the one he gave me. And as if hearing my thoughts, his hands left their hold of me and took a very different one. Meaning suddenly my back was against the window, with my wrists taken in his hands before he lifted them above my head, holding me prisoner in the most divine way.

I gasped and it was one he swallowed down as if I was as much of a drug to him as he was to me. The cold glass at my naked back wasn't enough to cool the heat building up in my core. I felt as if I was burning up for this man and the feeling was one I wasn't used to. Of course, I had pleasured myself, knowing the feeling of a building orgasm and the addictive gratification of its release.

But this…

Christ, it was something else entirely.

However, I knew this was just the tip of the iceberg, and I wanted more. I wanted it all! Everything in him, I wanted for myself. Every single thing he had to give me. Which was why I couldn't help but make my own demands, moaning the moment his lips made their way to my neck.

"More." His answer to this was a growl against my skin before his hands were put to better use than holding me pinned to the window. Hands that reached down and grabbed my ass, using this hold to lift me up, making me spread my legs open so he could step into me. I did the natural thing and wrapped my legs around him, feeling his length tucked to my core… and right where it needed to be.

However, there was one problem, one I was brave enough to point out…

"You're wearing too many clothes." At this he chuckled once before gripping me tighter and using this hold on me to carry me over to the bed.

"You're right," he agreed the moment he lowered my back to the bed. Then he stood above me, soon awarding me with the delicious sight of him unbuttoning his shirt, one I wished he would have just ripped off just so I didn't have to wait. But then, didn't the saying go, that good things come to those who wait? Fuck, I hoped so.

A proven fact when he finally removed his shirt and awarded me with the glorious sight of his naked torso. One that was a powerhouse of rippling muscles that weren't exactly a surprise to see, but knowing this didn't detract from the sight. Or the way I shamefully gasped, unable to help myself. He was utter perfection and it continued to get better as he unbuckled his belt, the act not only erotic but also dominating. The way he ran the length of leather through his hands as he pulled it free did things to me.

His thoughts soon became clear when he told me,

"Soon I will use this to tie you to me but, for now, I want both hands free for what I plan to do to you." His words naturally shocked me, making me wonder what he truly meant. But more than anything, I wanted to know if he would follow through with the sexual thought. Of course, it didn't take long for this wonder to leave me as he threw the belt to the pillow before dropping to his knees.

I was about to ask what he was doing, until it became quite obvious when he took hold of my ankles and dragged me to the very edge of the bed. Then he tossed my legs over his shoulders and spread me wide open for him. The embarrassment I felt must have easily shown on my face, because he smirked up at me as if he liked what he saw.

"I have never..." I tried to explain, soon transforming that smirk into a full-blown grin, one that looked as if belonged on a villain more than the hero he had been only moments before.

"I'm glad to hear it," he informed me.

"You are?" I asked, surprised, considering I was worried that my lack of experience would have been a turn off for him.

"Indeed, for now I know I will be the only one who knows the taste of you." I blushed at this, until his eyes lowered over my sex and then I gasped when he gripped the backs of my thighs, pushing my legs up against my belly and exposing me even further.

"Mine," he growled down at the core of me, before suddenly his head was there and his lips were kissing my quivering flesh.

"Oh god!" I cried at the contact, feeling something so foreign, so new, it was out of this world as his tongue explored every inch of me. I couldn't help but try and arch my back, but with his bruising hold on my legs, I felt helpless to anything but take the pleasure he wanted to give me. The delicious path his tongue took up the lengths of my soaked folds, before coming to tease that glorious bundle of nerves. But then when he took the sensitive little clitoris into his mouth, I cried out the second my orgasm erupted.

"Ohhh... oh... yes... I'm coming!" I shouted as it hit, making my legs start to shake despite his hold. But then as the feeling rolled away from me, the oversensitive feeling took me, making me try to pull myself free. However, my reactions were met with displeasure, and suddenly a strong arm shot out and landed on my center, pinning me down in a different way.

It was a dominate action that came with a warning growl.

"I am not done with you yet… my perfect meal."

CHAPTER 15
PERFECTION

"*I am not done with you yet... my perfect meal,*" he reprimanded, his tone both scary and a total turn on.

I might have spoken, might have said something to this, but then his large hand cupped my breast and pinched my nipple, making whatever was on the tip of my tongue, end in a loud moan. A sound that only continued when I felt his lips back on me, his tongue probing and fucking me like he was a man possessed. Of course, I had fingered myself before, but this... *this was something else!*

This was incredible.

But then soon, his tongue was replaced with his own thick finger and his lips latched onto my clit once more. Needless to say, this sent me hurdling off the edge like a fucking rocket!

"Yes... yes... yes... Fuck YES!" I screamed this time as it was more powerful than the first. But when he wouldn't stop, I knew I was hitting my limit, forcing me to shamelessly plead with him,

"Please... please... I can't... I..." However, his answer to this was to growl back over my soaked sex,

"I will say when you have had enough, for it will be of my choosing." I swallowed hard, nearly choking as I gasped straight after a second finger entered me. My ass flew from the bed as my back arched up. His hand quickly left my breast so he could plant a heavy palm over my sex, pushing me back down and pinning me once more to where he wanted me. Then he started to finger fuck me, thrusting into me and curling his fingers in a way that I felt it rubbing against something new inside me.

"Please... oh god... no, I can't... I can't... fuck, yes... don't stop, don't stop... DON'T STOP! AAAHHH!" I screamed, quickly changing my mind on him stopping as my third orgasm burst from me unexpectedly, this time making me shake from the force of it. I continued to pant, completely spent of energy and I felt as if I could have slept for a week. But then he finally released me, and I forced myself to look down at him, finding him sucking on his fingers as if the magic they'd created produced liquid candy. Fuck me, it was the hottest fucking sight I had ever seen in my life.

Well, that was until he stood up and started to rid himself of his slacks, pushing them down along with the waist band of his underpants. The sight it freed was one that had me sucking back a startled breath. But he must have seen the wide-eyed look of fear for himself as he took his length in his own hand. The length and girth were far more than I believed even possible to take. The size far exceeding his own large hand as he pumped his palm down this cock, one that looked more like a weapon for breaking virginial, naive girls.

"Don't worry, sweetheart, you were made for me," he said clearly, knowing exactly what I had been thinking.

"I beg to differ... *emphasis on the begging part,*" I said, making him grin, and it was purely bad to the bone. I even found myself shifting further up the bed, and I wasn't one hundred percent sure it wasn't to get away from him or not. Especially when I heard his shoes hit the floor, followed by the rest of his clothes, knowing what was coming next. I even flinched when I felt the bed dip, seeing now the way he crawled over me, like some predator defending its kill. Christ, he was glorious, all perfect naked skin over rippling muscle, he looked like someone had sculptured him out of clay. I was afraid to touch him, as if it wouldn't be allowed and God himself would strike me down for daring to touch such perfection.

His large shoulders and the bulk of his arms, including those powerful bulging biceps... well, it was no wonder he could pick me up with ease the way he did. But then, they looked to come in handy now, as he leaned all his weight on one forearm next to my head, so he was free to dip his hand down my body. I then felt him run two fingers between my soaked folds, making me shudder beneath him at the sexual contact. But before he could do more, his fingers left me and I was soon no longer questioning why.

"I want you to taste the perfection I have tasted... *open.*" He ended this on an order as held out his two fingers to my lips, a pair now dripping with evidence of my multiple orgasms. I had to say I was shocked enough that my lips parted. And whether it was an invitation or not, he took it as one, slipping his two fingers inside my mouth. I had to open wide to accommodate them and his eyes heated at the sight, as if he was imagining something else there instead. Something I knew without a doubt I would struggle to take. But then from the looks of him, that idea only added to the sexual kick he would get.

But I also found myself questioning why, despite my innocence in the bedroom, why did I find the idea so hot? Why did I find the taste of myself being licked from his fingers such a fucking turn on? Despite not being naive enough to know that it was a thing and that many people participated. A man's dominance over me in the bedroom hadn't been something I thought I would ever want.

But as for myself... *fucking addictive.*

So, I licked his fingers clean until he pulled them from between my lips, making me suck tighter around the digits. Doing so as if trying to give him a taste of what I hoped was to come the next time a piece of him came near my eager mouth. And with the way his eyes glowed a brighter shade of blue again, I would say he didn't miss the want in my actions.

And I didn't miss his.

Not when those same fingers threaded into my hair before making a fist, pulling my head back so he could consume my lips, letting me taste myself yet again. His kiss turned hard as I felt the weight of not only his body against my own but also the weight of his cock lying against my stomach. I swear the thing was pulsating in its own eagerness to get inside me, and the thought made me brave enough to want to take it in my hand and touch it. Something

I did and was met with a hiss of pleasure as he tore his mouth from mine to make the sexual sound.

"I am trying so fucking hard here," he gritted out, making my eyes widen in shock before braving to ask,

"Trying?"

"To go slow, baby," he answered, putting his forehead to my own, and I sucked in a quick breath at the admission. So, I told him softly, with whispered words over his lips,

"Fuck going slow." Then I pumped my hand down his cock as if to seal my words as being a promise. This made him growl before suddenly he was up, and I lost my hold on him. I thought I had said something wrong, that was until he started spreading my legs around him, now lining up the head of his cock with my dripping core.

"Relax, baby, I won't hurt you." I purposely did as he asked and when he felt my leg muscles relax slightly, he praised,

"Good, Little Bird… *that's good."* He hummed this second part as he started to push himself inside me, and I arched my neck back as the feeling of being deliciously stretched flooded me. But then I soon realized this feeling would only increase, because there was a lot more to go before being seated fully inside me.

"Soooo fucking good," he practically purred as he pushed the next few inches inside, making me suck in a quick breath. Then he ran his hands down my breasts, gripping onto them as he pushed further inside me and I was at least thankful he hadn't just slammed into me. Especially knowing now how that would have felt because it was on the cusp of being too much. But then he lowered himself back down over me and told me gently,

"I have to take your barrier and I cannot do that gently." I released another held breath and nodded, unable to say the words. However, in the end, it was the words he wanted,

"Tell me to stop, Evie." I shook my head telling him no.

"I want your words, Little Bird." I swallowed hard and told him,

"I... want... you." At this he closed his eyes as if this had meant the world to him. Which also meant that his answer made this one of the most beautiful moments of my life as his lips came to rest at my ear.

"I love you, my Siren," he whispered and the second he did, two things stole my breath, because his words of love were followed with him pushing himself the rest of the way inside me. Now taking my virginity in the most perfect way. My head fell back and my mouth opened on a silent cry.

"The pain will ease, my sweet girl," he cooed down at me, smoothing back my hair from my face and running the pad of his thumb across my freckled cheek.

"I'm... I'm okay," I told him, panting through the uncomfortable pain, making him place his forehead to mine. This was before he started moving once more and, this time, making sure to go as slow as he was able. An action that replaced the discomfort with a building pleasure that made me want more. My hand found its way to his ass, digging my nails in the fleshy muscle. This was at the same time I pleaded,

"More... give me more, Ryker." At this his eyes widened in surprise before they narrowed in a heated way. His animalistic growl ended up vibrating against my neck, with the flesh there being held in between his teeth. This was at the same time he started to move faster, making me uncharacteristically wish he would bite me for real, not really understanding where that primal thought came from.

Again, the feeling built inside me, only this time it was different. Not like when having his lips latched onto my clit but a different type of pleasure. One I felt more in control of, like I was the one who needed to let go of it and trust him with drawing it out of me. So, I tightened my legs around him and started to meet his thrusts with my own, being the one to chase the orgasm, until finally he told me,

"Let it go... trust me and let it go, Evie." As soon as he spoke, it was like opening the flood gates for euphoria to consume me.

"YES, RYKER!" I cried out as it waved through me, making me spasm around his length, one that was soon pumping his own release inside me.

"FUCK! ARHHH!" he growled, throwing his head back and roaring at the ceiling, the cords on his neck bulging from the strain. Witnessing his release was fascinating and I was riveted to the sight of his pleasure. But then he relaxed into me, held me tight, and sealed this moment like I was living in a dream...

"You were perfection."

CHAPTER 16
WET DREAMS

"I would ask where you got your skills at doing this from, but I am afraid I won't like the answer," I teased as he rubbed my shoulders and neck from behind with soapy hands. Hands that admittedly felt like magic.

"I can assure you, there has been no practice involved, for whatever skills I have, it is merely stemmed from the need to touch you," he answered, making me groan and I let my head fall back against his naked, wet shoulder.

"Seriously, how is it you always know the most perfect thing to say?" I only half complained, making him chuckle. But then I turned quickly just as he was about to speak and put my hand over his mouth,

"No, don't say it, I'm stopping you before the next Casanova sonnet comes out of your mouth." He grinned against my palm, before I felt his fingers wrap around my wrist so he could pull my hand away from his lips.

"I believe Shakespeare was better known for his sonnets and Casanova for his…"

"Yes, yes, I get it and, besides, you have already exercised that particular skill tonight, one I definitely know didn't come from the need to touch me." At this he raised a brow and gave me a skeptical look in return, before dipping his head closer to me.

"Mm... if you believe it stems solely from my past experience then answer me this, how was it that making love to you felt like the first time all over again, and was the best sex of my life, when all else before you pale in comparison?" I couldn't help but blush at that, as well as my heart doing backflips and high fiving all my other organs. Obviously, my sex got special recognition.

"Well, I doubt that's what the ladies thought," I replied, making him scoff a laugh.

"Are you mocking me?" I warned, wondering where this new playful side of me had come from. Although, one look at the wet naked body behind me, I could very well imagine. He just seemed to bring it out in me.

"I wouldn't dare, you are far too fearsome," he teased, making me splash him anyway, seeing as we were currently in his big bath together. This after he had carried me in here shortly after making love to me, telling me that it would help with the tenderness between my legs. Of course, he had been right, but as to when exactly he'd had chance to run the water during sex, was anyone's guess. It was impossible actually, seeing as the last time I had been in there, the tub had been depressingly empty.

So, the moment he placed me in the bath, I was shocked to find I wouldn't be doing this alone, as he soon slide in right behind me. However, my embarrassment didn't last long. Although it was long enough that when he picked up a cloth and started to clean in between my thighs I tried to take the cloth off him. To which he kissed my neck and hummed against my flesh,

"Be good for me and let me take care of you."

"But why? I mean, I can just…"

"Because it brings me pleasure, that is why… now relax, My Dove."

I couldn't help but do as he told me when I felt his hands all over me, and cleaning the mess he had made was just the start. He also insisted on washing me, rubbing soft soap suds all over my body in a maddeningly sensual way. And to the point I was near squirming against him. A fact he most definitely seemed to enjoy.

Not long after this and I did relax, getting used to his touch and his gentle teasing. I even started to feel confident enough to do the same back. Like now, as I picked up his hand and started playing with his fingers as we talked about lighthearted things. As if we were both purposely avoiding the serious questions, ones we knew at some point we would both have to face answering. But then Ryker clearly had something else on his mind.

"Tell me, for I am curious, why the Ingwaz rune?" he asked, rubbing the pad of his thumb over the tattoo on the inside my wrist. Of course, he knew that I had five of them, all in different designs, ones he had kissed or stroked not long after sex. Tattoos he had also washed too.

"Where there is a will, there is a way," I told him, sighing back into him as he hummed in acknowledgement.

"You play with this one whenever you're nervous," he stated, shocking a breath from me at the fact he noticed.

"It gives me strength and courage," I told him, and the arm he had resting at my belly pulled me tighter at that.

"Of course, it is also the symbol for knowledge but also for divine energy, something I have a feeling I will need a lot of around you, if our time in the bedroom is anything to go by." At this he chuckled, making me jiggle against him.

"I did wonder at the hospital if I would discover more of them painted on your skin," he mused, running his hand along the one on my hip.

"Ah yes the hospital… tell me, was this before or after your thoughts of kidnapping me, hmm?" I said in a teasing yet pointed tone.

"I am unsure, for I have had so many thoughts of kidnapping you since the first time I kissed you," he replied in a musing tone, making me turn to look up at him and ask softly,

"Then why didn't you?" he laughed at this and told me,

"It certainly wasn't through lack of trying." I had to grin at that.

"Ah yes, I did manage to elude you a time or two." A reply he growled at, making me chuckle. I was quickly getting used to the sounds and the differences between them.

"Yes, well it was not a skill I was praising you for having, that was for damn certain," he grumbled, making me bite my lip to stop from smiling. But because I needed to express how I felt, I did this the only way I knew how. So, I told him,

"Well, I'm not running anymore." To which I felt his hand come to my face before turning me to face him, and awarding me to a look that would have made my legs weaken. Because it was clear that saying this had meant a great deal to him. Something that was confirmed when he lowered his lips to mine and spoke over them, sealing his gratitude with a kiss.

"Thank you." Then once it was finished, I gripped onto his shoulders to stop him from going too far and told him boldly,

"I know how you can really thank me." Another growl I understood was my answer as his grip tightened on me. But despite the want I saw in his heated gaze, he still asked,

"You're not still sore?"

I shook my head, telling him no, I wasn't. Because despite the tenderness, it was nothing compared to the pain of wanting him and having to wait. Which was why I decided to be bolder still, this time turning fully so I could straddle his lap. His hands instantly came to my hips, holding me there as if he feared I would change my mind.

Like I would.

Like I ever could.

Not now I knew what it was like to be his. To feel this way. It was as if my soul was singing, my blood carrying that song straight to my heart. I felt powerful. I felt strong. But most of all, *I felt happy.* Truly happy, and not just the feeling I told myself I felt.

I felt like I was finally living a life.

Not a lie.

Because he was my truth. My anchor to this happy place I never wanted to leave. Which was why I needed to feel that deeper connection once more, just to assure myself that it hadn't all been a dream. A dream that wouldn't shatter the moment I opened my eyes, for this time the sight they saw was my incredible reality. A reality I could touch, starting with my hand dipping under the water between us so I could take his hard cock in hand. A steely length, more than ready to take me. Then I guided it to my pussy, one aching and needy for him.

"Gods," he hissed the moment my hand wrapped around him. I lifted myself up, keeping the head positioned at the ready to lower myself down over him. His hands gripped me tighter the moment I did, making us both sigh with pleasure.

"My insatiable girl," he hummed against my neck, before kissing his way down to my breasts. And as if it was the most natural response in the world, my back arched, pressing them further into his face. I was quickly rewarded for this bold behavior when he got the hint by taking a nipple into his mouth.

I cried out at the first bite of pain his teeth created as he rolled the hard tip between them. This combined with the way I lowered down over his hard length was enough to have me near coming in seconds. My hands at his shoulders tensed and my nails drew lines across his skin, making him growl against my nipple.

"Oh shit… I'm so sorry, I didn't mean…" I started to say when I realized I might have hurt him. But he left my breast and snagged the back of my neck in a tight grip, dragging my lips to his,

"Don't ever apologize to me again, not when you sit upon my cock and gift me with the pleasure it gives you," he ordered sternly, making me gasp at the dark, commanding edge to his voice.

"I…" I was cut off as he growled down at me,

"Now make me fucking bleed!" he snarled before kissing me deeper, at the same time gripping my ass in his hands and

taking over my movements by lifting me up and down over him. I moaned in his mouth as the pleasure built until only seconds later, and it ended in a scream as my first orgasm ripped through me. Which meant this time when my nails scratched across his skin, I couldn't help the marks I made, throwing my head back and crying out. He feasted on my breasts once more, creating one release to roll straight into the next.

I swear, I was near mindless as I continued to come, missing the exact moment he did, as his roar matched that of my screams. Our movements slowed and I let my head fall forward on to his chest, panting through the wonderful aftermath. His large hand cupped the back of my head, holding me tenderly to him. And as a result, I felt my eyes start to close.

Now falling asleep to the sound of his beating heart.

One that I knew…

Loved me.

CHAPTER 17
WHAT A DIFFERENCE A DAY MAKES

That night, falling asleep in his arms was one of the most blissful experiences I had ever had. I had never slept with anyone before yet, despite this, being held by Ryker I knew was on another level. Because, I had never felt so safe, so treasured before in my entire life.

It started when I woke up to find myself being carried from the bathroom wrapped in a large towel. I even found myself warning,

"We will get the bed wet."

"When it comes to my bed, the only thing I care for is that you are in it. Now ssshh and go back to sleep, Little Dove," he told me, making me smile as he lay me down. But then, when he didn't follow me, I sat up and found my hand reaching out to take his hand, stopping him from walking away. His reaction to this was to look down at my hand in his before his eyes rose to meet my own, the question there was easy to see.

"I will be right back," he told me softly, running a finger down my cheek and across my lips.

"Where are you going?" I asked in what I knew was a vulnerable tone I could do nothing to hide.

"I need to speak with Vander, to see how he has handled things," he said, looking toward the window. The hard lines of his jaw made it seem as though he was gritting his teeth as the memory of me being attacked came back to him.

"You mean… *your ex?"* I asked, approaching the touchy subject.

"She was an ex of nothing, Evelyn, please believe that." I nodded before asking the insecure question,

"Will you… erm… see her?" Then I looked him up and down in hopes to remind him that he was still half naked and only wearing a towel hanging low around his hips. At this he released a soft sigh before reaching out once more to cup my cheek before he told me,

"No, I will not see her, for I fear if I do then I will wring her scrawny neck." I scoffed at that.

"I merely wish to be assured that she has been removed from the estate," he told me, making me release a deep sigh that definitely held relief.

"Okay," I said, feeling assured that he would be doing just that.

"I won't be long, Little Dove," he said, kissing the top of my head before turning and striding from the room. Then once alone, I flopped back on the bed flinging my arms out to my sides and sighing in contentment.

"In the words of good old Dinah Washington, what a difference a day makes," I said smiling to myself, and I had to wonder if I also woke up smiling. Well, if not, then I certainly did after finding two things, one of which was the feel of Ryker holding me from behind. And the second,

He made good on his word, only instead of using his belt...

He had tied our hands together with a length of gold silk.

⚜

The next morning, I woke with the feel of someone stroking a hand down my face and instantly it made me yawn. My reply to this was a chuckle as I stretched out before opening my eyes to the delectable sight of Ryker who was unfortunately dressed. But this was one of the rare occasions that I was seeing him wearing anything but a suit. Light blue denim encased long, muscular legs, and a navy-blue knit sweater barely hid the rest. The outline of his powerful torso was hard to hide when you were as big as Ryker. He looked nothing short of dreamy, making me question my state of mind as definitely being awake or not. His dark hair was styled back, giving him that sexy clean cut authoritative air that would soon have me squirming again.

"Good morning, Little Dove," he said, smiling down at me before taking a seat on the edge of the bed next to me. However, when he placed a hand the other side of me and began leaning down to kiss me, I covered my mouth quickly. It was a denial that he didn't look pleased with as he raised a questioning brow and, damn, even that was sexy.

"Morning breath," I told him from behind my hand. And his response to this was to first shackle my wrist before forcing my hand out to the side, growling down at me,

"Fuck morning breath." Then he kissed me and by the end of it I had to agree with him. Especially considering by the time he pulled back, he left me breathless and needy.

"I brought you breakfast," he told me, encouraging me to look toward the sitting area where I found a tray on the coffee table.

"Wow, I didn't take you for the domesticated type," I said, winking at him and making him grin.

"Well, if by domesticated you mean ordering the kitchen staff to cook for you, then yes, I am most definitely husband material," he said winking back at me and making me blush. And well, it had nothing to do with the wink but all to do with the word *husband*. But then I remembered one of the things that woke me up in the night, and it was after discovering that I was tied to him.

"We need to talk," I stated, making him look amused and not in the least bit concerned by my tone.

"Oh?" he hummed.

"I think I better get dressed first," I said, making him stand and hold his arm out toward the walk-in closet.

"By all means, be my guest." I frowned at this, before lifting the sheet as if pointing out the obvious problem. However, when he didn't get the hint, I told him,

"Erm… I'm still naked."

"And?" His tone said it all.

"And I am naked," I repeated, making him smirk.

"A beautiful sight I have burned to memory, I can assure you." Again, my cheeks heated at that.

"Thank you but… I… well, it's the daytime and I don't…" At this he interrupted me on a chuckle before covering his eyes in a dramatic gesture, asking me,

"Will this help?" I rolled my eyes before warning him,

"Fine, but no peeking."

"I wouldn't dream of it," he teased with that bad boy grin

of his firmly in place and not likely to go anytime soon. So, I decided to be quick, tossing the sheet aside and running into the closet.

"Holy shit!" I shouted, making him ask from the bedroom,

"Is there a problem?"

"It's filled with clothes!" I exclaimed, making him laugh.

"That is usually the point of a closet... or so I have heard," he teased dryly.

"Yes, thank you, Captain Obvious, but they are all woman's clothes," I told him, raising my voice over my shoulder.

"And?" he asked like this meant nothing but obvious facts.

"And unless what you have to tell me about yourself is that you're a growly, cross dressing wizard with glowing eyes, then I would say this is a bit odd." I heard the burst of laughter coming from behind me, making me spin quickly. Then the second I saw him standing there, leaning against the doorframe casually, I reached for the first thing I could grab off the rack, holding it to myself.

"It's pretty, Dove, but a bit much for breakfast, don't you think?" he said smirking, making me look down at myself to see I was holding a red sequin cocktail dress in front of me.

"Actually, I always dress like this for breakfast... now as for dinner, well I'm normally a sweats and tank top, kinda girl," I retorted, making him grin.

"As long as you're a naked in my bed kinda girl, I couldn't give a shit what you wear, as long as I get to strip it off you." Once again, I couldn't keep the sappy grin off my face.

"Well, I just usually wear my clothes held up to me like this… unless of course I have been doing it wrong all these years," I teased back, making him unable to hold back the laughter again. But then he stalked closer to me until all that stood between us was a length of red sequins. Then he took hold of the hanger and told me,

"Not if all it takes to get your naked is this…" Then he threw the dress aside and yanked me hard up against him, kissing me once again. But then before he let it get to a place where we were fucking like teenagers on the floor of his closet as if hiding from our parents' downstairs (something my college roommate told me she did once), he told me,

"These clothes were bought for you, so you will find everything in your size and hopefully to your taste. So, get dressed, my funny little bird." Then he finished this with a slap to my ass, before turning around and walking out the door, leaving me looking at all the clothes with my mouth hanging open in utter shock.

He was crazy.

Well, at least I managed to walk out of there wearing a gold silk robe with an armful of clothes so I could get ready in the bathroom. Where, unsurprisingly, I found everything I needed, including what I wanted the most.

A new toothbrush.

After brushing my teeth, I blushed again at the thought of the underwear selection in the closet as I dressed. I went with something a little less 'sex kitten' when I grabbed a white lace set. Something I promptly covered with a pair of skinny indigo jeans that fit me perfectly and, I swear,m were the softest denim I had ever worn. To this I added a white crop top that showed part of my, belly and a tan-colored belt that had gold buckle of two interlocking circles. Then I grabbed a suede, lightweight waterfall jacket that was army green and hung open at the sides. As for my hair, I did what I usually did and plaited it to one side after brushing all the knots out from letting it dry naturally in bed.

"So, my things?" I asked from the bathroom, sitting on the toilet seat as I zipped up a pair of tan-suede ankle-boots. And I asked this because I was curious as to what he would say.

"Well, they aren't at that shitty motel you will never spend another minute at, that's for damn certain," he replied firmly, making me look at the closet when walking past, not seeing them there but ignoring this fact and instead commenting,

"So, this kidnapping of yours I see took a lot of planning." Then I walked closer, joining him by the sitting area where he looked to be drinking a cup of coffee.

"You look beautiful," he said the moment his eyes rose from the paper and scanned the length of me, making me blush as his gaze heated at the sight of me.

"Erm... thank you but the clothes, it's too much and I can't accept..." I stopped mid-flow as he placed down his paper and walked over to me.

"You can and you will," he said firmly.

"But..." I tried to argue but he quickly interrupted me.

"That night, you helped me despite what the consequences may be, and consequences were exactly what you found... *Because of me.*"

"Ryker, I..." At this he placed two fingers against my lips and stopped me.

"Your whole life was uprooted after you were attacked,

and I wasn't there to stop it. I wasn't there to protect you, despite knowing deep down that I should have been," he told me, and I couldn't help but near melt because of it.

"But you weren't to know," I reasoned after wrapping my palm around his wrist and pulling his hand down from my face.

"Perhaps not, but that doesn't mean that the fact doesn't weigh heavily upon my soul." I looked back at the closet and told him,

"I don't need compensation, Ryker."

"Good, because that isn't what that is," he established quickly, making me ask,

"Then what is it?"

"This is the beginning of me taking care of what's mine." His answer had me swallowing hard.

"What's yours?" I asked quietly, and at this he gripped my hips and pulled me into him before growling down at me,

"Yes, *what is mine."*

"Ryker, I am not a possession to be bought," I told him, hoping that this wasn't what he thought this was.

"No, you're the priceless treasure to be found… and guess what, Little Dove? *I found you first,"* he told me on a growl of words, making me shiver. It was a reaction that continued as he claimed my lips like he usually did when things between us became this intense.

"Now let me care for you… *please,"* he added once he had finished kissing me in favor of doing the same to my neck.

"Tell me yes, Evelyn." His whispered words against my skin were just not something I could fight against anymore,

and I found myself agreeing with a slight nod. One he had been waiting for as he took my hand in his and walked me over to where he had been sitting.

"Thank you... now come, eat, for you must be hungry."

"Well, I ate a buffet worth of food in your office building," I reminded him, making him grin,

"Yes, and at my request for I knew you had missed breakfast, as well as far too many proper meals to count." I frowned at this, asking,

"You have been watching me?"

"Are you really shocked?" he asked, and I admitted in a deflated tone,

"No, I guess not."

"Hey now, let there be no reasons for us to dwell on our turbulent past." I felt my face speak for me before my words followed,

"Easier for you to say when you were the one stalking me."

"That maybe so, but even you cannot deny the attraction between us from the very beginning." Okay, so he had me there.

"Then maybe you should have simply asked me out," I pointed out, and he laughed at that before reminding me once again,

"Ah yes, the thief and the runaway, tell me, Evie, when was I to have the chance?"

"Okay, so that's a fair point, I grant you," I admitted, making him smirk,

"But if you like, I would be honored should you grant me the pleasure of your company tonight, as I... *date you.*" I sucked in a quick breath and reminded him,

"But I didn't think you dated, least of all me... your words, remember?"

"You took my words to heart, I see, and most literal, but I should have explained better. I am not dating you, Evelyn." I couldn't help but frown at this.

"Then what is this?" I was almost too afraid to ask but then I was even more afraid of what he would say in return.

"I have claimed you," he stated as if it was that simple. As if I knew what that even meant.

"Claimed me... you mean sex?" I asked with a little shake of my head.

"No, sweet girl, I don't mean sex. I mean this is the start of you and me with no end-to-be in sight."

"I still don't understand," I admitted, quickly feeling as if life was spiraling out of my control and totally in his, with him standing at the center of all that was left of my life. And well, in truth, I didn't know if that was a bad thing or not.

"Evelyn, I don't want you as my girlfriend, I want you as my..."

"Ryker!" Van said, shouting his name, interrupting us when he flung open the door. The moment was lost and made me wonder what he had been about to say. As for Ryker, he stood quickly in front of me and growled,

"How dare you just...!"

"Come quick! There isn't time," Vander said, looking concerned, making Ryker react to this.

"Why, what has happened?" he questioned, making me gasp when we both received our answer...

"The front gates, they are under attack!"

CHAPTER 18
LETTING GO

Ryker gritted his teeth and told Van,

"I will follow, but I want no less than five guards at her door."

"On it," he replied, pulling a cell phone from his jeans' pocket and making my mouth drop,

"Five guards, that's a bit excessive, don't you think?" I said looking to Ryker, however, he ignored this and took me by the tops of my arms, before pulling me closer. Then he told me strictly,

"Wait here, I will be back for you."

"But wait, what about you?" I asked, but when he granted me a questioning look, I quickly admitted,

"I don't want you getting hurt." I knew the moment I said this that it must have meant something to him because his features softened.

"I know you won't understand the reasons why yet, but just know that nothing they do can hurt me." I frowned at this, unable to help my memories from resurfacing.

"But the bathroom…" I argued, making him close his eyes and say in a strained tone,

"That threat was taken care of."

"But…" Of course I tried to argue this, but was quickly shut down,

"No, no more worry for my safety," he stated firmly, making me point out in a small voice,

"But you worry for mine." And this was when he hit me with the truth, confirming what I already knew but was lacking the details on.

"Because you are human, and I… *I am not."*

I sucked in a quick breath, trying not to view his words as an insult. But then I had to admit, that it still stunk as he was classing being human as a weakness.

"Evie, please don't look at me like that?" he asked gently, making me turn my head away and step out of his reach.

"Well, that's the thing, Ryker, I don't know how to look at you considering I don't even know what you are. Or is it too hard for a lowly human like me to understand?" I knew it was a low blow the second I said it, but I couldn't help it. I was hurt. And from the looks of it, now so was he.

"Damn it, Evelyn, that's not what I meant!" he snapped, making me sigh.

"I…" I was about to apologize when he interrupted me,

"Look, I don't have time for this now, I have to aid my people in the fight. But I want you to stay here… no running from me, Evelyn." My head snapped up at this and I asked in shock,

"You think I would run now?"

"Well, we will soon find out, won't we?" he said, and

before I could retreat, he stepped into me and tagged me around the waist with one muscular arm,

"Why will we soon find out, Ryker?" I asked, making him sigh before telling me,

"Because you want to know what I am, and I can only hope that you're ready for it." I swallowed hard even as he kissed my forehead as way of goodbye. Then he made his way to the door and paused long enough to tell me the truth.

The truth of what he was at his core.

"I am a Demon, Evelyn... A Demon... *that loves you.*" Then after that he left, closing the door and locking it this time before I heard the stern orders barked from behind it,

"No one but me enters through this door, not even her... am I understood?!"

"Yes, Lord Greed," they all said in unison, leaving me standing on the other side with what felt like too much to process. Which meant it wasn't surprising when I backed away until I felt a seat at my legs as I also felt the tears falling down my cheeks. How could this be possible.

A Demon.

He was a Demon.

How could I have fallen in love with a Demon?

I asked myself all these same questions as I fell back into the seat and, instantly, my own reply was a montage of memories of every tender moment that had passed between us. Every single one had remained with me and, despite all the warnings I had run from, it had never been enough to stop me from falling in love with him.

So, the question now was... why did I care what he was? Why did I care when the foundations we both stood upon were as strong as we allowed them to be? Because I had seen him battle against humans that were rotten to the core, but I had never seen him hurt an innocent life. So, what did I really know about Demons, other than every human had the ability of the level of cruelty you would associate with Hell? So again, what did I really know?

The answer was nothing but the way I felt about one.

Which is why I found my voice, now saying aloud,

"I love him." Then I got to my feet and said it louder this time.

"I love him, and I don't care what he is!" But the very last thing I expected was to hear a reply to this…

"Well, how very touching." I froze the second I recognized the voice, one I really shouldn't have been acquainted with. But well, considering it hadn't even been twenty-four hours since meeting the bitch, let's just say I wouldn't be forgetting the murderous voice anytime soon.

Naturally, my fight or flight reaction kicked in and I looked toward the door. Then just as I opened my mouth to scream, taking my first steps toward the guards on the other side of the door, she was at me. She quickly covered my mouth with her hand and stabbed me with something that felt like a needle in the side of my neck. Then after this she dropped me unceremoniously to the floor, making me land hard just as my body quickly started going limp.

Then I watched as she opened a window and ripped off the bedding and started to knot it before fixing it to the ornate iron handle of the window frame. I started to get even more panicked by the inability to speak or move, I was left to just watch, praying this wasn't how she intended on getting me out of here.

However, I wasn't to find out, because by the time she

came back over to me, I could feel myself fading. She crouched low and I could just make out the evil smirk on her face getting closer.

"Shame they want you alive and I won't get so much as a dime for a dead Siren. Of course, with you out of the way, Ryker will find comfort in my arms once more, and all will be back to how it was before you came along. You stupid bitch, you could have ruined everything. Lucky for me, I know enough of Ryker's enemies. Especially when I have something to bargain with and it turns out, there are quite a few people in the market looking for a slut Siren just like you..."

She then leaned down, fisting my hair as she lifted my head so she could whisper in my ear,

"Have fun at the auction now, won't you?" Then she banged my head down on the floor so hard it was quickly...

Lights out.

The next time I woke, I knew it didn't look good for me because I didn't recognize where I was. In fact, it looked like I had been put in some dilapidate hospital room. One with nothing but a thin mattress atop a springy bed frame inside a room that held nothing else but the evidence that whoever was in here before me wanted out. I could tell that due to the eerie scratches at the door and along the walls. Walls that were also moldy around the window and had peeling paint hanging from the ceiling.

It was also as if, at one point, someone had gotten hold of a ball point pen and done a number on the room with it.

As if in their manic state they had been screaming while scribbling in the same spot over and over again. Then on the other side, random numbers in long lines, with sounds written underneath as if this was some evil tune they couldn't get out of their heads.

'Dum dee, dee, dee, dum.'

It was nothing short of creepy and only managed to add to my current nightmare. As soon as feeling started to flow back to my limbs, I sat up on the bed before attempting to stand, needing to brace myself against the wall. I then made my way over to the window, tossing the dirty, torn, once yellow curtains out of my way and praying this was my way out. However, I saw that not only did they not open, but they were also barred so trying to break them would have been pointless. That, and I was also up a few floors with no way of climbing down.

Not like last time.

I tried to take the time to access my situation and not give into panic, just like Arthur had always taught me to do. I rubbed my neck where I found it aching and remembered what she had said to me. Something about needing me alive and the mention of some sort of auction. Well, at the very least, that meant I had some time left. And if I was allowed to hope and by doing so go by my past experiences, then I knew time was all I needed for Ryker to find me.

My Demon protector.

But then I also couldn't help but think back to what else she had done after stabbing me with that needle. Because taking me hadn't been the only thing she had been prepared for, as I remembered her now opening a window and using the sheets as a makeshift rope. At first, I had thought she had needed this to try and get me out of it. But then it hit me that it had nothing to do with her escaping. But everything to do with *making it look like mine.*

"*Fuck,*" I hissed, remembering the last thing Ryker had told me. Admitting to me what he was. And now, well he would open that door and think only one thing again.

He would think that I had done another runner.

That I had run from him.

Which was when I ran to the door and hammered my fist against it, now screaming for Ryker. Screaming for him to come and save me, despite knowing in my heart how little good it would do me. Because now only one question remained. What would he do this time?

Would he hunt me down like always?

Or would he…

Finally let me go?

CHAPTER 19
A TIME FOR LOVE AND A TIME TO KILL
RYKER

"This doesn't make sense," Van stated, mirroring where my own mind was at.

"My thoughts exactly," I agreed as I looked at all the mercenaries now on the floor and begging for their lives. Of course, they had been easy to subdue, despite none of my men, me included, having the ability to control their minds. Just like it had been at the train station. But whoever was pulling the strings of these puppets surely would know that even without this ability, they would have been no match for the power of my men. And as for the mercenaries themselves, it was quite fucking obvious that they had no clue just what they were walking into.

"Something isn't right here, why go to the trouble of casting a spell over these men and using them like pawns... for what gain?" Van asked again, only this time, my mind was trying to calculate all the possible reasons this happened.

"I don't know but it was almost like it was... *a fucking decoy!*" I snarled the moment one of my men pulled back on the sleeve of one of the dead soldiers, and I saw the symbol for the Lega Nera tattooed on his arm. It was known as a Daemonis Cādūceus, which was Latin for A Demon's Herald Wand. A different version of the staff that was typically carried by Hermes, the Olympian deity known in ancient Greek religion and considered the herald of the Gods.

Of course, a Herald was essentially a messenger for a higher power, being either a King or the Gods themselves. Hermes was known as not only being one himself but also for being the protector over other Herald's as well. And not so unlike the Scepter of Dagobert, or should I say, the Scepter of Psychopompós and one I had been searching for, it had the same abilities.

Because Hermes also was known as a psychopomp or in our world, the more adeptly named, 'soul guide', who fundamentally is a conductor of souls, leading them into their Afterlife.

But as for this tattoo, it wasn't the typical symbol of Caduceus, being a short staff that was entwined by two serpents, surmounted by angelic wings. No, this Demonic version was a sword, with hissing snakes baring their fangs at one another at the top of the sword's hilt and with leathery, claw-tipped wings either side. It symbolized secrecy in all dealings when it came to the Lega Nera, with its messengers bound by their soul to take such a vow.

I quickly looked back at the house and snapped,

"They wanted the fucking scepter piece!"

"Well lucky for us, you had it taken to your vault." I released a deep breath knowing this was true, and that no fucker but myself could get into that... *not without my blood.*

"Have them all questioned, casting or not, they will not

withstand one of your interrogations." Van grinned and the ones that were closer enough to overhear started visibly shaking, with one going so far as to actually piss himself.

"Start with that one," I growled, making Van swear,

"Fuck but I hate the smelly ones."

I scoffed at that and started to make my way back to the house, just as Van was ordering his men to have them taken back to the bunker. One used solely as a prison and usually reserved only for my own kind. After all, every Enforcer needed one, as keeping the peace in our sectors was the main part of the job. One right now, that made me grit my teeth as I had far more important matters to be attending to.

Like my Siren.

Ever since I left her, I questioned why the fuck I had chosen that moment to tell her what I was. Of course, part of me knew, and it was something I didn't think I possessed.

It was cowardice.

I hadn't wanted to bear witness to her reaction to it, but instead hoped that time would have aided me. That it would have awarded me with a calmer situation to follow such a conversation. Because, in truth, I didn't know how I would have handled her rejection. How I would have handled the tears and the fear such an admission would warrant in a human?

So, I had taken the easy way out, telling her once I had her in a situation she could not run from. In a peaceful environment that I controlled. To give her the time alone to express her thoughts without me there potentially making it worse. Of course, I knew there would be questions, I was anticipating it and I would be a fool to expect otherwise.

But I also had to be honest with myself because I

couldn't help but feel as if a great weight had been lifted. I *wanted* her to know me. To know of my world and not fear it as one would no doubt do in her situation. I also didn't want her thinking that I had tricked her in any way, making love to her the way I had done without first telling her who or should I say, *what* I was at my core. In truth, I hoped it hadn't mattered and that her feelings for me still remained, regardless of what I was.

Of course, hope can so often be a cruel master for we were all slaves to it, just as I was now. Because after motioning for the guards to open the door, I walked inside, telling my second,

"I won't be long, for I wish to check on Evie before I join you for the interrogation." He nodded, before turning to the guards and telling three of them to get back to their original posts.

"Little Dove, I am back," I said when I briefly scanned the room and didn't find her. So, I walked toward the bathroom door and called her name softly,

"Evelyn?" Then I opened the door and hoped not to frighten her but when I was met with an empty bathroom as well, my heart started to pound in my chest faster. I quickly left and ran to the closet, the last place left to look… snarling in anger when I found it empty. Then after pushing off the door frame I had leaned my weight against when looking, I stormed back into the bedroom, this time seeing something that made my blood fucking boil.

"FUCK!" I roared, running to the open window and pulling the knotted sheet up, seeing now that she had fucking used it to escape!

"RAWHHHH!" I bellowed, making the windows shatter and Van rush inside.

"What's happened?!" he asked, but when his eyes scanned the sheet in my now Demonic hands, I snarled,

"She fucking ran from me!" At this I watched as he closed his eyes as if pained on my behalf. But of course, the fucker knew this would happen. As for me, I was torn halfway between being furious and between being fucking heartbroken! Because I had finally revealed myself, been honest and told her who I was and what had she done...? She fucking ran from me!

I told her I loved her.

But clearly, *she couldn't love a Demon.*

Hence why I grabbed the first thing I could get hold of and threw it against the wall.

"How the fuck did this happen?!" I shouted as tiny clock pieces scattered around the room. But even before the last piece had fallen, I was storming to the door and grabbing hold of the first guard I could reach. Then I quickly pinned the unfortunate soul against the wall hard enough the plaster crumbled around him.

"HOW THE FUCK DID SHE ESCAPE?!" he started to look panicked. shaking his head quickly.

"We... we didn't... hear anything, My Lord."

I snarled in his face, feeling my own changing just as my mouth opened ready to take a fucking bite right out of him. When suddenly, Van was there and placing a hand at my shoulder, one that had started to cover itself in my golden, Demonic armor as the change in me wanted to snap completely.

"Ryker, it wasn't him... let him go."

I snarled at my friend as the feeling of needing someone to blame other than her, pushed hard against me. But he was right. They had done their job, as none of us expected her to risk her fucking life climbing out the fucking window. So, I dropped him and stormed back inside the room, ordering him,

"I want every inch of the grounds searched!"

"I already made the call, Ryker, everyone is on it," Van assured me, and the knowledge should have eased my need to breathe... *but it fucking didn't!*

"She couldn't have gotten far!" I snapped, inhaling hard and trying to control my anger enough to fucking speak. But then I watched as Vander walked over to the window, now where only the frame and her escape route remained.

"She must have taken what happened at the gate as an opportunity to run," I gritted out, now dragging a hand through my hair hard enough it should have fucking hurt. But then nothing hurt like my fucking heart did right now. One I had been so convinced was stone cold and barely fucking beating. *But that had been before her.* Before she had breathed life back into it. Before she had cracked the hard shell of Greed and revealed beneath it a man who loved only one piece of treasure...

Her heart.

The one I thought I had been so close to conquering.

Oh, how fucking wrong I had been! I had never felt a bitterness like it. Like swilling acid and being forced to fucking swallow. I punched the wall in my grief, hoping the satisfaction would last. Needless to say, *that it fucking didn't.*

"I am not so sure that's what happened here," Van said, just as I was pulling my fist from the stone and plaster. Then that cruel master of hope was back, making me turn to him and bark,

"Explain!"

"Did you even see the length of this thing?" he asked, making me frown.

"No, why?"

"Because it's about ten fucking feet off the ground, girl scout is smart, she wouldn't have risked a fall like that. Besides, this was done in a hurry and the last knots left too much space in between," Van told me, making me storm over there to look, asking quickly before I got there to see for myself,

"What are you saying?"

"I'm not sure yet but I know a way of finding out for sure." I narrowed my gaze as he left the window and walked over to the same picture Evie had looked at when seeing my room for the first time. Then Van shocked me as he pulled it from the frame, showing me the hidden wires behind.

"Don't be pissed but I had a camara installed," Van informed me and naturally... *I... SAW... FUCKING... RED!*

"YOU WHAT?!" I seethed, storming over toward him.

"Easy, Ryker, I did it for your own good!" he argued. I grabbed him by the collar of his jacket and raised him up.

"You bugged my fucking room!" At this he closed his eyes before telling me,

"I didn't trust her not to try something... I didn't trust that she wouldn't run again." At this I forced myself to let him go, because he was fucking right. She had run! She had done the very thing he had tried to warn me about. But I hadn't wanted to listen. I had wanted to believe that she cared for me enough to stay.

I felt like a fucking fool.

"But, Ryker, I don't think that's what happened here." I whipped my face back to him and just as he tugged his jacket back down, he told me,

"I had Faron direct the feed straight to my phone, so it wasn't part of the rest of the security. I swear… fuck, man, I swear to you, I never watched it. I never intended to, not unless something like this happened. Ryker, you have to believe me, it was only done as a precaution, so that if she tried to run again, we may find her sooner." I dragged another hand through my hair before nodding, the bitterness still too strong to speak. But he took my response for what it was, as he quickly got his phone out of his pocket and started tapping on the screen.

"I am starting the feed from when we left the room, not before," he told me, as if trying to soothe my Demon's possessiveness, as he knew I would not have allowed anyone to see Evie the way only I was permitted to see her. Her perfection was mine and mine alone and I would tear the eyes out of anyone who dared to try and see it for themselves. I would kill anyone that dared try to take it from me.

Something I realized would soon be the case.

"Shit… Ryker, it wasn't her… she was fucking taken, look!" Van said, making me snatch the phone just in time to see that soon to be dead fucking bitch now stab her with a needle.

"FUCK!" I snarled, forcing myself to ease up on the phone so as I couldn't crush it before I had all the information I needed. I was seeing for myself how she had

tried to make it look like Evie had run. But she hadn't. She hadn't run from me.

She had been fucking taken!

"I will kill her this time," I warned, knowing now my mistake in just having her banished from my territory. Allowing her to convince me that she had no idea that she was my Siren. That she believed Evelyn to be a mortal intruder and nothing more. Damn my fucking weakness!

"Yeah, well that's a given," Van agreed, but then we watched as she pulled a glowing red stone from under the neck of her dress, one I instantly recognized.

"Fuck! She has the heart stone!" I snarled.

"The heart stone?" Van questioned, making me realize now that I had yet to explain what fully happened in the bathroom back in Portland, Oregon.

"It is a stolen piece of Annika Empusa's heart."

"Fuck! How the fuck did someone get close enough to steal a piece of your father's sorcerer?!" Van hissed, reacting just as I had.

"I don't know much of the details surrounding it, as she explained very little to me and, at the time, I was more concerned with getting back to my Siren," I told him, something that only managed to berate me with even more questions.

"You're talking about when you passed out, something you still haven't explained how that shit even happened, I might add."

"The fight back in Portland, it was Azhdar."

"Fuck, Ryker!" He swore through his teeth this time.

"When I walked in, I found him trying to drag Evelyn into a portal, one the heart stone managed to create. And before you ask, no, I have no fucking clue how. I only know that the big bastard had the piece of the heart and used it against me like a weapon." He frowned at this.

"A weapon?" he questioned, and like most rulers of our sectors and those who held positions of power, admitting what I did next did not come fucking easy for me. Even to my best friend.

"It had the power to overcome me, Van."

He hissed again, startled by the realization that there was something out there that could bring me down.

"Overcome you how?" Van asked, narrowing his gaze once again.

"I can only assume that being linked to my father's realm, it felt connected to me and not in a good way… as if it was draining my vessel of my Demon and trying to drag him back to Hell that way," I told him, going back to that day and almost shivering at the memory of that haunting feeling. It was as if the very essence of me was being stripped away, ready to leave a mere lost, empty shell behind.

"Shit, but how does something even wield a power like that?" he asked, making me shake my head.

"I don't know but it must have had a tethering cast upon it, as I saw Evelyn throw it back into the portal it helped create before passing out, and now it is still back in the wrong hands."

"One that bitch, Madison, is using now, forcing us to question, how did she get her dirty little gold nails on it?" I gritted my teeth at that, snarling,

"I don't know but I have a fucking good idea!" Van nodded in understanding before telling me,

"Well, whichever of our enemies she is now in league with, this is definitely how she got her out." I took a deep breath as that knowledge wrapped around my heart once more, forcing me to finalize it with words.

"She didn't leave me." At this Van slapped a hand to my back and told me,

"No, she didn't. And she wouldn't have…"

"What do you mean?" I asked, hearing something else in his tone. So, he took the phone from me and put the footage back to before Madison turned up.

"Watch," he told me, handing me the phone to find my girl sitting on the sofa, her head in her hands as if battling with herself. But then the moment some conclusion hit her, she raised her head and I didn't need sound to know what it was she said aloud,

It was a statement made.

"I love him." At this my heart fucking stopped before beating faster than ever before. It was as if those three fucking words had sent my body into overdrive. Because now it didn't just fucking beat… *it beat solely for her.*

"What did she say after that?" I asked, knowing Van would be able to lip read and I was right. Because she had stood up and declared something even louder this time, I could tell.

"She said… *that she loves you and she doesn't care what you are."* My breath caught and became prisoner to her words, her declaration, her affirmation. I looked to Van to find him grinning like a fool, whereas I was still dumbstruck. Then I found myself muttering,

"She loves me."

"Looks like it, Ryk… now let's find out how the hell we

get your girl back," he replied, jarring me back to the now and, in it, he was right. My girl had been taken.

Which was why I curled my hand into a Demonic fist and growled,

"And it's time to kill a lot of people."

CHAPTER 20
THE WRATH OF DEMONS

I soon had all my council sitting at the large oak table we usually conducted meetings around. Admittedly, with chasing Evelyn around the West Coast recently, it had been a while since our last one. However, as far as chasing Evelyn, well, that unfortunately hadn't changed.

I'd had Vander analyzing every second of the recording, trying to see what else he could lip read from that bitch, Madison. After lip reading all that he had been able to detect, this depending on the angle of her head, it had at least been enough to know what her motives had been to warrant such a stupid fucking move.

But then she hadn't been the only one to blame in this, as in my anger at her, before casting her out, I had made the mistake of revealing too much. Goaded into telling her that I had found my Siren and that she would be the only woman in my life that I would ever need.

I had wanted the pain to cut her deep and, well, it looked like I did too good a job at that. Because she knew how much a Siren would be worth to the Lega Nera. And she planned not only to cash in, but also held some fucked up belief that I would take her back if I believed Evelyn had left me of her own free will. But little did she know, that I would go to the ends of the earth to find her, and I wouldn't stop until I did.

So, our plan, it was as simple as it wasn't. Find my known enemies and known collectors that made their fortune selling to the Lega Nera. Because we may have not known where the next auction was being held, but I was hoping to find her before any exchange could happen. Because without a doubt, if a Siren was found, then that's where she was headed.

However, what I wasn't expecting was a phone call from another Enforcer and, this time, it wasn't Oblivion.

It was Wrath.

"I would ask as to what do I owe the pleasure, but I am too busy for pleasantries, so will come right out with it, what do you want, Wrath?" I asked the big bastard, one that I didn't only know as being another Enforcer, but also from his father who ruled over the realm of Wrath. He released a deep sigh which was unlike him to do, instantly putting me on edge. Because if something had rattled him, then it wasn't fucking good news.

However, the news he gave me... *felt fucking fated.*

"My Siren, she was taken... *fuck...* but my Halo, my Emmeline, I... I need your help, Ryker. I had the plane they took her in tracked to London International Airport in Ontario."

Van gave me a questioning look, so I held up a finger telling him to hold off and walked away so as I could take this call in private. For everyone in my inner circle knew of my own Siren, but I wanted to extend the same level of privacy in regard to Wrath's.

"Are you with those you can trust?" I asked, knowing he would do the same in return.

"My brother, Hel, is with me and no other," he replied.

"Seems you are not the only one who has found one of the Lost Sirens."

"You speak of Ward?" This surprised me as much as it didn't. Ward was a good man and like most Enforcers, as powerful as they came.

"No, I speak of Oblivion, although given the timing, I would not be surprised if there more and like us, we are keeping such knowledge close to our inner circles," I replied, making him guess,

"Fuck, you found your Siren?"

"I did but like you, my friend, she was recently taken from me."

He growled low, telling me that like myself, he was too fucking close to the edge of losing himself to his Demon. The only reason I suspected he hadn't, was also the same as myself, knowing we needed to maintain control enough to function or there would be no chance at finding them.

"Then we must speak in person, for what I have to tell you cannot be said over the phone, Greed."

I agreed to this, knowing that putting our resources together would achieve far more and have a greater chance at success when retrieving our Sirens.

"I will make my way to London and meet you at the airfield as I can do little but hope that, by then, I know more," I told him, making him respond in kind, before asking,

"We will be there shortly. Do you believe as I do that Lega Nera is behind it?"

"I have proof that it is, for the next auction must be soon and if your Siren has been taken to London, then I believe we also have the city in which it is being held," I replied, hopeful now that I was right, and the two Sirens were together.

"I know it is your territory, Greed, but I am telling you now, if I don't get my Siren back, I will tear the Gods be damned city apart!" he growled.

"And I will right there with you looking for my own, so don't question me on my loyalty, for you will find it matching that of your own when it comes to my Siren," I informed him, barely holding back my own snarled words.

"Good, then we are on the same page," he stated firmly, and the sound that followed I could image was from his fist pounding on whatever table was in front of him.

"Yes, we are. Now hurry the fuck up and get your ass here," I said, ending the call to the sound of his lasting growl.

"And?" Van asked with a raised brow.

"We have a location. Faron, get the helicopter ready," I ordered, as once again, hope bloomed inside me now that I had commands to make of my men.

"And where are we going?" Kenzo asked, making me answer before motioning for Van to join me.

"London, so have everyone ready." The siblings bowed their heads and left the room, quick to follow through with my order. Vander followed me off to one side and once we were out of ear shot, asked,

"And you know this how?"

"Because Wrath just called me, his Siren was also taken, and they tracked the flight to London Ontario. Coincidence? I think not," I told him, and naturally after anyone who had ever met the big bastard Wrath would say, Vander's first words were to question this,

"Wrath has a Siren?" The shock evident on his face made me scoff.

"And that is not all, Ward also."

Van whistled before speaking my thoughts,

"Fuck, but it seems the Fates have been busy."

"The prophecy is taking shape, meaning that with the more Sirens found, the more risk to them and greater importance for their Fated Enforcers to find them." He nodded at this, before I continued,

"I believe it is why the auction will be rushed. They will not want to miss the payload gained from such a prize and they will not want to risk our Sirens being taken before they can be sold."

"Yes, and with it lets hope they get sloppy," he said, making me wish for the same.

"We know the auction will be held in London, but the question now will be where, for we need to move quickly, as they no doubt will," I added, making him once more nod in agreement.

"And what of Wrath now?" he asked, no doubt hoping for the extra backup.

"He is meeting us at the airfield," I replied, making him grin this time.

"That's good, as we will most certainly need the extra man power." That we would, because if the auction was going down, then they would have with them a fucking army to ensure it went off without a hitch.

"Gather every man we have on the estate, as we won't have time to get everyone under my rule to London but at least with Wrath's combined forces, we shouldn't need them."

"I am on it." I nodded to my second but before he could go and convey my orders to the others, I grabbed his arm and stopped him.

"Give me your phone." He raised a brow in question but other than that, he didn't comment anything other than to hand me it and say,

"Just press play, its already loaded." I would have smirked knowing how well my friend knew me but, for now, I had more important matters until the helicopter arrived.

And that was…

Watching as my Siren declared her love for me.

CHAPTER 21

TO GUT AN ALBERT FISH

No sooner had I arrived in London, and I was getting another phone call, but this time from a different Enforcer.

"Oblivion?"

"Why do I get the impression you were expecting someone else?" he said in that overly-cocky tone of his and with his type of power, then it wasn't really surprising or misplaced.

"My Siren was taken, along with Wrath's," I told him, knowing that he too needed to know of the dangers to his own if indeed she had been found.

"Then it is good I called, for I have information you may need," he told me as I exited the car, now waiting for Wrath's private jet to land, knowing it wouldn't be long now.

"I reached out to Zepar and, guess what?"

I growled knowing of the Enforcer who was a High-ranking Duke of Hell. He was also the known Ruler over both Succubus and Incubus.

"He also finally found his Siren?" I guessed as much but

then if any of us ever did find them, it would be the dark bastard Zepar. As it was well known that he had been conducting his own search of her for decades now, perhaps even longer. And well, let's just say that his methods of doing so weren't exactly of the legal kind in our world.

Now just why the King of Kings chose to turn a blind eye to this I didn't know, but my guess would have been a blood oath of some kind. Either way, he was known to be obsessed with the idea of finding her.

"He did, and ironically not where he was looking, yet, in a way, the Fates didn't lie to him, for he got there in the end… this despite the literal means he took as being Demonic gospel turning out to be something else entirely." I scoffed a laugh at that, knowing of the once Angel that unlike most, had *willingly chosen to fall.* He had clearly felt as if Hell held a far more desirable life for him to live than the lies he lived by in Heaven.

"Yet this is not why I am calling," Oblivion informed me.

"You said you had information," I pressed, letting him know of my urgency.

"I do. The recent threat to his Siren led him to a lead I have been tracking."

"What kind of lead?" I asked, hoping this would be the missing piece I would need in finding Evelyn.

"You wanted me to hunt down the one responsible for illegal casting on the mortal minds you fought against at the train station."

"I have yet encountered more," I told him.

"I am not surprised, for he has been busy doing jobs for

an unknown enemy." I frowned at this, wondering just who else I would need to add to the fucking list.

"Unknown?"

"From what I have gathered, there is something bigger at play here and someone in the shadows pulling on the strings. But the rumor is that he needs all eleven Sirens for whatever he has planned, and is currently working as head of an underground organization that employs a startling amount of..."

"Mercenaries," I guessed, interrupting him.

"Yes, and not just mortals, but that of our own kind as well and from what my sources say, it's like a fucking cult. This group make the fucking Nazi's look like kindergarteners and the Gestapo like Preschoolers." I released a frustrated sigh, before inquiring further,

"And whoever he is, he is paying for this sorcerer to cast spells on them?"

"Exactly, now thanks to Zepar I finally have a name, as he has the asshole locked up and, well, despite the gregarious heads up, Zepar is not exactly eager to share in his vengeance... all things considered, I can't say I blame him."

I scoffed at this before wondering if there wasn't more to it than just blood lust of a Demon and the pleasure to cause pain.

"No?"

"His Siren got hurt and he is out for blood. But like I said, his name did get passed to me... where are you now?" Oblivion asked, as if he knew it may hold deeper meaning.

"London, Ontario."

"Now that is interesting," he said, soon confirming my suspicions.

"Why?"

"Because this asshole just so happened to spend a lot of time there in the 1920's." I narrowed my gaze, before asking,

"What is his name?"

"Albert Fish." As soon as he said the sick son of a bitch's name, I reacted.

"Fuck!" I snarled.

"Ryker?" Oblivion rightly questioned my outburst, clearly not remembering news of who the media dubbed as…

The Gray Man.

"I know the fucker!" I growled, before explaining quickly, "I think I know where they are holding the auction."

Because the only link I could make with London and Albert Fish, was the one place he had stalked decades ago.

"Then I will ask for the Gods to favor you in your killing and pray to Lucifer that you get there in time, Son of Greed."

"Thank you, Wye."

"Bonam fortunam, my friend," he said, wishing me good luck in Latin before hanging up the call just as Wrath's plane was coming into land. For I was pleased that at least now I was almost certain that I knew where I would find my Siren.

"Good news?" Van asked, making me nod and tell him,

"I fucking hope so," I told him, minutes before the sight of Wrath and his men walking out of the plane was more than a welcomed one. His large, tattooed frame strode toward me with purpose, and he looked as menacing as he always did. What with his Viking hair-style and piercing dark green eyes promising murder, he looked only a few heartbeats away from being at the ready to swing an axe in battle.

"Greed," he said, taking my hand and shaking it with the strength fitting for such a being.

"Wrath, I have news," I said, wishing to put him out of this new brand of Hell we both found ourselves in.

"Thank fuck for that, tell us we have someone to kill, namely any fucker that looks like me," Hel, his brother said, stepping up from behind him. I raised a brow at this, making Wrath add,

"It was how they got my Halo, a Manushya Rakshashu Demon. One who is possessing my brother's image." An image that could not be further from that of his brutal looking brother as Helmer, Hel for short, was usually seen wearing a full suit. Whereas Wrath preferred the comfort and practicality of jeans and a shirt. Hel had perfectly styled dark blonde hair cut short at the sides and longer on top, opposed to the razor shaved sides and twisted long hair that Wrath wore knotted at the back of his head.

But despite Hel's easy-going persona and devilish grin he wore like armor, he too was as deadly as his brother and twice as cunning. With those disconcerting turquoise eyes of his missing nothing and always at the ready to rip a person's throat out. Oh, and it was guaranteed that grin of his wouldn't leave his face whilst doing it, the crazy bastard.

"Come, there isn't much time, I will explain on the way," I told them both after offering Hel a nod of my head in acknowledgement.

"You have a location?!" Wrath asked, and it was easy to see that he was as rattled as I was knowing our Sirens were at such potential risk. So, he followed me to the convoy of

SUV's I had Faron secure for us, motioning for his own people to fall out and join with my own.

Then after Wrath insisted on driving, I joined him in the front whilst his brother and my second sat in the back.

"Turn right on Oxford Street East, the others will follow," I told him.

"Start talking, Greed, before I tear this fucking steering wheel off!" Wrath demanded, having to fix the indent he was making when gripping the wheel too tight.

"Albert Fish." As soon as I said the name, unlike Oblivion, Wrath recognized the name.

"That sick fuck serial killer who killed kids?" This was unsurprising seeing as many murders were committed in his own city of New York back in the 1920's and 30's.

"Also known as The Gray Man," I told him before going on to tell him the rest. That Albert Fish was a sick and twisted mortal who was a prime target for a Jikininki Demon. These type of Demons usually fed from dead human flesh, but this particular half breed went one step further. He possessed the sick and twisted mind of one Albert Fish when he was serving time in Sing, Sing prison for grand larceny. After that he came out of prison even worse, claiming to be hearing voices in his head. And not only was the apostle John speaking to him, but he even went so far as to say that Christ was as well. That it was his mighty Lord that asked him to commit these crimes and unthinkable atrocities. But his crimes that included anything from rape, child molesting, murder, and cannibalism, were what fed the Demon inside him. The voice in his head came from only one place as the Demon hung onto this mortal for years, feeding not only itself but also the sick nature of the man Albert Fish that was at his core.

A pure evil soul.

But being that he was also mentally sick, he was therefore an easy target, often giving into the Demon's need to punish that of his own vessel. He would even ask his own children to beat him, to paddle his buttocks with the same nail-studded board he used to abuse himself. He also went so far as to insert wool doused with lighter fluid into his anus and set it alight and, all of this, I believe was solely for the reason to inflict pain on himself in order to continue to feed his Demon.

Something that continued for the rest of his life. As even after finally being arrested, an X-ray found that he had at least twenty-nine needles lodged in his pelvic region. All caused from self-harm by pushing needles into his groin and abdomen.

As for my dealings with the evil soul, it wasn't long after he was caught trying to make two young boys his next victims. He had invited them to lunch and whilst making it, they accidently found his self-proclaimed 'instruments of Hell' hidden under his bed. This was basically his kill kit, which included a meat cleaver, a hacksaw, and a knife. Thankfully the boys escaped, but it was enough to get him sent to a psychiatric hospital. Although it was kept quiet at the pleading of his family, telling the authorities how sick he was.

He was diagnosed with many things, one of which was religious mania. However, it was whilst here that his Demon really came out to play and news soon reached me that he was conducting something that was referred to as a 'crimson dinner party'.

Unfortunately, back in those days, a lot of these hospitals were ripe with medical torture, often after doctors had been turned mad themselves and with only a little push from dark Supernatural means.

Which meant that having a poor unfortunate soul strapped to a table, with other possessed minds all gathered around like vultures. This so as a feeding frenzy could ensue and all under the guise of a medical procedure, which of course ended with extreme pain, hourly torture, and then the desperate release of death being granted.

"In 1929 I apprehended him for the part he played in orchestrating 'Crimson dinner parties', as well as turning the minds of mortals and feeding on them whilst posing as a doctor. He was taken in, and I had him imprisoned and awaiting judgement when he escaped," I told Wrath, as he too had dealt with his fair share of crimes committed in his sector. Kings Park Asylum being only one of them.

"Escaped?"

"He was last heard of terrorizing patients in Waverly Hills Sanatorium in Louisville, Kentucky, before its closure in 1961. It was also said that he was working with Gruen." Another known enemy of the King of Kings and therefore, his Enforcers.

"Fuck."

"Yeah, but he was no longer in my jurisdiction, so my hunt went cold," I told him, making Hel comment from the back seat,

"It says here he got the electric chair back in 1936, at

Sing, Sing." I glanced in the mirror to see him reading the facts from his phone.

"Yes, for the murder of a little girl called Grace Budd."

"Fucking good memory, Greed," Wrath commented, making me grit my teeth before telling him,

"You always remember those who get away. Besides, I like to be thorough when doing my research into those I hunt. The real Albert Fish may have died on old sparky, but the second he took his last breath, the Jikininki Demon that had possessed him all those years soon took his place, now having a vessel to inhabit."

"Fucking old vessel, the guy looked like a fucking corpse at his trial," Hel commented dryly, still reading what I gathered was an old article on who was duped as being The Gray Man.

"And now?" Wrath asked, ignoring this comment by his brother.

"Zepar has him. Turns out he has moved on and is now working for someone else, a common enemy we are yet to know anything about other than he is making a play to kidnap all Sirens."

Wrath growled at this, his hands starting to change into his Demon once more.

"We need to get there, so get a hold of yourself, brother," Hel suggested, and if there was anyone in the world he would listen to, it would be his brother.

"What does he want with them?" Wrath practically snarled.

"We don't yet know. Hopefully Zepar will discover more. Well, that is if he doesn't outright kill the fucker in his rage first," I commented with envy that I couldn't be the one to do so myself. I fucking loathed it when they got away.

"His own Siren?" Hel asked before his brother could.

"Found and, unfortunately, she got hurt in the process off the back of getting Fish apprehended," I told them both.

"I will kill them all!" Wrath vowed, allowing his Demon to seep through into his voice.

"We will," I amended, before telling him,

"All Enforcers that are fortunate enough to be gifted their Sirens will have to band together, for I fear that this is only the beginning." At this he looked my way and nodded the once before then asking,

"So where are we going, Greed?"

Which is when I looked out window looking straight ahead and told him,

"Where the hunt first began…"

"…To London Psychiatric Hospital."

Evie

CHAPTER 22
A LIVING NIGHTMARE
EVIE

At some point I must have fallen asleep and with little else to do, it wasn't really surprising. I didn't know how long I had been stuck in this room, only that when the sound of my door being unlocked woke me, I looked to the window to find it was now nightfall.

The man who opened the door wasn't anyone I recognized, although I wasn't sure why I would. He also didn't look like he would have much to offer in a fight, because he may have been taller than me, but he wasn't 'Ryker tall'. And as for his weight, if there had been a string bean weight in boxing, that was the category he would have been put in.

He had shaggy brown hair, a thin nose, and barely enough stubble to be considered anything more than face fluff. His dull brown eyes looked me up and down with nothing short of boredom. As if he had drawn the short straw in this chore and wished he was back in his mother's basement playing video games, eating Cheetos, and getting artificial cheese dust on his keyboard.

Oh, and he was also standing there now holding a garment bag in his hand.

"Come with me."

When I didn't move, he released a sigh as if this was all so very boring for him and he had a million better things to do. He also chose that moment to pull a gun from his back that must have been tucked into the waist band of his jeans. Because the second he pointed it at me, I knew this was threat enough to do as he said, knowing now why they trusted the skinny guy to threaten me.

"Yes, I thought so," he droned sarcastically.

"I thought you wanted me alive," I questioned as I stood in front of him.

"Not me, them, and I'm sure having a few holes in you won't mark down the price too much. May even get some bidders excited," he said, winking at me before ordering, "Now move it." To which he added the jerk of the end of his gun as he backed out into a dingey hallway, telling me to follow.

It didn't take long to realize that I was right, I must have been in some kind of hospital, and from the scratchy overkill and number work on the inside of my room, I gathered it was of the insane variety.

It also looked as if it had been closed down for quite a few years, or at least this part of it had because there was more paint peeling off the walls than there was sticking to it. I was just surprised that the place still had electric, or walking down these eerie hallways in the dark with this bored gunslinger for company would have been even less fun.

"What do you intend to do with me?" I asked, hoping for some insight to my immediate future.

"I keep telling you, it's them, not me. I am just the lacky," he admitted, surprising me.

"Then if you're not with them, why not just let me go?" I tested, doubting this guy had enough morals in him to do so. But still, I thought to at least try.

"Oh I am sorry, I should have said *paid lacky*, as in they give me money and I do as I am told. Which means so do you, now keep moving!" he snapped, nudging me in the back with the end of his gun. The hallways felt endless and really, each new space merged into the next with very little change in the unnerving interior.

"In here, this is a good as place as any." He nodded toward an open doorway, and I couldn't help but suck in a quick breath when I saw that it looked like an abandoned operating room. Although the moment I saw the big freezer-style door on the right-hand side, I gasped, realizing what this was.

"No way, it's a fucking morgue!" I shouted, making him grab my arm and push me inside, telling me,

"Yeah, well, it's where you're gonna end up if you don't hurry your ass up and get on in there!" I stumbled inside after being pushed, righting myself just in time before I went flying. Then he tossed the garment bag at me and ordered,

"Now get changed, and sort out your fucking hair, they want you presentable. And hurry the fuck up, they are waiting!" Then he closed the door, thankfully leaving me alone to change. Although being inside here wasn't great, at least I wasn't dealing with the asshole with a gun being waved at me. I decided to be quick, changing in hope that would give me more time to look around the room and maybe even find something I could use as a weapon.

So, I stripped off and unzipped the bag, pulling out a long white dress that was made up of a floaty material and had a corset style top that made me feel like a contortionist when pulling at the laces at the back.

I then put on the shoes, that thankfully were ballerina pumps that tied with a ribbon around my ankle and were, most importantly, flat without a heel. Which meant running without the worry that I would trip and break my ankle if I ever managed to escape.

I unraveled my hair and ran my hands through it before re-plaiting it to one side. Then after scanning the bare worktops and metal trolleys to find them all empty, I started to walk inside the next room. It was joined to the morgue and looked like some kind of office space, littered with discarded paperwork and old medical journals. Notebooks and folders that held the name, London Psychiatric Hospital. A place that at the very least, looked to be in Ontario, telling me that I wasn't that far from where I had been taken from.

I scanned the cupboards above and below, ignoring all the old textbooks and files, close to laughing at one that said 'dating and sex behavior in adolescence'. Of course, this wasn't exactly the time to be amused at what they classed as sex education from the 60's.

"Come on, Evie, if you can kill a guy with a TV then you can get creative with a... stapler... no, not that," I told myself, now looking back at the door and checking he wasn't just standing there.

"Fuck, there must be something!" I hissed as I opened draws and found nothing... that was until I closed it and the

metal handle fell off on one side. I frowned down at it, before pulling it off the other side, something it did with a little jiggling.

"Are you finished in there or what?!" I heard him shouting.

Knowing I didn't have much time, I quickly yanked the handle the rest of the way out, pleased to see that it had a great long nail attached to the two ends and an arch of smooth metal in between. Then I purposely put my camo green jacket back on and tucked it into the pocket, seeing as I didn't have anywhere else to hide it. But then again, I was hoping to use it before it could be discovered.

I spun quickly just as the door opened and the asshole behind it was telling me,

"Time's up."

I then walked toward him, not wanting to give him any reason to raise his gun up but instead lead him into a false sense of security, playing the good little prisoner. Although, I could have hit him right there and then, when he outrightly checked me out and let his eyes linger on my breasts. A pair that felt more smushed up thanks to the boning in the top part of my dress. But then I wondered if I could use this to my advantage.

"Lose the jacket," he ordered with hungry eyes that clearly wanted to see more of me.

"It's cold in here," I complained, trying to buy myself more time and knowing that if I was going to make my move, then the time would have to be now. So, I decided to give him what he wanted, hoping his gaze would be busy on my breasts and not on what I was doing with my hand.

"I don't give a shit, take it off!" he snapped, making me say,

"Okay, okay… I just need to adjust my shoes," I said, purposely taking a step closer so that he was within attacking distance before placing a hand on the wall and leaning down to give him a good view of my cleavage. Then while his eyes were perving on my breasts, I tucked my hand in my pocket and gripped the handle. Then I made a move like I was falling into him, purposely away from the gun by his side. This was at the same time bringing my unconventional weapon up to his neck and digging the nails into his skin.

Naturally, he froze, especially when I warned,

"Make one move and I will fucking kill you, do you understand?!" He gritted his teeth but nodded slightly, stopping when he felt the prick of the nail dig in hard enough, it caused droplets of blood to drip down his neck. He hissed in pain but despite the threat, tried to call my bluff.

"You don't have it in you," he gritted out.

"Oh yeah? Wanna tell that to the cops who are looking for me for murder? Of course, I could always say my TV accidently smashed him in the head," I told him because, well, at least some of it was true. I watched his eyes widen and, just in case, I dug the nails into his skin further, making him whimper.

"Now toss the gun, ass wipe," I ordered, making him grit his teeth, but in the end, he did what he was told. It clattered to the floor in front of us, but I didn't dare go for it because I knew that would give him the chance to make a grab for it, or me. Or it could give him chance to run and shout bloody murder. Either option would only get me in deeper shit than I already was.

No, the only chance I had was to knock him unconscious or lock him up somewhere. And lucky for me, even though I may not have had a baseball bat to hand to achieve the first, I definitely had something in this room to achieve the second.

"Now move!"

"Where the fuck are you... oh no, no fucking way am I going in there!" he complained the second I started to back him into the big open metal door.

"I could just stab you and dump another dead body in the freezer," I said, giving him the choice and making him shout,

"Okay, okay, fuck!"

Then once he was through the doorway, I pushed him in, making him stumble back far enough that I could slam the door. Then just as he started banging on the other side and before he could open it, I slid across the barrel lock. Thankfully, the door was that thick I could only hear a slight muffled scream of him begging to be let out. So, I knew that no one would hear him and come running.

Now just why they needed a lock on the outside, I didn't know, but at this point, I was just thankful that they did.

Which was why I grabbed the gun, and promptly made a run for it. Of course, running through an abandoned psychiatric hospital wasn't any less creepy, but at least now I had adrenaline on my side.

After running down what felt like an endless corridor, I finally found a map on the wall, seeing for myself the strange layout of the place. It looked like two stars connected by a bigger building in between, with what looked like a huge room attached at the bottom. One that looked like it could have been a hall or gymnasium.

Well, one thing was for sure, it didn't take a genius to

know that if there was some kind of shit show about to happen, then I would bet my skills as an escape artist that it was being held there. And with people selling illegal stuff, including actual people… well, I needed to stay as far away from that place as possible.

So, I started running in the opposite direction to where I hoped I would find an exit. I tried not to think on the rooms I passed and the poor souls that had spent their unfortunate lives in them. I tried not to think about the treatment room I passed, and words like 'Shock therapy' and 'waterboarding' went through my head. I only thought about what horrors awaited *me* in a place like this, one I was starting to feel trapped in. It was a bit like being a rat in a maze put there by some mad doctor conducting experiments.

And as if my mind was already on its way to being lost, just like the inhabitants of this forsaken place, I suddenly found myself seeing the impossible. A ghost of my past, and the one that I knew would forever haunt me. A pair of double doors opened at the end of a hallway and an impossible sight walked through them, making me skid to a frightful stop before falling on my ass. I scrambled back, saying over and over,

"No… no, it can't be… I… I killed you!" I shouted, making the man smirk back at me as I continued to drag myself across the floor. Fear outweighed all common sense other than telling me to run.

So, I finally managed to get to my feet, before pointing the gun at him as I continued to walk backward.

"Now is that anyway to greet me after all these years?" a voice I knew only in my nightmares said to me, making me shake my head again.

"You're not real… *not fucking real!*" Then I raised the gun in his direction at the same time walking back to the corner I had just come from. But just like that night, he looked unconcerned by the threat. It was a lesson learned seconds before his death.

"Then if it's a ghost you see, Evelyn Leucosia, perhaps you deserve to be in a place like this," he said in that same tone he had spoken to me that night. I was just about to open my mouth to say something when he nodded to something behind me. However, I was too late to react as I suddenly felt the blow to the back of my head, knocking me down and, more importantly, knocking the gun from my hand.

I cried out as I hit the floor and just before the world went black once more, there was still one last sight of my ghost left for me to see. A dark figure now standing over me, just like he had done that day my world had ended and, with it, my mother's life.

I was once more living a nightmare, as he told me…

"Hello again… my dear daughter."

CHAPTER 23
A SIREN'S CALL

I swear, my life currently felt like a never-ending nightmare of passing out and waking up to find myself still living it. It was like I didn't know what was real anymore and what wasn't. But I had to confess to being hazier than the last time I had been knocked out, remembering only snippets of it.

I think I had been running, having managed to get away but after that, I must have been found shortly after because what happened next couldn't have been real. It was that or I had been seeing a ghost. Perhaps I could have even been hallucinating. I just didn't know the answer, only that it couldn't have been real.

However, what was real was waking up as I was being carried somewhere, and from the pain in the back of my head, I could only hope at this point it was back to my cell. All I wanted to do now was lie down and sleep. I had to wonder if I was suffering from concussion, because I was feeling very sluggish. As if all fight to try and escape had been knocked right out of me.

Although that was until I saw where they were now taking me, it looked like a fucking big fish tank! Now, normally, this wouldn't particularly have been seen as threatening, but considering I couldn't swim, having a very real fear of water, I quickly started to panic. Because despite it not having water in it yet, from the looks of the pipes leading to it, it didn't take a genius to figure out what their plan was.

There were two tanks, side by side, being no bigger than ten foot wide. But as for the height, they were at least twelve feet tall with a barred latch above the enclosure. Inside them had been made to look like a human sized fish tank, with sand on the floor and a single plastic rock that I gathered was put there for us to sit on.

As for the rest of the room, this view had been cut off. There was a large red curtain that hung from a metal pole above, separating me from the villains I gathered were here to bid on me. I didn't even need to wonder how they were going to get me up into that thing because the big metal staircase on wheels was a dead giveaway.

Which was when my fight or flight response finally kicked back in, and I started to struggle enough that the man holding me had to let go. I fell to the floor, ignoring the pain and quickly scrambled to my feet before trying to make another run for it.

However, this didn't go so well this time, and I was grabbed from behind and tossed toward someone ready to catch me. Neither of which had any faces to speak of, because both of them wore masks as if I had been dragged into some kind of cult meeting. And unlike Ryker's mask, these were cold and featureless, being just plain matt-black.

Then I was taken by the arm and practically dragged up the steps and toward an open grate at the top.

"No, you don't understand! I can't fucking swim... I will drown if you put water in there!" I shouted, making the man chuckle as he roughly handled me, the tight grasp of his fingertips bruising my skin.

"Then you better hope you get bought then... *and quickly.*" Then I saw him wink at me through the eye hole before pushing me inside and making me fall to the bottom. The landing managed to knock the wind out of me, so I could do little but curl up on my side and try to catch my breath in the sand.

"Bring in the other one and, unlike this bitch, let's hope she wakes when inside the tank. It will be less fucking hassle that way!" he said, sneering down at me.

"Ass...holes!" I shouted between breaths, now trying to drag myself up and feeling the pain in my hip where I had fallen. But his response to this was to turn a lever attached to the pipe while blowing me a kiss with his hand. I, in turn, gave him the finger but then the second the water came flooding in I quickly got to my feet, nearly falling because of my hip.

I then hobbled over to the fake rock in the tank and started to climb up it as the water level started to rise. I looked over to the other tank next to mine and saw the water rising in that one too. The sounds of laughter at my expense came from behind me; they obviously enjoyed the sight of my panic. The bastards!

Thankfully, however, the water eventually stopped, and I gripped onto the perch of the rock in an utter death grip. Taking a bath was one thing but this, this was like my private version of hell! Memories of being nearly drowned as a kid came back to me, along with the abuse I suffered... the feeling of not being able to breathe... my lungs burning and crying out for me to just take that last deadly breath...

I was fucking terrified!

But then the agonizing minutes ticked by, and I watched as they carried another girl in. It gave my mind something else to be focus on. It gave me another to be concerned for, and I watched them carry the curly haired blonde over their shoulder, up the staircase that I could see had now been moved over to the next tank. It was clear she was still unconscious because she didn't even stir as they lowered her inside, doing so with a little more care, considering they obviously didn't want her to drown. Not like my punishment after trying to escape.

But I was more concerned now for the other girl, fearful that she would slip from where they had put her, and she would drown regardless. Because even the water lapping at her legs didn't manage to wake her, knowing that it was left up to me to try and do something.

I was worried about what they could have done to her. Whether or not she could be hurt. Had I seen her bang her head when they lowered her in? I couldn't remember, but as I looked down at the water in my own tank with fear in my eyes, I closed them and tried to breathe through it. Now telling myself I needed to help her if I could. So, I let go of my death grip with one hand, using it to scoot closer to her side of the tank and then when I assured myself I had a good hold, I banged my palm on the glass as hard as I could.

"Wake up!" I cried out.

"Fucking be quiet, the guests are arriving," one of the masked men hissed at me.

"Fuck off and die!" I shouted back, making him walk back over to the lever and just when he was about to pull it down, warning me with the obvious threat, someone else came and stopped him.

"Not yet, you know our orders," he said, making the man visibly grit his teeth before warning,

"Your time is nearly up, bitch, so go ahead, enjoy screaming while you can! Who knows, hearing your panic might make them spend more."

I ignored his threat and continued trying to wake up the girl. Christ, she was so small, she looked like a porcelain doll, with her riot of tight blonde curls and cute face.

"WAKE UP!" I screamed, banging harder on the glass than before and wishing I was as strong as Ryker, knowing it would most certainly have cracked by now.

Fuck me, I missed him, and not just how helpful his obvious strength would have been in this moment. But I simply missed him. Even in the short time we had spent together, I realized now how much I wanted more. How badly I could see my life with him, despite what he was.

I just didn't care; I had known the worst humanity had to offer and knew that the real demons of this world weren't just from Hell. Because Ryker was one man I knew would never hurt me, who would protect me and care for me. He had offered me but a glimpse of what it would be like to be with him. And now, I wanted more.

I wanted it all.

Hence the cruel twist of fate I was now facing... the irony wasn't lost on me. The moment I had decided that I was done with running from him turned out to be the very moment I was taken. Making me now wonder about the other girl, asking myself if she was in the same predicament. Did she too mean something to one of the men in Ryker's world?

Well, regardless, if she was or not, I knew I had to help her. So, I continued with my screams, my shouts, my banging, doing so until my palm was red and sore. It didn't matter, I wouldn't stop until my hand was bleeding by the knuckles and my voice was hoarse.

"You need to wake up! Oh, please wake up," I said, this time in a deflated shout, having done this for what felt like a small forever. But then finally she started to move, and I sucked in a quick breath of utter relief.

"Oh, thank God, you're not hurt," I said, trying to get closer, and when I nearly slipped, I freaked out as the water splashed up my legs.

"Where are we?" she asked, her voice strained and dazed as if she had been drugged, which given my previous experience, was more than likely.

"We are in a place called the London Psychiatric Hospital in Ontario. It looks like it has been abandoned for a long time. They dragged me in here, but you were already unconscious," I told her, already knowing a lot more of the place thanks to my time trying to escape. But then, it was doubtful she had seen what I had, perhaps coming straight from a cell like I had woken up in.

She was also wearing the same thing I was, meaning it was likely she had been forcibly changed. Perhaps after the experience they'd had with me, they most likely decided not to take any more chances.

"What do they want with us?" she asked after first taking the time to look at her surroundings, no doubt doing as I did and trying to find a weakness or means of escape.

"I don't know, but while I have been held captive, I've heard people talking about an auction," I told her, unable to help myself shivering now the adrenaline of trying to wake her up had left me. But then this wasn't surprising as the water was ice cold, and no doubt made me as pale as the other woman looked.

In fact, I was just about to ask her name and where she was from when a booming voice interrupted my thoughts.

"Silence!"

My wide eyes immediately went to the curtain-wall in front of us, waiting for the moment it would inevitably drop.

"Welcome, ladies and gentlemen. We start this year's auction with the long-awaited treasures of Heaven, I give you two of the Lost Sirens!" My mind whirled, now hearing what Ryker had called me more than once, wondering why the fuck everyone seemed to think I was one of these Sirens?

Of course, seconds later and like I knew it would, the curtain fell from the ceiling. I gasped at the sight of the sea of people now filling the hall, and I knew then that I had been right in thinking of staying away from this room when I had been running and came across the map.

Of course, my new friend and I weren't the only ones to gasp, because I suddenly knew what it felt like to be an animal displayed at the zoo. All those eager faces staring back at us, whispering among themselves like we were some rare creatures found in a magical lagoon.

The sight sickened me, making me focus on the room itself instead of the despicable people all here ready to bid on us like fucking prized cattle! But this was also when I saw it was no longer dark outside as daylight penetrated the dirty windows, or should I say, what was left of them. Broken floor boards had all been pushed to the sides so the space could be filled with what looked like hundreds of people all sitting on chairs. Each of them were wearing expensive finery, and holding paddles ready to give the auctioneer their number for the winning bid.

But then as I scanned the crowd, scowling at each one of these despicable people, I saw a certain face in the crowd and gasped. It was one it seemed I would never be rid of, and I couldn't help but close my eyes, shake my head, and mutter,

"Oh shit." It was a reaction heard by the girl next to me, and she quickly tried to offer me comfort, not knowing that I was once again being haunted by my past. Because there he fucking was, smirking at me from within the vile crowd.

"It's okay, we will be okay," she said, making me nod quickly, holding onto her words and letting them soothe me.

"Let's make this more interesting, should we, Randel? If you please," the voice boomed once more on the microphone somewhere out of sight. It was an order that made me tense as I looked back to my tormentor to find him there, winking at me once more before flipping a different lever up this time. The second I heard the gush of water I knew that they were only filling up mine this time, making me instantly panic.

"No! Stop... stop this!" the girl shouted on my behalf, seeing now that I was not dealing with this terrifying situation easily. It was as if she recognized the fear in my eyes as being her own. I banged my bruised fists on the side of the tank in vain, knowing it would do nothing but allow everyone to get a good kick off my terror. I scrambled up the rock as the water continued to rise, forcing me to soon get to my feet. Trying to balance on the highest bit. But even then, it wasn't high enough for me to escape because I couldn't reach the top.

"I can't fucking swim!" I tried begging for my life, hoping they would want me alive, but the auction just continued as if I had welcomed them all to witness the end of my life!

"This particular Siren is brought to you by our esteemed vendor, Gastin, one of the King's own Enforcers. Should we start the bidding at one million?" I gasped, my mouth dropping in utter shock, before I whispered,

"No way."

But then as the water started to reach over my knees, my protests continued, making me bang harder than ever before. This ended in me slipping and screaming as I was forced to scramble back up the rock and to standing.

"Someone, save her, for fuck sake!" the other woman screamed in my defense, but it was useless as the bidding continued. As if my drowning was nothing to them but daytime TV. But then just as the water level rose to my neck, I saw a dark figure rise from the back, as if he had just snuck in, now scanning the stage we were on. I couldn't see his features, but it was enough to make me scream for him, whoever he was.

"HELP ME!" This seemed to work as the man suddenly bellowed,

"One hundred million!" Making the crowd gasp at the amount. Something I would have done too had the water not

suddenly covered the top of my head, just as I heard the auctioneer shout,

"SOLD!" After this, I held my breath, watching through a watery gaze as the man stormed down the center of the aisle before getting close enough to act. He quickly leapt up onto the top of the tank, in an unhuman way, making my gaze go up. I would have cried out in utter joy at the face I now saw above me, but I also knew that doing so would have likely meant my death.

I then watched as he barehandedly ripped off the latch above and tossed it back, hitting into the assholes that had been the ones to taunt me. They flew back like pins in a bowling alley, and I would have smiled had I not been fighting for my life at the time.

After this, he quickly reached down and grabbed me, pulling me up just as I was about to run out of air. He then gathered me up in his arms, and I shivered against his hard chest, one I could feel breathing heavily, as if he was trying to control himself.

He then jumped down as if this was as easy as walking, jarring me only a little as his grip on me was certainly tight enough not to let me fall. But then, when I looked up, I couldn't stop myself from reaching up to his face, whispering the name of my savior,

"Ryker… you came… you came for me."

He tensed around me, holding me tight as if he feared I would get snatched off him. Then he told me,

"I will always come for you, my little Siren." Then as he started to walk from the room, I remembered my friend, hearing now the auctioneer introducing her. So, I quickly told him,

"No, we have to go back, we have to save the other girl!" At which he paused and gave me a tender look before telling me,

"Don't worry, she has her own Enforcer who has come to save her." It was a statement that made me ask,

"What's an Enforcer?"

Of course, the second I heard a loud and ear thundering roar from back in the hall, he grinned down at me and said,

"I am."

CHAPTER 24
GREEDY MONSTERS

Once I was assured that the other girl had definitely been rescued, I started to relax enough to realize that I too had been saved. And just in time too apparently, because Ryker's men had only managed to surround the building once the auction had started to take place. This was alongside another man's small army, a man Ryker told me was a friend called Wrath.

Someone I only got a brief look at and if I was honest, he was a man that would have utterly terrified me. That was, had he not had the curly blonde girl bundled in his arms like she was the most precious thing to him in the entire world. Just the same as I appeared to be in Ryker's, as I too was still held in his arms.

And for such a beast of a man, to see how he was clearly besotted with her made for a startling contrast. He fussed over her like he feared as if she would shatter any minute.

Again, this was very similar to Ryker and how he was with me, and it was a sight that tugged on my heart. I would have liked to ask her name or even ask if I could hug her. But in all honesty, I hadn't yet been ready to leave Ryker's arms, and he certainly didn't seem ready to let me. In fact, I had never felt so vulnerable in all my life and couldn't seem to uncurl my bruised fist from his tactical vest. He looked very similar to how he looked the first night we met and I had to admit, the sight was doing strange, needy things to my body.

He looked so fucking hot, I swear I was close to panting!

But as for the other girl, in the end, all I managed was a gestured nod in her direction, something she returned with a grin, as we were both carried to different vehicles. It also looked like a lot of people were being arrested, as others were clearly fleeing the scene while they still could. Expensive cars were flying out of there as if someone had let off a gun at the starting line.

"Did you find that fuck?!" Ryker barked out the second Vander walked over.

Vander looked over his shoulder at the sight of one man being dragged out and about to be thrown into a van.

"No, turns out Gastin wasn't even there but had another in his place ready to receive the payment. Information we learned too late as he also escaped," Vander replied, making Ryker grit his teeth.

"Tell me I have someone to kill," he growled, making me flinch. He noticed this and instantly looked guilty, before cooing down at me,

"Easy, sweetheart, I will try and cool my anger."

"The raid was successful enough that we have a few we can hold responsible, the bigger players, however, weren't in attendance," Vander told him, making his jaw harden before offering his own opinion and giving me a little bit more insight to what they were talking about.

"They most likely knew it was too risky, especially with how quickly they threw this one together."

"I agree," Vander said while looking back on the commotion of people involved still being rounded up. So, I decided to speak up.

"Erm, if it helps, I trapped one of them in the morgue when I was trying to escape." At this Vander laughed and commented,

"Of course, you did, Girl Scout."

Ryker smirked down at me before jerking his head for his friend to silently give us a minute. Vander grinned at us both before walking away and leaving us to talk. Ryker then carried me over to one of the cars that had its doors open ready and as he placed me down, I quickly told him,

"I didn't run... I promise that whatever you found that made it look like I had, it wasn't me and I know I freaked out when you told me what... what you are, but I didn't..." At this he pulled me in for a hug and cradled my head to his chest.

"Ssshh now, I know... *I know it wasn't you, sweetheart.*"

I choked back a sob, nodding into his chest where he held me, stroking a gentle hand down the back of my head.

"I thought you would see the sheets from the window and think I had done another runner," I admitted because this had been one of my biggest fears... *well, other than drowning that was.*

"I wouldn't have left you," I told him as he now ran that

soothing hand up and down my back, making me soak up his touch like a soothing balm to my soul.

"I cannot tell you how much that means to me to hear, Evie, but despite that being my initial worry, I soon discovered the truth. She will be punished… I promise you this," he said, confirming with this last part that he did in fact know who was responsible. He pulled back then and cupped my cheeks, asking me,

"Are you alright… are you hurt anywhere… did they…?" He never finished, as I covered his hands with my own and told him,

"I'm okay, you got to me in time."

"I didn't think I would. The auction started sooner than our intel believed it would and you were supposed to be the last two sold. We were just getting our people in place when we overheard the announcement and knew we had to act. Hence why people were allowed to escape." It was nice to know that the most important thing to him and his friend Wrath had been saving us. This despite it being apparent that catching these guys had been a big thing for him.

"I'm sorry they got away," I told him, making him scoff, and confirming what I already knew.

"I'm not, not if it means getting you back unharmed… now please tell me that I am right, that they didn't harm you?" he asked, dipping his head to my height so he could assess for himself if I was harmed or not.

"Nothing more than a few bruises and a few restless nights' sleep to come I imagine." At this he growled lower before, pulling me to him, gently cupping the back of my head once more.

"It never should have happened. I am there to protect you and so far, I have been the cause of…"

"No, please, Ryker, don't blame yourself for this," I told him, quickly interrupting his self-blame and looking up at him with what I imagined were big, pleading eyes. It was a look he couldn't seem to deny. Because he soon lowered his lips to mine, kissing me until the force of it transferred to his hands. And unfortunately, with it came an unavoidable flinch as he touched the lump on my head.

"Evie?"

"I… I got hit on the head," I admitted, making him growl,

"Fuck!"

"It's okay," I tried to say when his eyes turned murderous.

"It's not fucking okay!" he snapped before looking up and finding Faron close enough to bark an order at.

"Faron, I want you to call in a doctor, have them waiting for us."

"Ryker, I am…"

Ryker narrowed his eyes at me, stopping me in my tracks.

"I warn you, Little Bird, do not finish that sentence with the words fine or okay, or it will piss me off." I released a deep sigh before commenting wryly,

"I would say you're there already."

"Too fucking right, I am, they stole my woman, drugged her, hurt her, and tried to fucking drown her… now tell me, Evie, should I be anything but pissed off?" At this I sighed again and agreed,

"Okay, well, when you put it like that."

"Where do I send them to, boss?" Faron asked, already on the phone and clearly working fast.

"Send them to the estate, and get the chopper to land here…" He paused long enough to look down at me, running the backs of his fingers down my cheek when continuing.

"I want to get my girl back home."

The next few days that passed were admittedly a lot to take in. Of course, this wasn't just down to how my life had completely changed but more like my entire world. This was thanks to what Ryker started to share with me, something I had asked him to do the following day. But even then, he feared that I hadn't been up to it, quickly quoting the doctor who had examined my head and told Ryker to watch out for signs of concussion.

Meaning that Ryker took this as a very literal thing, not taking his eyes off me for even a second. Of course, I hit my limit when wanting to use the bathroom, snapping at him that I would rather sing on the toilet than let him watch me pee. He naturally asked how that would help, and I told him if Elton John started to get slurry, then he should come a-running. He laughed at this, but not as hard as he was laughing when he heard me sing *Rocket Man*.

"It wasn't that bad," I complained, making him smirk from where he was leaning against the wall just outside of the bathroom.

"No, but I wouldn't give up on being an artist anytime soon, as clearly, that's where your talents are." At this I grinned and told him,

"Oh, but I'm sure that's not where all my talents lie." Then I winked at him before wagging my eyebrows in a comical way, making him roar with laughter.

"And I look forward to discovering all of them but as for right now, back to bed with you." I giggled and told him,

"Funny, because I'm sure that's where to practice most of them."

"Yes, well as tempting as that is, such will have to wait."

I then gave him my best pouty face, making him chuckle.

"And as cute and adorable as that face is, you are bruised to hell and need your rest." At this I decided to try a different tactic, telling him,

"You know by denying me your body and my new found love of sex with it, you are letting the bad guys win." At this his lips twitched like he was fighting another grin.

"I am the bad guy, remember?" he teased.

"No, you're not, you rescued me, *remember...?* Which, in my book, makes you the hero," I told him as I walked back over to his huge bed, that I had to admit, was going to make it difficult to get out of in the mornings because it was seriously the stuff of sweet dreams... *just like Ryker was.*

"I also was the one to kidnap you... *twice, remember?"* he said, repeating the theme of the word 'remember' and making me grin.

"Yeah, but I secretly liked it and besides, it worked out well for the both of us, and my newly lost V card certainly thanks you for it." He laughed again and told me,

"Quit being cute, Little Dove, and get in the bed."

"Now there's an offer I can't refuse," I teased, making him sigh with a grin, shaking his head as if he didn't know what to do with my horny little self. Well, I knew exactly what he could do, he was just refusing to.

"Since when did you get so sassy, eh?" he asked, gathering me in his arms from behind and nestling me in between his legs, playing with my hands in front of me. But then I pulled away so I could turn in his arms and look back at him.

"When I started to sleeping with a Demon who vowed never to hurt me and basically just did this totally bad ass move by leaping onto the stage and saving me from drowning." At this, mirth played in his eyes before repeating,

"Bad ass, huh?"

"Yep, totally focus on that part," I quipped, and again, he laughed at that but then he focused on the first thing I said and told me,

"About that... I know I should have told you sooner."

"Told me?" I questioned.

"Before I made you mine," he added, giving me more insight as to why this was coming up now... *he felt guilty.*

"Just wondering, does sex always come with some kind of claiming element for you guys or is it just special cases?" I asked, making him smirk. Then he leaned in closer and told me,

"Only the most special cases," he teased.

"Oh, I bet you say that to all the girls," I teased back.

"Only the one who ever mattered," he replied, and I swear I would have swooned had I not already been in his arms. Instead, I kissed him, letting what his words meant to me be heard in my actions. Until I pulled back far enough to ask,

"So, about that Demon thing..." He chuckled at this before shaking his head again, mocking,

"Oh, this is going to be fun."

I ignored this and told him, "I think it's time we have the talk, don't you?"

"Not really, but I suppose there is only so long I can force sleep on you," he replied wryly, making me grin.

"You can tie me to the bed if you like," I said, holding my hands up like I was ready for the handcuffs.

"Gods but I have created a monster," he teased, making me laugh.

"Yes, one who wants feeding but considering you have denied me that, then I would say you better start talking." At this he covered his eyes with his arm in a dramatic way before groaning,

"Can't I simply claim I have a headache and that be the reason for both silence and momentary celibacy?" I laughed again, pulling his arm down and loving how funny he could be.

"I don't know, do Demons get headaches?"

"No, but we can lie about them." I giggled this time, and it was a sight he seemed to adore. But then I asked him in a serious tone,

"Are you really afraid of telling me?" At this he released a heavy sigh and told me,

"No and yes." My cynical look said it all.

"I have never cared about what another living soul thought of me... *not before there was you,*" he admitted softly, making me melt into him before whispering in his ear,

"Then trust me when I say that whatever it is, if it's a part of you, then I will accept it."

"Alright, then I ask for you to give me the night and, tomorrow, I won't just tell you, but I will show you."

"Show me who you are… but how? Just who are you, Ryker?" I asked, frowning in confusion before he pulled me close and whispered,

"I am Ryker Wyeth…"

"…Son of Greed."

CHAPTER 25
THE CORE OF GREED AND HIS SIREN

The next day, Ryker kept his word and once I was awake, he asked if I still wanted to see the real him. Of course, I said yes, if not a little apprehensively, seeing as I had no idea what that would truly entail. Especially now that I knew a bit more about his world. Because thankfully, he hadn't just dropped this bombshell on me without explaining what it truly meant. It was a conversation where I admittedly spend most of my time with my jaw slack and my mouth open. Which was a fact he teased me about whenever it happened. To the point when he growled, gripped my chin, and yanked me closer before warning,

"Sweetheart, keeping opening your mouth like that and I am going to be tempted enough to fill it." I blushed but because he seemed to like this new sassy side of me, I braved to say,

"Is that supposed to be a threat? I love hotdogs." Then I winked at him, making him roar with laughter.

"Good to know." He smirked, his voice sexy and full of

humor. But then these moments between us were the only thing that kept me sane during these heavy conversations. Like I kept needing to be reminded that despite all he had told me, Ryker was still the man I had fallen in love with. Not just the son of the mighty Mammon, his father was ruler and King of the 4th realm of Hell, making him not just a Demon but Demon freakin' royalty! A Demonic Prince of Greed, with legions upon legions of Demons under his command. A being that had been in countless battles and who fought unruly Demons and Angels by night and wore a business suit by day.

It was as terrifying as it was fascinating!

But then being an Enforcer wasn't the only thing he told me. Because as soon as we were on our way, headed to wherever it was he wanted to take me, I then got up enough courage to ask about Sirens. Mainly why I had been named such, not only by him on numerous occasions, but at the auction as well. As if my being one was some well-known statement in his world.

In fact, we hadn't long arrived at a place called La Cloche Mountains and hiked for only a short distance from where the convoy of cars had dropped us off, when Ryker started to talk about it in more detail. And he started this off by telling me a mythological story about the ancient Greek Gods.

How there was once eleven Angels known as Sirens, who were created for Zeus's amusement and were known for their beauty and enchanting voices. However, despite caring for his creations, he used them as scapegoats so blame would not be cast his way, when he made a deal with his brother, Hades (not Ryker's head of security, as trust me, I asked after first gasping in shock). This was for the Lord of the Underworld's loyalty and there was only thing Hades wanted in return...

Zeus's daughter, Persephone.

But now as for her mother, Demeter, who also happened to be Zeus's older sister and, at this point, my disgust wasn't something I could hide, because eeew... well, she did not approve of the match, being overly protective of her daughter. Zeus conceived a plan. He ordered the Sirens to lure Persephone beyond the protected barrier of Mount Olympus and into a secret garden. A place where Hades would be waiting for her. To which she was promptly kidnapped and taken back to the Underworld with him. Something that I was quick to comment about, muttering wryly,

"Hmm, I wonder how that feels... oh no, wait, never mind." Ryker gave me a teasing look in return before yanking my hand to pull me closer and growling down at me playfully,

"Behave, Little Bird." Then he kissed me, leaving me breathless before pulling back to nip at my lips as his teasing continued.

"Mmm, looks like my prisoner can be easily tamed with my lips." I grinned before giving him some of my new found sass back.

"Tamed, yes, but if you wanna see me purr, well, I will need more than a kiss, handsome." Then I winked at him and walked away. Or at least I tried to as he snagged my hand, yanked me back, and this time his growl of approval was rumbled over my lips with my back firmly pressed against the nearest tree.

Needless to say, he only continued with his story about ten minutes later after a heavy make out session.

"So, what happened to the Sirens?" I asked once we continued walking, coming to what looked like the base of the highest peak of the mountain range.

"Demeter cast blame their way, despite where their orders had come from, and Zeus cast them out, but Demeter placed a curse upon them before being banished to the human realm.

"That bitch!" I shouted, being well and truly invested in the story.

"Yes, well, she wasn't exactly known for her kindness, nor having a rational mind. She whispered to them as they fell, *'be gone and search for my daughter the world over'*. After that, each of the Sirens became human," he said, pausing in front of a bolder that looked like any other. I was about to ask for more when he reached inside a crevice in the stone and activated something I couldn't see. I heard the motions of some mechanism release from behind the rock, one that was easily the size of a car. After that it became clear that this wasn't just part of the rest of the rock formation but instead a secret doorway. He reached to the side of the boulder and swung it open like a door. And just watching the way his muscles tensed with the strength needed to do this, well, it made it hard to swallow past the sexual lump that had formed in the back of my throat.

As soon as it was open, it revealed yet another door, making it look like there was some hidden bunker behind it. Off to one side of the metal reinforced doors, was an access panel, where he put in a code, scanned his face, and then finally spoke into it, speaking foreign words I had no clue what they meant.

I had to admit, I felt a little trepidation here because when Ryker had told me he would show me what he was, this wasn't exactly what I had in mind.

"What... what is this, Ryker?" I asked nervously.

"You will soon see... come, trust me," he said, looking back at me with his hand held out, waiting for me to show him that trust. And because I didn't want to let him down, I did as he asked, placing my hand in his. He opened the door, and this must have activated the lighting system because bulbs in metal cages all flickered to life, illuminating the inside of a cave. It also must have activated the main bunker doors to close as well as the bolder to swing back into place, and the sound made me shriek out in fright. But more than that, the lights showed me what looked like industrial elevator doors, like some black cage I knew we would soon be getting into.

"Don't suppose I could wait down here for you?" At this Ryker gave me a soft, tender look before gripping my hand tighter and pulling me toward the thing. Then after slapping his hand in another scanner, the doors opened with an echoing clatter of metal before he pulled me inside.

"I guess that's a no then," I muttered as Ryker hadn't answered me. No, he just smirked like he found me sweet and endearing. So, in order to take my mind off the weirdness of it all, I asked,

"So, being called a Siren is in memory of the Sirens that fell to the earth that day?" As soon as I asked this, Ryker released a sigh, and it wasn't a sound that gave me comfort about what else he was about to say next.

"The original Sirens turned into mortals, yes, but they carried with them the latent gene over into the female offspring they were each destined to have. This continued throughout generations of daughters, and each one was thought of as a chance at getting back their wings and reclaiming who they once were. But this didn't happen and wasn't going to happen until…" He paused as if he didn't know what I would think of this next part. So as the elevator continued to make its way to, I had no clue where, I nudged him.

"Until when?"

"Until each of them were destined to meet their Fated Enforcer." I gasped at this, utterly shocked by what he was saying.

"Their Fated Enforcer?" I muttered because suddenly it all started to dawn on me. Why he had fought so hard to find me, to keep me. He believed this was all Fate.

As soon as the elevator came to a stop and the doors opened, I was out of them, needing to walk away and get some space. A space that was something right out of a damn fairytale. Christ, it looked like we were now standing outside some castle doors, and beyond them I would find an angry King sitting upon a throne of gold.

Or such a King who was standing outside them with me now.

Ryker growled angrily behind me and snapped,

"So out of everything I have told you, it is your birthright that offends you so?" he asked frustratingly.

"No! What *offends me* is now knowing the real reason you want me." At this he narrowed his dangerous gaze at me and warned,

"I suggest you rethink your next words, Little Bird, or you may not like where this temper of mine is headed." I frowned at that and snapped back,

"Oh, and just what are you going to do, gag me until I obey you?"

"Gagging you will only be a small part of what I do to punish you, if you continue down this path," he warned and, Jesus, half of me wanted to push for it and the other half go running off screaming in fear! But then, I still knew despite all of this, he wouldn't hurt me physically, which is why in the end I stayed and pushed.

"And what path is that, Ryker, hmm? The one that says *you have to be with me because it's Fated?!* What if I had been some crazy hobo, living in the wilderness, eating nothing but mushrooms and talking to a stump I had named Burt? What would you have done then?!" I snapped, making his lips twitch as if he found this amusing.

"Or what if I had been some sea fairing fisherwoman with a beard that smelt like trout and big hairy legs to keep me nice and toasty, despite having a ship full of fishermen to keep me warm because I was a big hairy slut?! Huh? What then?" I asked, and at this he could contain it any longer, now leaning against the wall and grinning at me. But then as I opened my mouth to speak again, turning away from him and having my next contender for his chosen Siren all lined up, he must have hit his limit.

"And what if I was..." At this I was spun around and forced to stop when he held me by the tops of my arms, now looking down at me.

"But you are you, Evelyn," he replied earnestly, making me swallow hard.

"But what if…"

"No… no what ifs. You were always Fated to be mine, regardless of the life you lived or the past you endured." I flinched at that and looked away, telling him in a small voice,

"But how can you say that when you don't know…" Once again he cut me off,

"I don't need to know, for there is nothing that you could tell me that would ever change the way I feel about you. About the girl I fell in love with, *not the Siren."* I looked back up at him when he said this, feeling the tears fill my eyes.

"Do you really mean that?" At this he cupped my cheek and ran the pad of his thumb under my eye, catching the first fallen tear,

"That night, I kissed you not because I knew you were my Siren, Evelyn, but because for the first time in my long life, *I had the want, the need, the desire to kiss my first human.* You tempted me like no one ever had before and had I known you were my Siren at that moment, I would have snatched you away there and then." I sucked in a quick breath at his words, letting them settle deep and affect me to my core.

"You didn't know?" He shook his head at this and told me,

"No, something I deeply regret not knowing. But, Evie, even the day after, I was still thinking about you. About the girl who captured my heart like no other. And that was all you, not some prophecy or some foregone conclusion written by the Fates. *It was all you.* With your big brown sugar eyes, your dusting of freckles I find myself itching to touch."

"You should probably get that looked at," I joked, making him smirk before continuing,

"Your delightful wit and the strength of your character. Your fearless determination, Gods, I have never known anything like it, despite cursing it a time or two." I laughed at that, knowing the hard time I gave him in looking for me. But then he looked down my body and pulled me into him on a growl.

"And let's not leave out this fuckable body I fucking crave to consume, to have writhing under me, calling out my name for hours... *for days.* The only man you will ever know claiming you, to feel entering your body and making it my own. That is not fucking Fate, Evelyn..." He paused so he could rest his forehead to mine before whispering the sweetest words,

"...but it is all you." After this, I thought he was going to kiss me, but instead he turned me around to face the castle doors.

"And now it is time to discover just who I am..." he said walking me toward the entrance to what I knew was something far greater than just a mountain. But then, I soon discovered that the doors themselves were far more than those you could just push open. Because I watched as he left my back and walked over to what looked like a gold alter. But then as I walked closer, I realized that atop of it was a black charred bowl that looked as if it had been forged in Hell.

It was all twisted up like clawed hands were cupping the charred dish, as if a moment in time had been frozen by the crashing wave of lava. The base to the alter was waist height to Ryker's tall frame and had connecting symbols all joined with swirls carved in the gold. This created a thin channel all the way down to the stone floor, continuing the design.

I quickly gasped when I saw Ryker raise his hand to his lips before biting down hard into his flesh. But before I could ask what he was doing, he lifted his crimson hand over the bowl, and I watched as thin ribbons of blood dripped down, filling it. Then the macabre scene continue, and the blood filtered down to the front of the alter, soon filling the channels and highlighting the symbols in stark crimson against the gold as the blood travelled.

This then activated another mechanism of sorts, as well as creating a shimmering veil to be seen covering the doors, for mere seconds. This was before it started to disappear, as if breaking down some magical barrier, like acid eating away at paper.

I jumped back when the doors then started to separate, feeling the strength and bulk of Ryker stepping up behind me, placing his hands at the tops of my arms as if to prevent me from running away. But then as the doors opened further, I couldn't help but gasp in utter astonishment and awe. The glow of so much gold was near blinding. It sent a beam of light straight through the opening, like a pathway to Heaven, before landing directly on me.

This was when Ryker finally finished off his sentence,

"...For this is the true nature of the Son of Greed."

CHAPTER 26
A GOLDEN MOMENT

As soon as those doors opened, the very last place I expected to find myself twenty minutes later, was in a fantasy bathroom staring at myself in a floor-length mirror wearing a dress. But it soon became clear that Ryker had plans for me, and showing off his treasure horde had not been one of them...

Of course, the moment I saw the endless cavern of treasure, with more gold and jewels than I even thought existed, I found myself stunned to silence. Meanwhile, Ryker simply walked past me, taking hold of my hand as he strode into what I soon discovered was a hollowed-out mountain.

The main part of it was a vast and seemingly endless open space where I could not even see the ceiling, it was so tall. Inside, different levels had been carved out of the rock, and each seemed to hold a different cave room or collection of treasure. As for the main part, the walls were lined with piles of gold in the form of anything from coins to jugs, jars, pots, necklaces, plates, caskets... you name it, if it could be covered in gold or forged into it, it was there.

I half expected a mighty dragon to uncurl its body and reveal itself from within the sea of gold. Down the center was a clear path, where the floor beneath the treasure gleamed like it had been made from black glass. This to the point that it almost looked like liquid and I was nearly afraid to step on it.

But then the gigantic doors behind me closed and the sound echoed through the space with a loud, deafening boom, making my echoed scream the next to follow it. Ryker laughed at me, looking more devilish than I had ever seen him, now he was surrounded by his greedy horde of treasure.

"Come, let me help you relax," he told me, holding out a hand for me to take because he wanted to lead me into a cave of sorts. One that was framed by an arch of... yep, you guessed it, *gold*.

Because I was curious to see where it led to, and too in shock to do anything but do as he asked, I put my hand in his and gave myself over to his will. Which ended up with me gasping once more in shock because it now looked like a golden living space. Everything looked old and something I would expect to find in a pharaoh's tomb. Priceless pieces of furniture were set out just like a living room, and period dramas of kings and queens filled my mind.

Elaborate gold framed sofas with deep-red velvet buttoned upholstery were positioned in front of a fireplace carved right out of the rock. One big enough to stand in, with large roman style pillars at the sides. With merely a flick of Ryker's hand, a fire erupted inside it, soon filling the large space with a crackling sound.

But as my eyes continued to scan the treasure-filled space, I found there was too much to even take in. People-sized vases, with painted gold garden scenes, small round tables that were topped with gold, and its design made it look like a giant-sized gold coin was fixed there. These held gold fringed lamps with black lacquer bases, encrusted with mother of pearl. There was a tall grandfather clock, intricately carved with gold accents. Even the rugs looked as if they had once graced the floors of some Persian King.

"I think I have just guessed your favorite color," I teased, needing something to say. But then he pulled me closer and told me,

"Your eyes."

"Sorry?"

"That's my new favorite color..." Then he growled low before telling me directly over my lips,

"...Fuck the gold." My mouth opened in surprise, which ended up being something he took as an open invitation to deepen the kiss and taste my shock for himself. Which meant that there we stood, in the middle of his golden room, kissing like I wasn't just standing in Aladdin's cave, internally freaking out about everything he was sharing with me. I wondered if that was why I clung onto him so hard, curling my fist in his jacket like it had the power to save me from a tornado.

"Mmm, fuck me, but how I do love this mouth," he hummed down at me after pulling back enough to do so and, admittedly, making me feel like swooning again. Speaking of swooning, suddenly he bent down and swept my legs out from under me, making me squeal in shock at the quick and jarring action. But he ignored this and walked past his extended horde of treasure into another cave that was connected to the living space.

It made me wonder how big this place really was and if it was a honeycomb of treasure rooms just like this one. However, what did shock me was finding a bathroom, only unlike one I had ever seen before. Because unlike the room before it, where the walls had been made to be smoother and more square, this was all left natural. Not a single even space, it looked more like the practical elements of a bathroom had been molded to fit the walls and not the other way around.

The bath for example, had been carved out of smaller mound of rock, with the outside left raw and jagged. Whereas inside it had been carved smooth before being painted gold. I had to wonder just where did the water come from, which lead onto other questions, like why it wasn't freezing cold in this cave or how did it have electric and obviously, plumping?

There was what I assumed to be a toilet off to one side behind another large rock sticking out, with some sinks sitting on a rock shelf that were large golden bowls. I didn't see a shower but seeing as there were lots of other rocks I could have looked behind, it wouldn't have surprised me to find one there. But that wasn't all the bathroom was, as there was even comfortable seating in here, in case you wanted to have a conversation with someone while in the bath. I can't even lie and say I didn't know where that thought came from because it made me wonder if the night would end there.

Hell, forget the night, I could have moved in here and lived quite happily. Well, that was until the sight of so much gold started to hurt your eyes.

Ryker put me down and watched me as I continued to study the room. As if he was silently happy to do this, as I felt his eyes following me as I walked around the space. But then I soon stopped dead, because there in the very corner of the room, was a mannequin and on it was... *the dress.*

My dress.

The golden dress I had been wearing that night, now gracing the curved lines of a white marble body. One that I swear could have been the mirror image of me, if I had ever been frozen in time. To the point that I found my hand reaching out toward it but pulling back at the same time, as if too afraid of what would happen if I did.

"Is that...? No, surely not." I was about to ask, then stopped myself, feeling foolish to presume. But then I felt him walk up behind me.

"I admit the resemblance is remarkable but not nearly as perfect as the real thing," he told me, running his hands up and down my arms, taking with it the open zip-up sweater I wore and slipping it from my shoulders. At this I could barely speak, but when my confusion continued to rise, I forced myself to ask,

"It's... it's me?"

"It is." My heart started hammering in my chest at this before I turned around and looked at him.

"But... but... how?" I stammered out, making him grin.

"Let's just say I had a lot of pictures of you... *left over from my stalker days,"* he teased, but my mind was still stuck on the fact that he had a marble statue of me!

"But that's... that's..."

"A masterpiece?" he offered, making me blush.

"Insane!" I shouted instead, making him laugh.

"If you haven't already noticed, Evie, I am not a normal man." Jeez, he had that right!

"Yes, but you had a statue made of me," I stated, trying once more for him to see how crazy this was.

"I am also a collector of the rare and beautiful, so yes, I had a statue made for such a dress when it holds such a memory needed to be showcased amongst my treasure, and that dress is only to grace the figure it was made for. So, I naturally wanted it in my collection," he told me, as if this was the most normal explanation in the world.

"But… but…" At this he grinned because I clearly still struggled for words.

"Buts are for the unsure and by now, you should be anything *but* unsure of my intent for you," he replied, making me close to actual swooning this time.

"Am I… part of your collection?" I braved to ask, and this time his grin was more like I would have expected from a Demon named Greed. But then he yanked me hard into him and told me one of the nicest things anyone has ever said to me before.

"*No… you are the gift I would give it all up for.*" At this I practically fell into him, holding him tightly and saying his name on a breathy sigh,

"*Oh, Ryker.*" He wrapped his arms around me as I hugged him, resting my cheek to his chest and closing my eyes as I let his beautiful words sink in deep and stay there. But then when I felt him pull back, I looked up, prompting him to do what he seemed to always want to do, which was cup my cheek. Then he asked,

"Will you wear it for me?"

"You want me to wear it now?" At this, a deep purring sound rumbled from his chest, as if I had just stroked a wild beast.

"I want to worship you in it." A sexual shudder ran through me at that, stealing my words and giving me the only option to nod.

"Thank you. This means a great deal to me," he said before walking toward the statue, one that was on a plinth high enough that removing the dress would have been a struggle for me alone. Something he already thought of, because as soon as he had the long, golden fabric in his hands, he laid it gently over the sofa in the room.

"Now take all the time you need. I had some feminine items stocked here in case you needed anything."

"Feminine items?" I questioned with a grin, making him lean close and whisper,

"Girly shit." I laughed at that and playfully pretended to be offended, hitting him on the arm.

"I bought these things in hopes of bringing you here one day, as I would like us to spend the night here, if that is alright with you?" he asked, making me look around the place and say,

"This place is incredible, why would I not want to spend time here?" At this he grinned, and it was in such a lighthearted way, I knew that my words had meant something to him. Like this was his secret place and he had been worried I wouldn't like it.

"But just so you remember, the human girlfriend still needs feeding... right?" At this he laughed, walked over to me, and said,

"The human girlfriend will get fed." Then he kissed my forehead, something easy for him to do given our height difference, and then he walked toward the door.

"But wait, what will you be doing while I'm getting ready?"

He smirked before cryptically answering me,

"Oh, but I might have something in mind." Then after granting me a knowing wink, he left me to get ready, making me look to the dress and say,

"Time for round two."

CHAPTER 27
RIBBONS OF GOLD

olden thoughts and golden moments.

Something which brought me back to now and how I was standing in front of a gorgeous full-length gilded mirror, close to asking myself who was the fairest of all. And I hoped the answer was at least giving me a seven out of ten.

Of course, the dress was a knockout, but knowing he'd had it made with me in mind, then I didn't even want to think of how much it cost. But then one glance at the marble freakin' statue of me, and again, enough dollar signs flashed up that I didn't even want to think of the cost of that either.

But then again, here I was, standing in his golden horde, so clearly money wasn't a big deal to someone like Ryker. But to me, it had always been a struggle. Which was why being here now, like this, was both out of my comfort zone and out of my reality. However, one thought back to the way Ryker had smiled at me when I told him my thoughts, and it was enough to calm my nerves. Because clearly, he wanted me here and now it was time to find out exactly what he had planned.

So, after one last look in the mirror, checking my hair, that I had pinned into barrel curls over to one side and tried to apply the same make up as last time, I braved walking to the door. The long, slim ballgown that flared out at the skirt in a mermaid style, had me holding it up as I walked just like last time. The heavy weight of the exquisite demask pattern in sparkling gold sequins was one I remembered. Its sweetheart neckline, with little shoulder strap sleeves meant wearing a bra was out of the question, instead I just grabbed just a pair of sexy lace panties and left behind the bra to match. The dress fitted me like a glove and made me feel amazing. I hoped that Ryker liked it this time just as much as he had the first.

Which was why I was hoping that I looked similar to how I had done that night, because it was clear Ryker was trying to recreate a moment. Also making me wonder if what he had planned for me was how he would have hoped that night in the club would have gone... had I not run from him and instead woken up with him by my side.

Of course, being able to recreate that night hadn't just been thanks to the dress, because Ryker hadn't lied when he told me I should find everything I need, including a new pair of gold strappy shoes to match. It also made me wonder how long he intended for us to stay here, as I had to confess, the idea of being locked away with Ryker made my body shiver, and not in a bad way.

More like I was now living in a sexual fantasy, kind of way.

But then this became even more real and closer to being

just that, when I walked out and found him ready for me. And when I say ready for me, what I really focused on was the bed of gold now situated in the very middle of his horde. It was like some kind of sacred shrine, and I could only imagine what we would soon be doing on it. Or should I say, what *he* would be doing to *me* on it.

Speaking of the man, he was standing there, now holding a glass of champagne, the bottle I recognized as being the same I had enjoyed before. An endearing fact he kept remembering and therefore it was one I continued to receive. But then the champagne was the very least of my thoughts right now, seeing as I was more mesmerized by the man who held it. Especially as he was now dressed in the same dark suit he had that night, looking even more handsome because now I could see his face.

Of course, I could also allow myself the time to really admire the look of him, because before he had scared the crap out of me. But that was back when I had no idea what he wanted with me and when I believed him to be some mob boss or something. Who knew I would find him being a Demon more appealing?

As for right now, well I wasn't the only one drinking in my fill and his eyes scanned the length of me just as his motions became slow and more predatory. Then with only two words and a jerk of his fingers, I became a puppet in the skills of this master.

"Come here."

I did as I was told and tried not to look like a combination of uncool things. Like nervous, clumsy, too eager to please, or the worst one, *self-conscious*. But then this was easier said than done in sight of such a man, which is why self-conscious and nervous took center stage.

"That night, you looked exquisite," he told me, making me blush when his hand came up and he ran his thumb over my freckled cheeks, ones I didn't try to hide under make up because I knew he liked them.

"But now without the mask..." He paused to take a breath before telling me in earnest, *"...fucking perfection."*

He growled just as his hand slid to the side of my head, embedding his fingers in my hair and pulling my face up to his as he kissed me. This time it was hard and all consuming, like he was trying to brand not only the sight of me to his memory but the taste of me to that of his Demonic soul. I couldn't help but let my head fall back, where he cradled my head to deepen the kiss from above.

"Gods, girl, you drive me wild for you," he said, before lifting me in his arms and carrying me over to the bed, one that I could see better now.

It was unlike anything I had ever seen before and not just some gaudy bed painted gold. But it looked as if it had been made with the Gods in mind. As if some sorcerer had commanded an ocean of gold and while casting his hands outward, it had created two waves and remained frozen like that. This then left a space in the center for the actual bed part to go.

Although surprisingly, the sheets were black silk, making it look like liquid flowed over the mattress and between the sections of the wave design at its lowest. But this wasn't all, because there was also a golden canopy, like four bare twisted trees had been dipped in gold and positioned at each corner. As if the golden flood had flowed around the roots of them. Then from where all the branches entwined, there were hundreds of lengths of thick golden ribbon acting as curtains either side of the bed.

It was incredible and like something straight out of a fairytale.

"That's not a bed, that's art," I told him, making him grin, telling me,

"Not yet it isn't, but it soon will be." This was cryptic to say the least, and only managed to add to the anticipation and my nervousness. But then as he lay me down on the bed, he rose back up and just stood there and watched me.

"I... erm..." I made a sound because I was unsure what to do.

"Easy, sweetheart, I am just taking in this moment so as I may always remember the beauty before me," he told me, making me blush. But then after I started to squirm under his heated gaze, I pushed myself up, leaning back on my arms, so I wasn't lying flat.

"Are you... are you going to come join me?" I asked in an unsure tone and again, he seemed to be feeding from my apprehension.

"I will indeed but first, I have to ask if you trust me?"

I frowned at that, wondering where this was coming from. Or more like why?

"Let me be more specific... do you trust me when it comes to your body, Evelyn?" I swallowed hard and thought back on how he had taken such care with me for my first time. How he cared about my pleasure and not just taking his own. How well he seemed to know my body already and the way he treated it as if it was precious to him. So, because of all this, naturally, I told him,

"Yes, I do." At this he grinned and told me,

"Good, then I want you to prove it by letting me have my way with you tonight." I swallowed hard before repeating uncertainly,

"Your way with me?" At this he looked down at his cuffs and pulled at them, while explaining,

"I have certain… tastes should we say."

"You mean kinks?" I asked, and his grin was bad enough that he didn't offer it to me this time but focused on his cuffs again.

"You could call them that, yes." I swear anyone looking at me then would have no doubt called what I did next a comedy gulp.

"Will… will it hurt me?" At this he finally looked up at me, his eyes flashing with that inhumane glow before telling me,

"Never. I would not allow such a thing. No, for the most part it will be… *restricting.*" Okay cue for another comedy gulp, one he didn't miss this time as he homed in on the action. Damn that handsome evil grin of his.

"You want to tie me up?" I asked, continuing with my brave questioning. But then his answer to this was confusing at first.

"You ran from me for a long time, longer than I would have ever thought possible." He paused, running his hands down the lengths of ribbon, watching the gold as it glided through his fingers. "Therefore, I have had a long time to imagine all the ways I would punish you for the offence."

"Punish me?" I nearly squeaked, making his head snap up and his eyes burned into mine.

"There are many forms of punishment, Little Bird, let me

show you," he said, his eyes glowing before he took a step back.

I would have asked him where he was going, but he stopped and raised his hands up while looking at the bed. I ended up crying out in shock as he started to forge the gold around the bed like he commanded it!

I looked all around me in utter astonishment with my mouth hanging wide open, gasping at the unbelievable. This was because the gold turned into liquid once more and started to take a new form, shaping itself around the bed I sat on. It was a sight that startled me enough to make me quickly go scrambling into the center on my knees, afraid it would touch me.

The gold started to stretch and separate into long lengths, raising up like bars of a cage. They were now reaching up and arching over where some of the ribbons fluttered down on the bed, raining like streamers from above. Then bursts of golden flowers began to bloom as golden vines grew from beneath. Now wrapping themselves around the bars and creating a floral design on what now looked like giant bird cage.

My eyes shot back to Ryker to see his eyes now simmering down back to the navy-blue I knew best, whereas mine were wide and full of questions.

"Ah, now that is better for my lovely Little Dove," he said as if congratulating himself.

"Ryker?" I said his name in a fearful tone, now seeing the cage I looked locked to, with no door to speak of.

"It is more fitting, don't you think?" he said, his voice taking on a strange tone, as if something else was trying to break through.

"Ryker, what is this?" I asked, about to get to my feet when suddenly, I cried out when with a flick of his wrist, the ribbons moved and started to restrain me. They wrapped around my torso, crossing over and pulling tight against my breasts. Long lengths then sought out my wrists, wrapping around them, the same as others did with my ankles.

Then I cried out as everything tightened, before they pulled me toward him, shifting me along the bed with ease thanks to the silk sheets. Only stopping when I was where he was waiting for me. I was still on my knees but despite being on the high bed, his dominating presence still towered in front of me. His hand then came through the bars and stroked down my face, his enjoyment clear to see.

"Easy, sweetheart, nothing I do to you will hurt, but you will let me have my fun now, won't you?" he asked in a seductive tone.

I found myself unable to do anything other than nod slightly.

Then he praised,

"My good girl..." However, he paused long enough to pull my face closer to the bars so he could growl over my lips,

"...Good little pet of mine."

CHAPTER 28
BIRD IN A CAGE

"*Good little pet of mine.*"

He praised again, before letting me go and reaching back with his hand. I gasped when he made the gold table slide toward him, the glass and the bottle in the crystal ice bucket not even so much as losing a drop. This was done so he could reach back without letting go of my face, now bringing the glass through the bars and to my lips.

"Drink," he ordered, making me do as I was told, feeling strangely like this game wasn't only turning him on but doing something to me too. I felt that knowing wetness between my legs, and the feeling of being his pet, of belonging to him, was an intoxicating experience. It was also a spell I didn't want to break, needing to see where the end would take me.

So, when he pulled the glass back and exchanged it with lifting the lid off a dish, my eyes went wide. Chocolate covered strawberries were dusted with edible gold leaf, making them look even more decadent, and clearly, Ryker had thought of everything.

"I know you like these, for you always saved them 'til last whenever eating a particular dessert in the coffee shop you worked," he told me, surprising me with how much detail he had taken in of my life when stalking me. Again, another thrill shuddered through me at the thought of him watching.

"Open," he ordered next after plucking one from the pile and holding it out to me. But when I raised my hands up to take it, his other hand shot up before slashing down. This made the ribbons around my wrists tighten before they yanked my hands down by my sides.

"Ah, ah, ah… my rules, remember… now lean forward and open your pretty mouth for me," he commanded after the reprimand. So, I did as I was told, leaning forward and opening my mouth as he held out a chocolate dipped strawberry for me. I bit into it, and it was so juicy that I felt it drip past my lips and down my chin.

His eyes locked onto the red fruity drip as I chewed the delicious treat. But as I opened my mouth ready for more, his hand was suddenly taking something instead of giving, as he gripped my face and pulled me closer so he could kiss me through the bars. He then licked up from my chin to my lips, catching the juice before sucking the taste from my mouth, making me moan at how erotic an act it was.

"Fucking delicious," he growled, pulling back and now licking his lips, making me wish that talented tongue of his was still licking me. But then he pulled back to feed me more, and so the game continued. A sip of champagne, a bit of a strawberry, and then a kiss for my owner. Which

meant that I was near dizzy from how stimulating it all was.

But then when he was finished playing this game, he gave me one last drink of champagne before he set the glass down for good. I was on the edge, questioning just what he intended to do next, because he seemed to have a definite plan in his mind. I knew that for certain when he flicked his wrist and the ribbons tightened once more before pulling me back. I cried out in surprise at the sudden action, one that continued to pull at me, until I was lying flat on my back.

As for Ryker, he lifted his hands, creating steps up onto the bed that he walked up, and just before I could ask how he would get inside the cage, he ended up astounding me further. His clothes started to strip away, as if now nothing more than dust floating behind him, leaving behind the utter perfection that was all him.

A body so breathtaking, I found it hard to breathe, and not just because he started to walk into the bars. The gold lengths actually merged into his body, as though he was momentarily becoming a part of the gold itself. Like he didn't only have the ability to control it but had the power to absorb it as well.

Again, the sight of my utter shock was one he seemed to enjoy, and a grin played at his devilish lips as he took the last few steps to bring him inside the cage completely. Then as he stood over me, he waved a hand down my body and slowly, the same thing that happened to his clothes started to happen to mine. The dress started to disappear, making me wonder where it went and was it no more? Had it been destroyed completely never to be seen again, or was it back on the marble statue of me.

But then thoughts of the dress were no more, and I soon realized that all that was left, was the lengths of gold silk ribbon that bound my body in so many places. As for Ryker, his eyes started to glow that brighter blue as he scanned the length of me like a hungry wolf.

"Gods but how I am going to enjoy this," he told me like a vow, and I swallowed hard in view of him. His muscular body on show, standing over me like a God ready to take me to Heaven. Or perhaps his sinful version of Hell was more like it. Either way, I knew I would go regardless. His large cock was also a sight I could barely look away from because it stood firm and ready for action. Which was why when he finally did drop to his knees, I released a relieved breath. The wait had been making me squirm.

"You look like my most treasured gift ready to be unwrapped… but unwrap you I will not," he told me, making me frown and, in turn, the sight of my confusion made him grin once more.

"You won't?" I questioned, daring now to speak.

"No, not when I have far more important uses for your bindings," he answered before proving this with another flick of his wrist. This time one that commanded even more ribbons to fall from above and wrap around my breasts this time. This before pulling tight enough, that it made me gasp.

However, I didn't have long to question it as another ribbon made its way around my neck. In fact, too many to count all came at me, and soon I found myself tied up, with my arms spread out to my sides. And as for my legs, these were pulled up in the air before being spread wide open. Oh and with Ryker knelt between them, moving his hands like he was conducting a masterpiece.

But it was when the ribbons snaked between my legs that I started to pull against them. Especially when they started to spread open my sex and embed themselves in the crack of my ass, forcing me up and hovering above the bed.

"Ryker, please... I..."

"Easy now, just relax and don't fight them," he cooed down at me, his arm reaching down the length of my body and stroking two fingers along my jaw line. Then when I did what he asked me to do, he let that same hand travel the return journey, now playing special attention to my tied breasts that were perked up, looking twice the size as usual.

"Now as for these beautiful breasts of yours, lets decorate them, should we? For such a bounty deserves to be painted in glittering jewels," he told me, pulling at my nipples and making me cry out at the sweet pain that shot straight to my very exposed sex. Then once my nipples were hard enough, he ran a palm over the top of them and revealed the decorations he spoke of. A pair of golden clamps in the shape of diamond encrusted starburst were now gripping onto my erect nipples, each the size of a large gold coin and covering the whole of my pink areolas.

Again, the sight must have turned him on, because that same glow ignited momentarily before shimmering down. As for the clamps, they bit into me but, thankfully, weren't unbearable to take. No, instead they only managed to heighten his touch, as he soon started to pay my sex a visit, this time staying there.

However, so he didn't have to hunch over, he jerked his fingers up, making the ribbons yank me further up, until part of my back was now lifted off the bed as well.

"Ah!" I shouted, as the jerk of my body caused my

breasts to drop and hang closer to my chin, and therefore the clamps bit down with the movement. But then this complaint ended quickly when he dipped his head and started making a meal out of me. His tongue licked long strokes up the length of my folds before latching onto my clit and sucking hard before flicking it. He then continued to alternate between all three, making me near mindless.

"Please! Please, Ryker…!" I begged, because he would bring me to the brink before changing his focus and leaving me gasping to come.

"Mmm, yes, little bird of mine?" he hummed against my quivering thigh, and when I opened my eyes, it was to find him smiling against my flesh looking down at me. My leg held firmly in his grasp, as if ready to take a bite out of it. Navy-blue eyes turned more Demonic in nature, and the thrill of white fire seen in them was enough to have me panting as fear and lust merged into one. It was a powerful concoction, and enough that the next time he teased, I came like a fucking explosion of sensation. But first he wanted me to beg.

"Please… please make me come?" I asked, giving him reason for that grin to grow before he bit my thigh, making me cry at the sting of his teeth. However, he didn't break the skin, but it did mean that when he went back to my clit, I came harder than ever before.

After this, he left me panting and the lower half of my body swaying in the ribbons. Then he positioned himself between my legs, making the ribbons drop me like before, so only my legs were held up and open. Again, the sudden motion made my nipples zing with pain, morphing it quickly into pleasure.

"You beg so beautifully, Evelyn… so perfect, *every fucking inch of you,*" he said, growling this last part before shocking me on a desperate cry as his cock slammed into me without much warning.

"AAHHH OH GOD!" I screamed as he seated himself inside me, his big heavy cock stretching my sex and adding to the pain-pleasure dynamic.

"Fuck, but your hot, wet pussy is made for me. Made for my cock, for my desire… *for my seed,*" he said half with gritted teeth, as if his own pleasure was building far faster than he intended.

"In fact, let me show you how beautiful your submission looks. How beautifully owned you are," he said, now lifting a hand up over him, and at this I watched as the roof of the cage started to change. The gold merged together and soon I found myself staring back at myself as he created a mirror of gold, clear enough for me to see our reflection.

But then he leaned over my body, and whispered in my ear,

"Watch as I fuck the beauty I own." Then he started moving, and I cried out as that euphoric feeling quickly built once more inside me. I closed my eyes, the glimpses of him fucking me too intense to witness. However, the second I did, he was growling down his next order at me,

"Open your eyes and don't you dare fucking close them… open them and watch as I possess you!" They snapped back open at this, not wanting to disobey him, and now I forced myself to watch as he fucked me hard and fast. My breasts were slapping up and down, even as the ribbons tightened their hold. The clamps biting down with every bounce, making me moan and writhe against the restraints.

"Yes, yes, yes… fuck, Ryker, yes, I'm going to…"

"No! For we find it together!" he growled down at me but then as he lowered himself over me, I found him whispering at my ear,

"But not before, I claim you for all eternity." Then I watched in fear as his Demonic face started to show.

Starting with…

His Fangs.

CHAPTER 29
GOLDEN QUESTIONS

I didn't get to question this change, because suddenly the ribbon around my neck was ripped away, at the same time his hand was fisted in my hair. He yanked my head to the side and dove into my neck, before biting me there and making me scream.

Pain shot through me as I started to struggle, the ribbons tightening instantly. However, what I thought started off as a nightmare ending to making love, suddenly made me scream with the most intense pleasure. I came like I never had, making all before it shadow in the wake of this new sexual experience. I kept my eyes on the sight of him ravishing me, drinking my blood and making me his meal like some wild beast.

At the same time his hips bucked into me, and he continued to thrust his cock, pounding into me and dragging out the orgasm for what felt like endless minutes. But then he suddenly tore his fangs from my throat and bowed his body back, roaring at the mirror as he came. I became transfixed by the sight of his pleasure, his muscles tensed like solid steel and the cords on his neck straining against the skin. The sight of my blood pooling at his open mouth before dripping down his chin and onto his hard, wide chest shouldn't have turned me on the way it did.

He looked like an uncontrollable Demon feeding from his victim, and again I had to question why these thoughts only added to my erotic desire. One that was winding down for both of us. I now felt beautifully fucked raw. As for Ryker, he dipped his head to my neck once more and I tried not to flinch. Something I didn't manage to succeed in as he eased my fears,

"Calm, sweetheart, for I will not bite you again, I only wish to clean the mess I made, as I have already sealed the wound."

"Why... why did you bite me?" I braved to ask as soon as my ragged breath returned enough to speak.

"All in good time, Dove, but first, let's release you of your restraints, should we?" Then he took his time carefully freeing me, as he pulled at the ribbons, releasing my body and making me wonder if he received enjoyment from doing it himself. Because he didn't use his power to move them like before, so I could only assume that he now took pleasure in taking care of me. His hands stroked against the slight red marks made by the ribbon, kissing the darker imprints found on my skin.

Then came the nipple clamps, and he warned me,

"Take a deep breath." The second I did, he removed both at the same time, making me hiss with the spike of pain as blood flowed back into my nipples. But then his mouth was soon on them, sucking gently and soothing the pain there.

After this, he bundled me up against him with the soft silk sheets covering my now shivering body.

"I don't know why I am…"

"Ssshh now, it's just the adrenaline, it will pass, just let me hold you through it." And pass it did… and in the most wonderful way, because being held in Ryker's arms was like a dream. One I would have stayed in if the burning question about my blood had not been as persistent as it was.

"So, you like to bite during sex… good to know," I said, making him scoff.

"Trust me when I say, you are the first and will most definitely be the only."

"Also, good to know." I felt him grin at this, as he held me from behind and dipped his lips to where he had bitten me.

"But seeing as we are on the subject, there is something else we must discuss," he said, making me tense in his hold. His tone told me this was something important.

"Is this where you tell me you will need me to slit a vein daily for you to feed like a Vampire?" He scoffed at this before muttering,

"I am no fucking Vampire."

"You mean those exist?!" I said, turning around to face him and making his eyes soften at the sight of my curiosity.

"Yes, they exist, but any warped cultural notions you have of them needing to drink blood in order to survive is misguided, just as it maybe with your thoughts on Demons."

"Oh phew, for a second there I thought I would have to…" He swiftly interrupted me,

"Become my daily meal… no, Little Bird, but I will become yours," he replied, making me frown in question.

"What do you mean?" At this he raised his wrist to his lips and before I could stop him, a pair of those same frightening fangs extended and he bit down hard into his own flesh.

"Ryker! What are you…!" I never got to finish as he brought his bleeding wrist in front of me, his blood dripping all over the sheets. Then he lifted it to my lips and gave me one last order,

"Drink." I swallowed hard and shook my head a little.

"No… I can't do…"

"Drink, Evelyn, this is not a request," he said sternly, and because I was still in the aftermath of playing the part of his pet, my mouth opened as he brought it closer.

"Good girl, now lock your lips around the wound and suck… *drink me down, my Siren.*" He purred this last part the second I made contact with his open flesh. His blood filled my mouth, and I swallowed the first taste of him, discovering it wasn't as I thought it would be.

Not. At. All.

In fact, I couldn't help but moan as my tastebuds sang in pleasure, something that quickly traveled to my sex, making it flutter. Then much to my embarrassment, I found myself coming again, the moment I heard his deep and guttural growl of gratification coming from behind me. However, the moaning scream I did around his wound was echoed by his own release, and I felt the jets of come shoot up my back as he too found his sexual release from having me drink from him.

But then when I pulled away, his hand cupped the back of my head and pushed me back to his wrist, one held firm and locked to my lips.

"More," he ordered on another growl. So, I did what I was told, drinking down even more of him, now doing so until he was ready for me to stop.

"Alright, my claimed, that should be enough… for now," he said, pulling his wrist from my lips and I watched as the wound started to knit back together instantly. *It was fascinating.*

"Will I… have to do that often?" I asked quietly, feeling vulnerable for asking.

"It is my hope that you will want to, yes." His reply made me turn in his arms and nod, as that was the only answer I could give him. However, his smile told me that he was happy with this, and he brushed his thumb across my heated cheeks.

"Now, how about I feed my girl?" he said, making me grin, before inviting sassy me back to play by licking my lips and telling him,

"I think you just did." At this he grinned big and teased down at me, making me giggle,

"Damn… but I did create a little monster."

⚘

A little time later and I was dressed once more, but this time in a satin and gold nightgown. It was beautiful, with most of the top being a sash of gold material, I didn't even know the name of. But it looked like it had been spun straight from the precious metal into the finest thread.

It covered most of my torso, including one breast and dipped off the shoulder with its sleeves. The other breast was black satin, which joined the long flowing skirt, that had a slit off to one side and was edged in the same gold.

My hair was down and in loose curls around me, thanks to Ryker ridding me of all the pins I had used earlier. We were also lounging in the bed, eating from the tray of food he seemed to have plucked out of thin air. Perfectly sliced fruit, cheese, meats and nuts were all laid out on a big golden platter that we both picked at. As for Ryker, he busied himself feeding me, and dipping his fingers in my mouth at every opportunity.

It was perfect.

Because while we did this, we talked more about his world, and let's just say that the Vampire comment was not one I was willing to let go of just yet. But we also talked about his origins and his father, who ruled down in Hell and acted as Lucifer's treasurer of souls. Needless to say, it was all as fascinating as it was mind blowing.

But then we spoke about other things also. Like he asked about my art and if it would be something I would like to pursue. This lead on to me telling him about all the art I sadly left behind. This before I started to question how I would even begin to start again. It was a conversation which soon prompted me to ask exactly what the future may look like for us both. And a question that soon made him tense.

In fact, I thought I had said something wrong, especially when he abruptly shifted from the bed and got to his feet. One that shortly after all our sexual exploits, he had changed back to one more conventional looking. I swear I had been almost sad to see the bird cage disappear.

He then held his hand out to me once more and told me,

"There is something I wish to show you." I didn't

question this, I simply put my hand in his and let him help me to my feet. But then when he started to lead me further into the mountain and along the snaked path through his treasure, I couldn't help but ask,

"Ryker, where are we going?"

"You'll see," he told me, squeezing my hand as if to try and easy my nervousness. One that only mounted as we came to a tunneled cave, one glittering with gold just like the rest of the place. Thankfully, this part was still lit up like the rest of the vast space, with gold lanterns showcasing the modern age of electricity.

"Not much further now," he assured me and he was right, because a few seconds later and the cave opened up into another large room and, this time, what decorated it was art I recognized.

"I keep the most important treasure back here," he told me softly the second after I gasped at the sight.

"My... it's... *all my paintings!*" I stammered as I looked around the room, shocked to see them all displayed on golden easels, like his own personal art gallery.

"You kept them! Oh, Ryker, you don't know what this means to me!" I said, throwing myself in his arms and hugging him, making him hum down at me,

"Not nearly as much as they mean to me, for they were created by the woman I love." I melted into him, before lifting my head and going on my tiptoes to kiss him. Something he appreciated as he quickly deepened the kiss. But then when I pulled back, I whispered,

"Thank you, honey." His eyes heated at the endearment I braved to make, telling me I had done the right thing.

"You're welcome, sweetheart," he replied, now kissing

me on my forehead. But then I stepped back so I could face all the small canvases displayed, telling him,

"I still can't believe it... thank you for showing me this."

"That's not all I wanted to show you, Little Bird," he said, making me turn back around to face him and, this time, my shock didn't just continue, it nearly made me fall to my knees.

However, there was already one of us on our knees and the second he lifted a box up and flipped open the lid, I gasped just as he asked...

"Marry me, Evelyn."

CHAPTER 30
THE QUESTION OF TRUTH

"Marry you?" I repeated, and I wasn't sure why, seeing as he had a ring and everything. But I think my utter shock was easy to see, along with my panic. He didn't answer me, but simply pulled the ring from the box and started to put it on me, which was when I pulled back. Something I hated to do seeing as the hurt was easy to see on his face.

"Yes, Evelyn, marry me," he repeated, making me shake my head and tell him,

"But we haven't been together longer than a few days and you... *you don't even know me.*" At this he frowned before getting back to his feet and telling me,

"I know everything I need to in order to know this is what I want." After this I really started shaking my head.

"No... you don't, and you can't say that," I argued, making him narrow his gaze down at me.

"The fuck I can't. I love you, Evie, that's all that matters."

"But... but you don't know me enough to..." Again he cut me off, asking,

"Do you love me?" I startled at this, realizing I hadn't said it yet. But I knew the second I did say it, then he would find even less of a reason not to marry me. And I couldn't let him do that. I couldn't trap him this way. Not when he didn't know the real me.

Not when he didn't know what I had done.

So, I did the cowardly thing and turned away from him, telling him as I did,

"Why can't we just carry on the way we are?"

"Evelyn, do you love me?" he asked again, ignoring the way I tried to steer the conversation away from admitting that I did, knowing he would use it against my weak reasons.

"Ryker, this all too fast, we barely know each other." At this his jaw hardened and his eyes narrowed before he looked away.

"I see," he said firmly, and just the way his voice changed, I could hear the hurt I had caused.

"I see," he said again, and I actually winced from it. But just as I said his name, he promptly left, now walking out the door.

"Ryker, I..." This trailed off into a curse... "Fuck!" I hissed, grabbing my head and hating what I was doing to him. Because if I was honest, saying yes to marrying Ryker felt so fucking right! Being his for as long as I was alive, seemed like the most natural decision to make in the world. But the girl he was asking, wasn't the girl he knew. I wasn't the Evelyn Parker he was asking to marry him.

I was Evelyn Leucosia.

Murderer.

But then as I looked around the room, the evidence to the love he had for me cried out to me. It was showcased everywhere in the artwork he had saved. So, I had to question what his reaction would be to finding out about my past. He was a Demon after all, perhaps he wouldn't care.

Perhaps when he said he knew all that mattered to him, he was being truthful. And well, in reality, if he couldn't accept it, then wasn't I better knowing now? Before he had the chance to break an even bigger part of my heart the longer I stayed? Because only one of two things was going to happen. He would either say that he didn't care about my past crime, or he would ask me to leave.

Now the question was, would I be willing to risk it? Because if the only reason I wouldn't marry him was because I didn't want him to trap him. To allow him to enter into such a relationship without knowing who and what I had done. Then wasn't dating him just the same thing? Foolishly allowing him to believe I was one thing, when I was in fact another?

So, I had to ask myself... *what was the difference?*

I was being deceitful either way and I could now make a choice. I could continue pretending to be who he wanted me to be, or I could confess to what I had done and hope that he chose being with me regardless.

Because Ryker could have done the same thing. He could have continued to hide who he truly was from me for fear that I would want to leave him. For fear that I wouldn't accept the real him. But he hadn't done that to me, and I knew that he deserved the same in return.

"Fuck it!" I groaned before running out of the room and down the golden hallway.

"Ryker! Ryker, please… please, don't go… I'm sorry… I am not who you think I am!" I shouted the moment I saw him still walking back the way we came. He was near the center of the cave where the bed was and he froze as soon as I said this, now looking back at me over his shoulder.

"Do you love me?" he asked before turning to face me, making my shoulders slump before admitting with tears in my eyes,

"Yes… yes, I love you. Of course, I love you. How could I not, Ryker? Other than Arthur, you are the best thing to ever happen to me and despite everything that happened, all the running I did, in truth I was just scared. Scared because for the first time in my life, I knew what it was like to love and fear what it could do to me. Because honestly… *I have loved you ever since our first kiss.*" At this he closed his eyes, as if trying to deal with the rush of emotions my words brought him. As if this had meant the absolute world to him. Which was why when he started striding his long legs back to me, I put my hand up quickly to stop him.

"But there is more, Ryker."

"And I told you once before, sweetheart, there is nothing that could change the way I…"

"I killed my mom." I blurted it out on a desperate sob, making him pause his steps.

"What?" he whispered, and I bit my lip to try and stop it from quivering. But knowing that I had so much more to say, and while there was still distance between us, I rushed to carry on,

"I didn't mean for it to happen, but he was hurting her again."

"Who?" he gritted out venomously.

"M-my... my step-dad," I answered on a stuttered whisper, making him look pained, closing his eyes for a few seconds before asking me firmly,

"What did he do, Evelyn?" His voice was as hard as granite when he said this, but I knew it wasn't aimed at me.

"What he always did... he ruined everything!" At this I broke down and just as I was falling to my knees, Ryker was there to catch me. He lifted me into his arms, and I curled into his hold and sobbed.

I cried out all the years of pain. The shame and the heartbreak. I poured it all out like it would never stop. Because it never did. It never went away. Day by day it ate away at me, one small piece at a time.

"Ssshh, it's okay... I've got you... I've got you now," he soothed down at me as I sobbed my heart out, crying what felt like years of held in emotion. I had locked that night away for so long, that now it was free once more, it was like reliving the past all over again. I felt Ryker sit, knowing we had made it to the bed, and I was positioned onto his lap. He stroked back my hair from the side of my face as I soaked my tears into his shirt. But he just let me cry, knowing that I needed to get it all out. Only asking me for more details when I had calmed enough to speak again.

"Are you ready to tell me what happened, baby?" he asked tenderly, making me nod. So, I shifted off his lap next to him, and folded my legs up, hugging them to my chest.

"He had a drinking problem but even when he was sober, he was an asshole. Like he didn't know how to be anything else, you know?" Ryker nodded and told me,

"Men like him don't deserve to have a family, and they

don't deserve the love of a good woman." I swallowed hard and nodded.

"No... no they don't," I agreed, rubbing my nose on the back of my hand because there was nothing else. Well, until Ryker suddenly tore some of the silk off the sheets, making me jump.

"You didn't have to..." He gave me a pointed look and asked,

"What happened when he drank, Evelyn?"

"At best, he was verbally abusive, at his worst, he became violent," I admitted, holding myself tighter as I remembered what he put us through. Ryker gritted his teeth and looked like he wanted to kill him all over again.

"I begged my mom to leave him, but she was terrified he would find us, and it would make it so much worse when he did. But she would always protect me, whenever he turned on me, she was always there, taking the hits, the punches. Then he would leave, and I would be there holding the ice packs to my mom's face or cleaning up the blood, feeling guilty it was her and not me," I told him, needing to wipe a fresh stream of tears.

"Baby, no, you were just a child," he told me softly, pained by my admission.

"I know but at the time, I just wanted it all to stop, you know? I just thought if he went away, so would all the pain, all our problems. It would just be me and my mom again, dancing on Sunday mornings to the radio, eating pizza on Fridays watching gameshows together. All the stuff we used to do before he came into our lives," I told him, trying so hard to hold onto those memories I had of her. The ones that didn't have him tainting our lives.

"She sounded wonderful," he said, making me grin despite the pain.

"She was... she was the best mom... the best she could be under the circumstances, you know?" He nodded, making it easy for me to continue.

"It's why I'm afraid of water, she found him once punishing me." At this Ryker had to force himself to keep control. I could tell when his Demon growled and cursed,

"Bastard!"

"I won't go into what he did, but it was bad, Ryker... so bad that I nearly didn't... *make it*... not if my mom hadn't saved me." At this he held himself so still, so tensed I thought he would any minute burst out of his skin.

"I would have killed him... I would have ripped him apart!" he snarled angrily, making me put my hand on his thigh, trying to bring him back with my touch. Especially when that white fire transformed his eyes from the blue depths I loved into the Demon I was still getting to know. However, my gentle touch seemed to work, because it brought him back enough to ask,

"Tell me what happened to him, and I will pray it was the painful death he deserved." I took a deep breath, finding strength in his words, knowing now that I had nothing to fear.

"The night it happened, he rang my mom, drunk at some bar, wanting her to pick him up because they wouldn't let him drive. I remember wishing that they had, that he would have just crashed his car that night and been the only one to die," I said bitterly, turning my head away and swiping angrily at the fresh tears that fell.

"What happened, Evie?" he pressed when I was silent for

long minutes after this, knowing what came next was the hardest part.

"She didn't want to leave me in the house alone, knowing that I got scared. So, she told me to dress in my warmest clothes, and we left to pick him up. But before we did, I took something, something I had found in the closet a few days before."

"What was it?" he asked, and I swallowed hard knowing I was near the part of the story I would come to regret for the rest of my life.

"A gun," I told him, making him release a breath before he placed a hand on my knee and tenderly gave me courage.

"Oh, sweetheart."

"I hid it under my sweater, hoping I wouldn't need it. That it would be one of those rare times where he would just pass out and not cause too much trouble. But I needed to protect my mom, I told myself enough was enough." He nodded, as if really understanding this, and it gave me enough strength to continue.

"But it didn't happen that way. He started arguing the moment he got in the car. My hands started shaking, I could feel the gun heavy in my lap, just waiting for me to use it. I'd seen enough cop shows to know how to check that it was loaded and it was, but... *I didn't know about the safety,"* I said quietly, looking up at Ryker through a watery gaze. At this Ryker tensed as if this was as hard for him to hear as it was for me to say.

"He started shouting, God, it was so loud. Then he hit her, making her swerve the car and then he hit her again because of it. She kept crying out, begging him to stop or they would crash the car. So, I pulled out the gun and pointed it at him. He was so shocked, his face... fuck, I would never forget his face, Ryker... I... I had never been so scared," I told him, which was when he hit his limit, and he pulled me into him, letting me cry once more into his chest. Then he stroked the back of my head, his other arm wrapped around me, making me feel so safe, so secure.

"It's okay, baby, it's okay... we will get through this, just take it slow... *breathe with me,*" he said when my sobs grew louder, making me focus on his voice and doing as he asked.

"That's it... good girl, that's good," he praised, making me sniff and use the silk in my hand to wipe away my tears.

"I think that's enough for today, sweetheart, I think we should continue this another..."

"No... I... I want to get it out. I *need* to tell you what happened." He released a deep sigh before he nodded at this.

"He must have realized the safety was still on, because he didn't even flinch when he told me to shoot. So, I did. I pulled the trigger, but nothing happened. Then he snatched the gun out of my hand and stomped on the breaks over my mom's foot, making the car slam to a stop on the bridge. The next thing that happened was he grabbed me by the hair and dragged me through the front of the car. I remember my mom screaming, begging him not to hurt me, trying to grab me, but he was too strong."

"The fucker!" Ryker hissed, his fists turning white by his sides.

"He dragged me out of the car and threw me to the floor, then I heard the gun cock, and I knew that was it, he was going to shoot me. He called me so many names, shouting them over and over again, but all I heard was my mom. She was calling my name and I looked up to see her running toward me. But then the sound of gun went off and I closed my eyes and waited for the pain. But it never came... *it never came, Ryker."* I added this last part in a small voice, looking up at him and admitting,

"I wish it had. I wish I had taken that bullet." He looked the most pained by this, taking hold of my face, framing it with his big hands as he told me,

"No, Evie, please don't say that."

"But then she would still be alive," I told him, my tears now slipping over his hands.

"And you would be dead, and she would have had to live with that pain until the day he killed her anyway," he told me what no one else ever had.

"She died because of me... I opened my eyes, Ryker, and there she was, right in front of me. She had thrown herself at him, knocking the gun from his hand and taking the bullet herself. But if I hadn't brought the gun in the first place, then it wouldn't have happened." I sobbed this time, unable to hold it back once more.

"No, but then you all might have died in a car crash when he caused it by hitting your mother. Or it may not have happened that night, but maybe a week later. Perhaps not a gun, but a knife or a fire he started by falling asleep with a cigarette... my point is, Evie, that everything happens for a reason, and that night your mom chose to sacrifice her life for that of her child," he told me, and just as I opened my mouth to argue against it, he placed a thumb across my lips and stopped me, so he could continue.

"You should not taint that gift, that utterly selfless act, that heroic moment by shrouding it in the guilt you feel. She would not want that life for you. She would have died knowing that now you had a chance of freedom from that dark place she felt helpless to get you out of herself," he told me, making me cry against him, now wrapping my arms around his neck and whispering his name,

"Oh Ryker."

"It's okay, baby, I'm right here and I am not going anywhere," he told me softly, making me grip on tighter, making his words a reality.

"How did he die?" he asked, making me pull back after my tears eased so I could tell him the bitter end.

"I picked up the gun and shot him." He didn't seem surprised by this, no, in fact, he seemed relieved.

"Good, I hope the fucker experienced a slow and painful death." At this my eyes widened, and I pulled back a little in shock,

"Ryker, I shot a man dead. I killed him, that makes me a murderer."

"No, it makes you a survivor, there is a vast difference, Evie," he stated, making me shake my head a little before telling him,

"Not in the eyes of the law."

"Do I look like a fucking policeman to you?" he asked, making me admit,

"Well, I did start to think you were one with the way you kept trying to chase me down."

"And we will come back to that… but my point is, I don't give a fuck what the law says, he got only some of what he deserved, for if it had been me, I would have made him bleed for weeks." I swallowed hard at that, seeing now that he was not exaggerating.

"Er…"

"I am a Demon, sweetheart, what do you think I do to people that wrong me?" I pulled back a bit, starting to see this murderous side of him and it was making me nervous.

"Okay, and I was worried you would think differently of me when you knew." At this he looked as if I had just lost my mind and well, after his last statement, I could now see why.

"How could I possibly think differently of you? Other than already knowing how incredibly brave you are and just having had it proven again, but at a much younger age, how could you ever think I would judge you for your actions?" he asked, clearly astonished.

"Well, said like that, now I don't know and feel foolish," I admitted, making him sigh.

"Good and so you should, for had you not killed him, then that would have certainly been next on my to-do list." My eyes widened at that.

"Wow, just like that?" I asked, not sure if I wanted the answer or not.

"Yes, sweetheart, just like that... nobody hurts my girl and gets to live another day," he stated firmly, making me quick to point out,

"You didn't even know me back then."

"No, but even if years had passed, the offence of hurting you and your mom, is still one I would have punished him for. One I would have killed him for, no matter how much time had passed between," he told me, and I would have been yet another fool had I not taken him seriously.

"Well, I made sure he wouldn't come back, because I shot him until he fell backward over the bridge. However, that doesn't seem to stop me from having waking nightmares about him," I said, feeling free now to talk about those times.

"You still dream of him?"

"Yeah, but it's when I see him when I'm awake that's the worst. Like he's a ghost stalking me." At this he frowned and asked in a stern tone,

"You have seen him in the day?"

"Yes, but it's all just in my head, my mind playing cruel tricks on me," I said, trying to assure him, only this didn't exactly happen.

"Since when?" he asked, and his tone started to worry me.

"The last few months. Before that, they were just dreams, nightmares I would wake from. Now they have obviously manifested into something more." Ryker didn't like the sound of this, I could tell the second that tick was back in his jaw like he was grinding his teeth.

"And you're sure he died that night?"

"Ryker, I shot him right before he fell off a bridge," I pointed out.

"Into water?" he added, making me tense because I knew what he was trying to get at.

"Well, yeah."

"So, you didn't see a body?" he questioned, pressing me further and I knew it was because he wanted to be sure.

"Well no, but... come on, you don't really believe..." I let this trail off as the possibility he was leading me to started to take hold.

"Oh god, what if you're right?!" I started to freak out at this, wondering if all those glances of him, him stalking toward me in the hospital, what if it hadn't been in my head at all!

"Easy, easy now, I wouldn't let him get near you again... wait, was is it... Evie?" he asked the moment he saw my panicked eyes lock to his.

"At the auction... he was there. I was so scared, I was running, and it was creepy and I just thought I was going crazy! I got hit in the head and woke up believing it hadn't been real. But then after that I thought I saw him, sitting in the audience... Shit, what if he had actually been there, Ryker... *what if he's still alive!?*" I was about to scramble to my feet, and off the bed in my panic when his big arms stopped me. He picked me up and put me in his lap again, holding me to him as he tried to silently soothe my fears. But then with deadly calm, he told me,

"Then he gets to die all over again and this time..."

"...By a Demon's hands."

CHAPTER 31
STOLEN MOMENTS

Soon after Ryker said this, he left to make a phone call, because, well, I doubted cell phone service was any good inside a mountain. Which left me to explore after first getting changed. I found a pair of stone wash jeans and a burgundy ribbed knit sweater, with a boat neck style that had batwing sleeves. I wore a white tank top under this for some added warmth.

As for Ryker, he looked gorgeous as always, in a pair of dark jeans, a white shirt left open at the neck, and a winter wool overcoat in a trench style. One that was dark gray, had a lapel unbending at his neck and was single breasted, with black buttons running down one side.

Now as for my wandering, what I found took me straight back to the night I had first met my thief.

The golden bird.

I don't know why, but like that night I first unboxed it, I found myself taking it in my hands, as if something was compelling me to do so. It was about the size of both hands combined, and felt weighty enough to be made from solid gold. It also didn't look like any bird I had ever seen, with its large talons seemingly missing whatever it should have been gripping onto.

However, like the last time, it didn't take long before a bizarre feeling started to wash over me and, this time, instead of dropping it back in its box, I held on tight. I held on, despite now seeing the shadows on the floor trying to reach for me. I don't know why, but it was as if some other force was trying to speak to me. Trying to compel me to hold on through my fear long enough to listen. So, I closed my eyes, ignored the shadowy Demonic hands trying to reach me, and took a deep breath.

One that was quickly stolen from me, as vision after vision assaulted my mind and played out one after the other. It was like a flicker book of the future, and I was just trying to slow it down enough to make sense of it. But the part I didn't miss was what terrified me the most.

It was the end.

My life was being held in the hands of another, a man I had never seen before. An axe's blade held at my neck, ready to rid me of my head. Ryker's furious face turned to one pained at the sight of my life about to end. A long golden scepter held in his hands, as if a deal was being made. My soundless words, telling him goodbye, as if I knew the risks. Behind us all, a great chasm, glowing like some giant portal was at the ready to split right open and allow for Hell on Earth.

It was all there, like a disaster movie showing the volcano about to erupt or the cracking of the Earth just before the earthquake. But that wasn't all, because Vander was there. He looked as if he was trying to reason with

Ryker. But his friend's sole focus was on me, his mind made up. I knew that when he tossed the scepter at my feet, making the exchange. After that, I was forced to pick it up and the moment I did, I was pushed toward the portal, the threat still real at my back. Then an order was given, and I looked down at the bird at the top, focused on those claws, and turned it left so its talons lined up with the world the hand below it held.

And then everything changed.

The talons snapped into place, clutching the world, crushing it like it was symbolic of what would really happen, before the huge portal exploded outward, the veil of protection obliterated. After that I could see the Demonic army there, waiting to invade the mortal realm.

"Ah!" I screamed the moment I felt hands touch me, making me drop the bird and sever the connection.

"Did I scare you, Little Bird?" Ryker's voice helped break it even more as he had stepped up behind me. I looked down at the golden scepter piece now lying back in its box, my heart pounding and still trying to make sense of what I had just seen.

"Evelyn?" Ryker said my name with concern, and I forced myself to shake off the last of the visions. I didn't want him knowing what I had just seen, going so far as to question myself as to why. I couldn't explain it, but just something deep down was telling me not to. As if I had a choice and it was one that held the weight of the future in my hands. So, I cleared my voice and forced myself to comment as light-heartedly as possible.

"Well, clearly, I am not the only little bird in your collection."

"No, but you are the only one who owns my heart." At this I melted back into him, before turning my head side on and looking up at him.

"Thank you."

He smiled down at me and cupped my cheek, as was his way, before running his thumb over my freckles, telling me,

"You're always welcome to the truth of my feelings, Evie." I closed my eyes and leaned into his palm before turning to kiss it, making him rumble with pleasure.

"Speaking of birds, why did you steal it?" I asked once our tender moment had passed. Which was when he openly told me about the Scepter of Dagobert. The scepter had been created as a way to open large portals to allow for much greater numbers of souls to be delivered into Hell. When I asked why something like that would be needed, his answer was simple, he asked me just how many people died on the Titanic, or how many lives were lost in a single day of battle when a country was at war.

Of course, this made sense, until… well, it didn't. Because he went on to tell me that, unfortunately, when the gateway was open, it ended up causing an even greater threat. Because the portal allowed not just souls to pass into Hell, but it also allowed those on the other side to cross over into the mortal realm.

Which meant only one thing…

Demonic chaos.

Hence why the scepter was thought to be too dangerous and was broken down into three pieces. He went on to tell me how it was stolen from his father's realm and found its way here. And ever since, Ryker had been charged with finding the missing pieces and returning it to the Realm of Greed for safe keeping.

"So, it could be used as a weapon?" I asked, already knowing that it could thanks to my visions.

"Yes, and one that in the wrong hands could bring chaos through from my world to that of the mortal realm."

"That sounds bad," I said, shivering at just the thought.

"Yes, indeed. But as long as even a piece of it remains here, then I can prevent that from ever happening... what?" he asked when he must have seen the way I shook my head.

"Nothing."

"Evie." He said my name as a gentle warning.

"I just wonder when, if ever, I will get used to it all."

"Used to what?" he asked in concern.

"Used to all this," I said, looking around and trying to see this new world through his eyes. But I must have given him the wrong impression as he asked,

"Used to my gold?"

I granted him a look of horror.

"No... of course not that... that's all yours, I just mean your world. When hearing stories like the one you just told me becomes fact to me and not just some unbelievable tale. I keep asking myself when it will actually become something real to me... it's just a lot for a girl to get her head around, that's all," I added after I realized I was blabbing on.

"First of all, as far as I am concerned, all of this is now yours as well," he said, gesturing his arm out to all of his gold, making me balk.

"Ryker, be serious."

"I am... *deadly serious.* But, even if my words are not enough to deem it so, then our marriage certainly will."

Again my shock was easy to see, before I decided to point out a little fact he was missing in all of this,

"Er… I didn't exactly say yes."

"Do you love me?" he asked again, as if this was the key to everything. Yet despite knowing what he would take from it, I still couldn't deny it and therefore told him,

"Yes, of course."

"Then that is all the answer I need." And yep, there it was.

"But…" I tried, but was swiftly cut down because, clearly, I was dealing with a stubborn Demon who liked to get his own way.

"No buts, I now know you love me, as you so sweetly put it earlier, and that is all I need to know. Now as for my world, I promise you it is a lot to take in right now, but it will get easier."

"Easy for you to say," I grumbled, making him smirk as he pulled me closer.

"In case you haven't noticed, I like to get my own way." Ha, he could say that again. I had only been with him like this for a few days and already I knew so much about him. But then again, he wasn't known as the Lord of Greed for nothing.

"What, you? Nooo… shocking that," I commented sarcastically, turning that smirk of his into a full-blown grin.

"And when it comes to you, I will admit to being Greedier in nature than ever before…" I had to say, that made me feel all kinds of good.

"But that being said, I will agree to doing this at your pace and if that means waiting a few weeks before I get to make you my wife, then so be it…" My mouth dropped at this.

"A few weeks?! What were you thinking of doing if I had said yes, flying me straight to Vegas from here?" I asked in astonishment.

"No, but I do have a rather nice island in the Caribbean that I was thinking would make a good destination wedding."

"Ryker, be serious," I said after rubbing a hand down my face and trying to get my head around it all.

"And like I already told you, I am… *deadly serious,*" he growled low, making me sigh.

"Well, Arthur doesn't like flying," I said, making him grin and this time it was big one… *like a winning grin.*

"Then stateside it is," he stated with a nod.

"Well, I have always wanted to see the Grand Canyon," I mused, but this turned out to be a mistake because Ryker took this as an absolute, declaring with a tone of finality,

"Perfect. Then it's settled."

"Er… no, it isn't," I tried to argue, unable to help laughing at his eagerness.

"I think you will find it is," he argued back.

"This is crazy… besides, places like that are going to be booked up for months, maybe even years, we can't just…"

"Look around you, sweetheart, I could fucking buy the Grand Canyon if I wanted and still bury half my horde left over within its rock. Trust me, if I want a wedding there, I will fucking get it." I scoffed a laugh at this.

"Alright, Mr. Moneybags," I commented dryly, making him laugh,

"Good, I am glad you agree, soon to be, Mrs.

Moneybags." I groaned at that just as he pulled me into him for a hug, then he told me, all joking aside,

"I want to make you my wife, Evie, more than anything else in the world. More than all the gold you see, keeping you in my life is all I could ever wish for, could ever hope to dream, and could ever be thankful enough to receive... *there is only you."* Again, his tender words of love made me melt into him, which meant that when he tipped my chin up and said,

"So please make me the happiest Demon alive and say yes to becoming my wife... *and soon."* He added this with a grin and, this time, it was an answer I couldn't deny giving him. So, I lifted up on my tip toes, framed his face with my hands and pulled his lips to mine, at the same time telling him,

"Only if you say yes to being my Demon husband."

This time his growl of approval was one I tasted.

A little time later and it was time to leave this magical golden cavern of his, with assurances that we would come back again sometime soon. Then he teased me by whispering in my ear,

"After the wedding."

I couldn't help but smile at this, unable to keep the happiness from my face and the warmth from my heart. But then I knew it was too good to be true because that happiness was soon shattered and replaced by stone cold fear.

Fear that this time was for another.

Because the moment we made it outside of the mountain,

after Ryker had locked the doors the same way he had opened them, with his blood, we found we were no longer alone.

"Vander!" I shouted when I saw him bruised and bloody, as if he had been beaten with something that had been burned into his skin. Glowing red slashes like runes or ancient symbols were red raw and bleeding from the center of the burnt edges. His torn clothes showed this had been done all over his body, and I instantly found tears in my eyes in sight of such brutality.

Two men were holding him, one with old burn scars on one side of his face, that twisted and puckered his skin to the point that all his features were lost. Even his eye was white and looked out of use. But as for the other side, it showed high cheekbones, a sneering grin, and an eye the color of a stormy sky.

The other guy was much bigger in size and had long messy hair hanging from a ponytail. He had a small beady, dark eye and a thick red neck that was proportionate to his larger frame.

"They followed me here… Ryker man, I…"

"It's okay, Van, everything is going to work out fine," Ryker said after pushing me behind him and protecting me. Then he took a threatening step forward, his hands already starting to change into something horrifying and Demonic. A pair that thankfully looked strong enough to tear these assholes limb from limb because they looked like they were being taken over by some dark entity.

"Careful, Greed, we could just slit his throat right here and now, he might not die, but his vessel would be no more," the one I was calling Scarface threatened, and now I could see the wicked looking blade held under Vander's neck.

"Fucking do it!" Vander snarled, making Ryker hold up his hand to stop them from following through with the threat on his friend.

"Well, isn't this a touching scene?" A new voice spoke, coming from around the corner. The sound of authority laced every word, and I could hear the clear contempt he had for Ryker.

As for the way he looked, he was tall and made to look bigger through the layers of clothes he wore. His chest seemed to be covered in some kind of armored jacket, with thick leather straps buckled diagonally across his chest and abdomen. Underneath this I could see a black shirt and tie that matched his dark trousers.

But the item of clothing that made him look bigger was the over jacket, one that was long and finishing at his knees. This was left open with the large triangular collar folded back at the sides, resting tall at the back of his neck and head giving him the appearance of a magic-wielding warlord. The sides of his black jacket edged with silver buttons like this was some kind of military attire and he was getting ready for war.

As for his face, the best way to describe him was pure arrogance, like it was dripping from every pore. The sides of his head were shaven and the black long lengths on top slicked back. He had deep set eyes, like burning coals, black edged and glowing fire at the centers. These were made to look even more menacing with the slash of his brows set as if he was permanently scowling. His sneering lips were framed with thick black hair in a trimmed goatee. Just everything about this man screamed villain.

"Hector," Ryker snarled before stepping forward and stopping when Vander screamed.

The smell of burning flesh filled the air and making me feel sick. But then we saw the cause because the man held up his hand and the glowing red stone was clutched between his fingers. He was the one doing this to Vander, and I felt the bile in my throat I wanted to spit at him like acid.

Naturally, Ryker stopped once more in his tracks.

"Recognize this, I see. I stole it back from that fucking snake, Gastin, after he had given it to one of your whore cast offs because, clearly, nothing comes close to fucking a Siren," he sneered, making Ryker growl dangerously.

"Of course, she didn't put up much of a fight when I broke her neck, but then, I guess I did you a favor seeing as word around is you had a bounty put on her head for stealing your Siren for Gastin." I swallowed hard at this knowledge, knowing that she was intended to die at Ryker's hands.

"One less problem for me to face, Hector, but I doubt you came here for fucking payment," Ryker snarled, as if seconds away from losing it.

"Oh, but I did, Son of Greed, and I fully intend on collecting!"

"She is mine!" Ryker snarled Demonically and, this time, it wasn't a side of him I had heard before, telling me now that his Demon was closer than ever to breaking through.

"Yes, well the Fates may think so but after tonight, she will be tied to me whether she wants it or not." This time I found my own anger lashing out.

"Never, asshole!" I snapped, making him grin.

"Mmm, I do like them spirited. Of course, at first, I thought to only use her as bait, to lure you into opening your vault so as I could retrieve the last part of my scepter... but now I scent that I am being offered something far greater." Ryker stepped closer and threatened,

"It's not your fucking scepter, Hector, and you know it! Now as for my Siren... SHE IS MINE!" he roared, making me flinch back as the Demon's anger erupted from him. As for Hector, he didn't seem to show even the slightest bit of concern.

"Well, I hold two of the pieces and will soon hold the last, so your thoughts on ownership matter little to me."

"Over my fucking dead body!" Ryker snarled.

"Yes, but what about hers?" he asked, smirking and making Ryker grit his teeth. When Ryker took another step forward, he paused when Hector raised his hand and said,

"I wouldn't, if I were you, for I could quite easily give your claimed a little taste of what I am putting poor Vander through here." It felt as if every muscle in Ryker froze hearing this, making him growl viciously.

"Now imagine my surprise when turning up at the auction, where I could bid on a Siren, only to find two for sale and one of them, the little bitch, I had been trying to use against you. Now I would call that Fate, wouldn't you, Ryker?"

"I will fucking burn you to ash, *Baal Zabu*, for I know that is who you truly are at your core, his fucking puppet! And let it be known that I swear this, you will die by Greed's hand!" Ryker vowed Demonically, at the same time something was changing within him. It started as the material on his gray jacket started to split, and black spikes tipped with gold began to push their way through at his shoulders. I looked down at his hands that started to elongate, his skin turning to black with gold dusted at the knuckles. Long wicked talons pushed his trimmed nails out of the way, the cuticles framed with tiny spikes.

"Yes, well I think that's going to be pretty hard to do from where you are headed... after all, it seems like I no longer need you, Ryker Wyeth," he said, but before either of us could put a stop to this threat, a portal was suddenly appearing behind us both. I screamed as Demonic arms came from within it, reaching out and trying to grab Ryker. However, I was too close, making Ryker react to save me, pushing me aside just as they grabbed him instead.

Then before I could do a single thing, I watched in horror as they pulled him through, instead of touching me.

"RYKER, NO!" I screamed, helpless to do anything but watch as they dragged the man I loved...

Back to Hell.

CHAPTER 32
CURSED GOLD

I screamed as Ryker was dragged through the portal, making me fall to my knees as he was stolen from me. Tears streamed down my face, as I cried out my loss, ignoring the mocking and evil laughter that had sealed my fate. But I ignored everything but my pain, my utter heartbreak as the man I loved was ripped from me. Because I didn't know enough about his world to know what this meant. Whether he had survived being pulled through or whether he was in danger on the other side. I didn't know if it meant he was now trapped in Hell and would never be able to find his way back to me.

I just didn't know.

That was until I heard a commotion, and Vander broke free from the men holding him, so as he could make his way to me. I felt his arms go around me, before telling me quickly,

"It's okay, he will make it back. Trust me and trust him, he will come back to you... he will always come for you." I nodded through my tears as he cupped my head, holding me to him in a protective hold, making me try and breath through the painful memory. But I clung onto his words, hoping and praying that he was right. That Ryker would be okay and would make it back to me.

If I survived what was coming next.

"Oh, how very touching... now grab the bitch and let's get this done, as I will need much more than her blood!" the evil bastard named Hector said, ordering his men to first grab Vander off me, making him try and fight his way back to me. However, the second I was grabbed by Scarface and forced to my feet, Vander doubled his efforts.

"Get your fucking hands off her!" Vander roared as I was roughly pushed through the metal doors and back into the mountain. One that had been left open since Ryker hadn't even had time to close the security doors. They hit Vander, knocking him down and making me cry out,

"Leave him alone!" Although, little good it did me, because the asshole who had once held a blade to his neck now grabbed him by the hair and yanked his head back before asking,

"And this one?"

"Bring him with us, I don't want him escaping so as he can alert anyone, and he may continue to be useful to us yet," Hector said, before entering the cave.

"He has been reduced to nothing but a mortal blood sack, what use could he possibly have?" The larger man sniggered but Hector snarled back at him,

"One who means something to Greed and, therefore, the little Siren will have no choice but keep him alive, something she will only achieve as long as she does everything I fucking say... now bring him!" I gritted my teeth at that, knowing he was right. I couldn't risk Vander's life. I wouldn't. So, I let them drag me back inside the mountain and inside the elevator. Which meant that I was soon back to facing the colossal doors that was the entrance to Ryker's treasure horde.

"Now if you would be so kind as to do the honors, my dear," Hector said before jerking his head and giving Scarface a silent order to let me go. Something he did by pushing me toward the door.

"I can't open it, only Ryker can," I argued.

"Sure you can," Hector stated confidently.

"Only his blood can open the door, asshole!" I snapped, but this caused me nothing but pain because Hector walked toward me and back handed me, making me fall to the ground. The impact of his hand burned against my skin, making me force myself to hold back a pained whimper.

"Ryker will fucking kill you all!" Vander snarled, earning himself a punch to the gut and a kick to the ribs once falling to his side.

"Now as I was saying, you can and you will open that door, or I will come over there and slit a fucking vein myself and watch as I paint the fucking door with your blood!" I looked to Vander with pained eyes, and Hector saw this, so decided to use a different threat on me. He nodded to the brute with a ponytail, making him pull free his blade, flipping it out like he spent most his life playing with it. Then he used this to threaten Vander's life once more.

"Now show me where the blood lock is." I looked to Vander with tears in my eyes, and watching him mouthing the word 'don't' nearly broke my heart. He obviously knew the risks because, clearly, Hector was here for only one thing.

The bird.

But the bastard noticed this silent exchange between us and snarled,

"If I slit your throat and she ends up being useless to me, then who do you think is next and, as a mortal, there won't be any coming back for her… is this what you want for her, Vander?" At this Vander lowered his eyes before nodding, and for a moment I thought he was agreeing. That my death would be worth it. Of course, if it came to inviting Hell on Earth, then yes, we both knew that it was. But then he surprised me by saying,

"Show them, Girl Scout."

"But what about…" I argued, making him interrupt me quickly.

"Do it!" he snapped, making Hector grin.

"Oh, how self-sacrificing of you. Now show me the fucking lock!" I swallowed hard and nodded, knowing I had no choice. So, I walked toward the alter, making Hector clap.

"Ah of course… Grim, help her with your blade." I shot panicked eyes to Scarface as he walked over to me with an evil fucking grin. One half puckered and twisted due to half of his lips unable to lift into a smile.

I tried to step away from him, when he just grabbed me by the wrist and held it out over the same bowl Ryker had bled into. I tried to tug myself free, knowing it was going to fucking hurt and unable to help my reaction to want to flee. But despite the guy not being as big as the others, I was still no match for his obvious strength. He then used the tip of the curved wicked blade of his to draw a line across my palm, making me cry out as my flesh was cut.

"Fucking bastards will pay for this!" Vander snarled from where he was being held down on the floor, panting into the dirt.

"I doubt that," Hector replied confidently, not taking his eyes off the sight of my blood as it snaked its way down the symbols just like Ryker's had. Half of me hoped it didn't work but then I knew that our fate rested on those doors opening.

And open they did.

"Excellent." He grinned as the entrance was soon flooding with a golden glow beaming from down the center. One that got bigger and spread out as the doors continued to open. Then he clapped, a booming sound that echoed in the cavernous space ahead of him as he walked inside.

"Look at all of this..." He whistled then, creating another echo to travel through the mountain.

"I must say, I will be keeping your blood on ice if this is what it unlocks, for after I have taken possession of this mortal realm and forced it to its knees with my armies, then I will most certainly be coming back for all of this... for this... now, *is this truly is a thing of beauty,*" Hector said, grinning like some evil villain out of a movie. A villain who wanted all he saw for himself, and he quickly turned the second Scarface reached out and tried to take some of the gold.

The red glow in his hand snaked out just like it had in the bathroom that day, and the second it touched his scarred hand, he started howling in pain. One glance and I knew why because it looked like his fucking hand was melting off!

"Keep your fucking hands off it, for all you see here will soon be mine," Hector warned, but at this Vander started laughing, pushing free from his bigger captor, doing so easily now that Ponytail's mind was on was the treasure he couldn't touch. Not if he wanted to end up like his friend who was clutching his burning hand. Meaning Vander was the last person on his mind.

"This will never be yours, Hector, for only the blood of Greed can touch his treasure."

"Explain!" he hissed, now looking back at him as he limped closer to me.

"It's hexed," Vander stated, just as he made to me and slumped down on the floor with his back to a pile of gold coins that tricked down the mound with the movement.

"You lie!" Hector snarled, making Vander grin.

"What? You really think that the Son of Greed would simply hide his horde away with only a blood lock between it and a thief?" Hector paused to think about this, giving Vander enough to time to crush his doubt.

"No, Ryker had everything in this whole mountain touched with a hex, a death curse to anyone that does not hold his blood. A thief's name to appear on a death dealer's list is one that never gets erased. And well, we all know how those prompt fuckers can be. So go ahead, be my guest, activate the curse by taking the whole fucking lot from this mountain because, no doubt, I will soon see you down in Hell anyway," Vander said in a pissed off, carefree tone as if mocking Hector and how little he knew.

He snarled in anger and said,

"Then maybe I claim a Siren for myself and keep her alive and kicking, as with his blood in her, she will not be affected. Speaking of which, it's time to show me to the last piece of the scepter!" I looked to Vander and heard him tell me,

"It's okay, Girl Scout."

"But if he…" Vander quickly cut me off, telling me,

"Trust me, okay? I have a plan."

"Does that include getting us both killed?" I asked, making him grin.

"Let's hope not."

"And Ryker?" He didn't get to answer this because Hector had clearly had enough, and gripped me roughly by the arm before tossing me forward and telling me,

"Get it for me!" I looked back to Vander to see him nod one last time, so I decided to trust him because what other option did I have? I walked to where I had held it not long ago, and lifted off the lid, revealing the golden bird nestled there.

"Ahh, there it is. Magnificent. Now hand it to me." I gulped before doing as he asked, picking it up and, this time, it showed me much more than just a glimpse of a vision… *it showed me it all.*

It showed me my Fate.

I tried not to let him realize this, holding myself still until the vision ended, the very last piece I would need if ever I got the chance to end this once and for all.

So, with this in mind, I handed it over and while he was busy motioning his two lackies over, one of which I could see now carried a duffle bag on his back, I made my way back to Vander. Because now I knew he was the only one who could help me. I needed to speak with him while I had the chance.

"You're the one who spoke with Arthur, aren't you?" I guessed.

"Yeah, I know sign language, why do you ask?" he replied, but I ignored his question to ask him another,

"Vander, you love Ryker like a brother, don't you?" I asked the moment I could, now keeping one eye on the enemy. As for Vander, he looked at me in question.

"I would die for him," he answered, making me continue.

"Would you kill for him?" I knew what the answer would be before he said it.

"Yes," he stated firmly.

"Would you kill me?" This question took him off guard, and for the first time, I heard something other than my nickname coming from his lips.

"What is this about, Evie?"

"More specifically, would you let me die, if you had a chance to save only one of us?" I asked, now hoping this would help in making his decision. I was wrong, because he questioned me further.

"I don't understand?"

"Just answer the question, Van, we don't have much time," I urged, looking up to see Hector pulling the other pieces of the scepter out of the bag, ready to fit them together.

"Yes, I would save my friend," he finally admitted.

"Good. Then I need you to keep that promise to me," I said firmly.

"What promise?"

"When the time comes, you need to trust me. You need to get Ryker out of harm's way by any means possible, do you understand?" I pressed further but, again, he wanted more details. And not that I could blame him because I would have been the same in his shoes.

"Evie, what do you know?"

"Please… you have to trust that I know what I am doing here. I just need to know that when the time comes, if you have the means of getting Ryker out safely or not?" I replied, swallowing hard and praying that he did.

"I can get him out, but only if I get my powers back," he finally admitted, making me hope this was easier than it sounded.

"Good, then if we both make this part out alive, and what happens is what I think is going to happen, you have to be at the ready," I told him, hoping he was taking me as seriously as I sounded.

"He will kill me if I let you sacrifice yourself," he replied, talking now about Ryker. I released a heavy sigh and argued,

"He won't if I made you do this, if I made you swear to grant mc my last wish."

"And that is what?" he asked, his bruised face frowning down at me side on from where we both sat.

"To save the man I love and the world he lives in," I told him, just as I saw the last piece of the scepter being placed on top.

"At last, the power of Psychopompós is in my hands!" Hector shouted out, his booming voice echoing once more. Telling me our time was up as he walked back down the pathway lined with gold, now holding the golden scepter in his hands like it held the power of the Gods and from what Ryker had told me, it most likely did.

"He's got the Scepter," I stated the obvious with gritted teeth.

"Yes, but he doesn't think he can take all of it out of here… the bird is cursed, remember?" he said, winking at me just before I was grabbed roughly by the arm and handed the scepter.

"Now let's hope you have enough of that bastard's blood in you that you won't die before we get to the portal gate," Hector said, and I was forced to look down at the heavy weight in my hands, afraid of the power this thing could hold. And now that it was complete, I could see the same as what was shown to me in my vision. That the bird would be turned left to latch onto the Earth at its feet, symbolizing the end.

"Let's go, Siren!" Hector said, pushing me toward the exit, just as Vander was forced to do the same. However, the moment we made it back outside, this was where the problem with my plan began because Hector had one last order to make, when the one I had named Scarface asked,

"And what about him?" To which Hector just smiled that evil grin of his before telling him,

"We don't need him anymore…"

I cried out in horror, but it was no use, and Hector grabbed my arm, held me tight, and dragged me away as he issued the final blow…

"Kill him."

CHAPTER 33
BETRAYAL AND TREACHERY
RYKER

The moment I was pulled in through the portal I erupted into my Demonic form, roaring into the hot air and making steam rise from my body like a fucking dragon building up fire!

My foreboding form of black, tight leathery skin, half of which was covered in deadly spikes and my skeletal face were soon covered by summoning my armor, leaving me ready for battle. Plates of stone carved from my home realm interlocked around my body's spikes, leaving me the freedom of movement. My helmet covered most of my head and was a far more Demonic version of the mask I wore the night I first met Evie. Large golden tipped horns rose high above my head, and matched that of my armor, for each sharpened edge was also dipped in the precious metal.

It also didn't take me long to realize where I was and what I now faced. I was in the realm of Treachery, the ninth level of hell and closest to Tartarus. Meaning I was faced with what many mortals would have believed impossible to find in the pits of Hell, for this was a world of ice. Mountains of black ice could be seen as far as the eye could see, standing in lines like jagged towers, each one over a thousand feet tall like giant sentries. For they remained the same diameter at the base as they did at the top.

The frozen black lake I now stood on would, at the very least, make for a dramatic end to the bastard's life who had dragged me through here. For it was filled with the lost souls of Treachery, and those who had committed the sin against their fellow mortals. You could see them, rising to the surface like moaning phantoms, trying to reach a taste of the living they once had. One touch and they would strip you bare, consuming everything they could get their razer pin teeth on.

But the fury within me at being ripped away from my Siren was pumping an evil essence through my veins and making me hungry for the blood of my enemies. At the very least I had something to kill, as I came face to face with the one who fought me in my office building. The one who had tried to take my Siren. And all of which had been capable from that fucking stolen piece of Annika's heart stone! Although, at the very least, the fucker I faced now didn't have it and this was now a fair fight. Oh, but who was I kidding? I was about to tear this fucker into pieces and there would be nothing 'fair' or equal about it.

I would fucking destroy him!

"Time to die, Azhdar!" I growled venomously at the reptilian creature, who was hissing at me. Yet despite this, I could also see him backing away, as if the Demon knew that he wouldn't be able to take me. Not without his weapon that I knew was still in the hands of that fuck, Hector!

In the end, I didn't wait before I charged at him, summoning my favorite weapon known as my Colossus Killer, the sword, Zweihänder. Because as much as I wanted to make his suffering last, I knew that time was not on my side. I needed to get back to the mortal realm and hope that I wasn't too late to save my Siren. And also, the life of my best friend.

So I held my blade high, lifting its heavy weight with ease in this form, for I was twice my mortal size. The creature had no choice but to fight, trying to dodge my swing and ended up losing the first of its limbs for the effort. After this, the defeat easily followed, and soon it was crawling along the frozen lake without a leg to match his missing arm. But because I didn't have time to make it last, I decided a more fitting punishment should be the slow death of being eaten by the souls beneath us. They followed our every move, as if waiting for their chance, and that someone would crack the ice and fall.

So, I granted their wish.

"No! please! I know where he is taking her... spare my life and I will tell you!" he pleaded as I stood over him, now with my sword raised high for what he thought would be the killing blow.

"Then you must think me to be a fool, Azhdar, but then... this is the realm Treachery after all..." I paused long enough to crouch low and tell him,

"So, I am sure you will fit in nicely." Then I raised my sword and hammered it down, the blade running through his belly and into the ice below. Of course, it wasn't enough to kill him but then I had never intended for it to be. No, that came when I twisted the blade and cracked the ice beneath him, creating a hole big enough for the souls to quickly drag him under.

"NOOOOO!" he roared as I stepped back onto solid ice so as not to end up with the same fate. I then walked away, leaving the sight of him being eaten alive as they dragged him down into a watery grave.

Of course, in my rage I didn't have a chance at leaving him alive long enough to question him. But then, why would I even bother? I knew exactly what that fucker Hector wanted with my Siren. Gods, but just the thought of what he could be doing to her now, it was little wonder why I had taken my frustration and rage out on Azhdar.

I was worried to the point of blind fucking panic and needed only one thing to happen… and that was to get back to my Siren! Hence why I quickly ran toward the edge of the lake, one that was nothing more than frozen dirt, and I roared the name of my father's summoner! Then I gritted my teeth as I dug a talon into my own chest. After this, I carved it in deep and straight into my heart, knowing that all I needed to gain was just a few drops of blood straight from the source of my Greed.

It was the only way.

I roared with the agony this caused, and the anger forced me to go deeper, as deep as it would take until I had what I needed. Then once I was sure my claw had enough blood cupped inside, I yanked my hand free and tossed the blood to the icy ground. It sizzled the second it made contact, burning the earth and turning it black. This was seconds before I saw a hand reaching up through the blood that had spread out, like it was now eating away at the frozen land.

Knowing this Demon I summoned was from my own realm and wasn't yet a soul of Treachery, I reached down and grabbed the one still trying to claw its way up through the portal. The only one I had the power to create, being that I was connected to the only place I knew could help me now.

My home.

"I am the Son of Greed, now get my father's summoner!" I ordered once the Demons skeletal head was lifted far enough for him to understand me. Then I dropped him, making him slither back into the portal.

Waiting felt like a fucking eternity, despite it only being minutes. But that was the catch, minutes here could mean far longer in the mortal realm, and seeing as I didn't even know much about the level of Hell I was in, I had no concept of how much time could have passed.

I could be too late.

"NO, I will not think this!" I bellowed at myself. Something that was heard when the summoner opened the portal I had made bigger, and rose from it far more gracefully than the Demon I had dragged up by its burnt skin.

"Lord Greed." Annika bowed her head.

"I need you to link to the essence of your missing heart stone piece," I ordered her quickly.

"A portal was created?" she asked, making me grit my teeth.

"Yes, and I need to get back to the exact place, can you do this?" I snapped, talking quickly.

"I can, my Lord," she said in that eerie calm tone, and one I wanted to fucking scream at!

"Then do it! Everything relies on this moment, and I have no time to waste!" I barked like some rabid dog.

"No, I believe you are right," she agreed, before opening up a portal and connecting with the stolen power that was a piece of her. But then as I was stepping through, I thought I heard her saying something, but it was only later that I would really understand it. As for now, the second I stepped through, the sight I saw made me not even think twice before I reacted. My mortal vessel was capable of doing the same amount of damage to this soon to be dead fucker.

"I'm going to enjoy killing you, you cocky fucker!" said the scarred man now standing over Vander, who was on his knees facing the asshole with the knife. But then his eyes flashed to me, and he grinned in the face of death. And rightly so as he suddenly had a lot to fucking smile about. Then Vander told him,

"Not as much as I am going to enjoy watch my friend kill you first." Then he nodded to where I stood, and Hector's lacky turned in time to see me strike. I rained down blow after blow, until Vander had to stop me, reminding me,

"Fuck, don't kill him yet, not before I have drunk my fill of his mind and got my stolen powers back!" Then Vander grabbed hold of the guy's scarred head, one now bloody and beaten by my fists, and covered his eyes. He tried to fight this, but I snapped his legs with a twist of my hands, forcing the break without even touching him.

"Like a fish on a hook." Vander grinned before his eyes went black and he locked onto his victim's mind, this time ridding his victim of fucking everything! I knew that when I heard the man screaming, as if he was forever now stuck in his own customized horror story, eternally running for his life from his greatest fears.

I then watched as Vander stole back the powers he had been robbed of, watching as the magical castings burnt on to his skin now turned to black before all that was left was gray, flaky ash that brushed off his skin and floated away. Then we left the tortured man on the floor to his deadly fate.

"Evelyn... where is she?!" I asked in my panic.

"Hector took her. He has the bird. She had no choice, or he would have killed her." I let go of a relieved breath, and told him,

"As long as she is still breathing, that is all I care for."

"Yes, and thanks to what I told him, he wouldn't dare kill her now." I frowned in question until he told me,

"I made up some bullshit about the gold having a hex on it, some death curse that meant any treasure he removed from the mountain would mean their name on a death dealer's quoter or some shit like that." I scoffed at that and muttered,

"Idiots."

"Yeah, well now Hector knows your Siren holds your blood, then he also knows that he needs her to handle the scepter if he is to use it to open the gateway between our worlds," Vander added, making me thank fuck for the quick thinking of my second.

"You did this to ensure he spared her life?"

"He needs a Siren for some reason, but the way he was talking, he made it out to be an expendable need. I just ensured that if he wanted the added bonus of your treasure, he would need to keep her for a lot longer, seeing as she is the only one that could get it out of the mountain without the curse taking effect." At this I grabbed him to me by the shoulder and hit him on the back, telling him,

"You're a fucking genius!"

"Well, let's just hope he doesn't have someone who can call my bluff until we get there, as at least we don't need to guess as to where he is taking her." I looked off into the distance and growled,

"No, we know exactly where and soon…"

"The fucker will die there!"

※

Entering into another Enforcer's territory could always be a precarious thing, but none more so than the Enforcer Torn Wilder. This was because he wasn't just a Demon, he was practically considered a God. In the Inuit religion, Torngarsuk, Torn for short, was known as the God of the sea, of death, and of its underworld. One of the more important deities in the Inuit pantheon, he is known to be the leader of the Tornat. A group of protective gods that sit at the royal table in his realm. Fuck, but he was practically a God of the Gods.

But there was a problem.

He had gone rogue long ago.

The story behind why, was hazy at best, but it was said that he had spent too long in the mortal realm after refusing to go back to his underworld. Something he should have been doing on a regular basis. But something had happened there, making him refuse to do so, and in the end, it had sent him mad, unpredictable, and completely enraged. Meaning his people had no choice but to lock him up until Fate intervened.

And as for the territory he ruled over, it was still his, but now being maintained by people he trusted, people on his own council. All of which were living each day in hopes of bringing back their King.

"I take it Torn is still…"

"Locked in a bunker and still a crazed beast…? Yeah, why?" Van answered whilst we waited for the helicopter and the rest of my men to show up. Something Vander had set into place the moment we made it back from my mountain.

"Because there are only two places Hector could bring through an army and use the scepter. In the portal where I landed there was no army in sight, which means he will not be using the heart stone to aid him, for now we know it will only lead to the Realm of Greed or the Realm of Treachery," I told him, knowing now his options were limited.

"Which means he will be using the one in the Northwest Territories, gotcha."

"Contact Torn's people, let them know what has happened and ask if they would be willing to assist."

"You think they will?" he asked with a skeptical look.

"They may be loyal to their own King but with his mind lost, they are also loyal to another, which means they have a responsibility as acting Enforcer," I told him, feeling assured by this knowledge.

"So yeah, okay, when you put it like that," Van replied before he was on the phone once more. Which meant that in no time at all we were on our way to Hidden Lake Territorial Park, along the Ingraham Trail. As suspected, Torn's people met us a little away from the cave site, one not known to mortals for obvious reasons.

We exchanged pleasantries as I shook hands with Torn's known second in command, and who was now essentially running the show. She looked native to the culture, as her vessel was that of an Inuit. She was short, being no more than five foot tall and quite stocky in her build. Her beautiful Asian facial features held a hint of mischief about her, and her long black hair was worn in the typical style. It was spilt down the center and was plaited each side, with her cheeks looking rosy from the chill in the evening air. Her dark eyes scanned the length of me in my tactical gear, before looking around to find my men all dressed the same.

As for her own people, they all looked dressed for the cold weather and nothing else, as they could have come ready for a night drinking in a tavern rather than about to go into battle. But in truth, as long as they could fucking fight, then I didn't care. The plan was simple, they create a distraction, drawing out Hector's men from the cave whilst Van and I crept inside unnoticed.

After that, it was really anyone's guess as to what would happen next. My only hope was to get to Evelyn and rescue her above all else. Because I couldn't give a fuck if it was selfish or not, I wanted my Siren back and if the whole world burned around us, then so be it, I would just find a way to take her back to my own Realm of Greed.

Which meant I was soon ready to give the word, having some of Torn's men go in first to draw them out. Thankfully, this part of the plan went off without a hitch, as pretty soon, Hector's men were running into an ambush. The rocky terrain that led to the Cave's hidden entrance was a perfect place for Torn's men to hide behind before springing their trap and surrounding them. Yet despite being faced with this obvious defeat, they fought like Demons just as we all expected them to.

So as chaos ensued, something that Torn's men looked to revel in, it offered us the perfect distraction to sneak inside, making our way through the twisted cave system. The few guards we encountered were easily dispatched, as once more I called forth my favorite weapon. The Zweihänder made short work of relieving them of their heads, and Vander only needed to touch them to rip their souls right from their vessels.

Which meant, before long, we were right where we needed to be, as the last jagged tunnel opened up into a huge cavern big enough to hold a small army. One I was relieved to see was not yet filled with Demonic life as the portal was still closed... *for now.*

Although Hector was now stepping up to the singular piece of the rock formation, one that was arched and out of place from the rest of the cave's interior walls. It was bigger than the doors to my horde and must have been at least three stories high. The Sumerian symbols were etched in a boarder around the edge, just waiting to be used for the first time in over a thousand years. Its ancient lure pulsated in the air as if it could sense the scepter.

Even the Mayans of Central America knew of these gateways, for it was why they built temples over caves or even went so far as to build them to look like them. Because they knew that caves were the entrance to the underworld. It was a version of Hell I was going to try and prevent invading the Moral Realm. But first, my eyes scanned the space looking for my Siren, finding her being held further away from the portal by the big bastard that had beaten on my second.

She was also holding the scepter, as Van's threat of a hex was obviously still one that stuck, and clearly, Hector wasn't taking any chances.

"We need to get closer," I told Van from behind the rocks we were crouched behind, making him nod. So, we got as close as we could until I could finally catch Evie's eyes, something that unfortunately alerted the big bastard to us as well. However, she reacted quickly, now using the scepter as a weapon, bringing it up and hitting her captor in the face. However, before she could get far, he was on her, and I was too far away to get to her first.

"EVIE!" I shouted, but it was too late and as if knowing her fate, she was free enough to throw the scepter toward us.

"RYKER, RUN!" she screamed, trying to save me and the fate of her world by having me leave her.

Something I could never do.

So, I picked up the scepter and told her,

"I am not going anywhere, my Siren." At this she looked pained as she stopped struggling against the soon to be dead Demon that had hold of her. It was as if the realization of our situation made the fight go right out of her.

"Then… *Archízei,*" she said sadly, making me narrow my eyes as if trying to understand where I had heard that being said before.

"Annika." I said the name without context, making Van question,

"What has she got to do with…"

"Archízei, that was what she said to me before I left the

realm," I told him, knowing he would understand this more than most considering his extensive knowledge in languages.

"It begins," he repeated, translating the word from Greek.

"So, it does," Hector replied, now coming up behind my Siren as he had the time to take in the situation for himself since hearing me calling her name.

"Let her go, Hector!" I demanded, allowing my Demon to edge each word with murderous intent.

"Um, I think not, for we seem to be at an impasse. For you have something I want, and I know I have what you want…" he said, pausing so as he could grab Evie to him, and quickly holding a blade to her throat.

"…So, tell me, just what is she worth to you, Ryker?" At this I was forced to witness as his blade pressed in hard enough to draw blood, making me fucking panic when she screamed.

"Alright! Alright! Fuck, just let her go and I will give you the scepter," I told him, making him fucking tut at me like I was some unruly child.

"Oh, but I think not. You see, this good little bitch here is going to open the portal and live to tell the tale."

"You won't kill her!" I stated, knowing that if he was to get what he wanted, then he couldn't. However, he called my bluff, as he told me with a sick fucking grin,

"No, but that doesn't mean that I won't start cutting pieces off her fuckable body… tell me, Ryker, what are your favorites…? These, perhaps?" he said, now moving the blade from her neck and to under her breasts, making her inhale sharply.

"Or is it obviously lower…" he said, making the dagger

snake in between her breasts, snagging on her sweater as it travelled down her stomach and get closer to her sex.

"Fuck! Alright, just fucking stop!" I snapped, knowing I had no play left here. He had me backed in the worst fucking corner possible.

"Mmm, well there we go, my dear, looks like we found it. Now toss the scepter at her feet, or we will see how many pieces I can toss to you as a fucking souvenir!" he growled, making me want to burst out of my fucking skin at just the thought of her being harmed. The drip of blood trickling down her neck was already fucking with my mind.

"Ryker, you know you can't..." Van said, making me snarl before raising my hand to him and growling,

"Shut the fuck up! Alright, Hector, just don't hurt her," I said, seeing the tears in her eyes, after she told me,

"You can't... *please, just let me go, Ryker.*" I gritted my teeth, knowing that she was trying to sacrifice herself for her world and mine combined. But I couldn't let her do that, making me say,

"It's okay, baby, it will all be okay." But then her eyes went to Vander's, and she started moving her hands, making me narrow my gaze at her. What the fuck was she doing? However, the moment Hector pressed the dagger to her side, and she yelped, I knew I was out of time. So, I tossed the scepter close to her feet.

"Pick it up!" Hector demanded, pushing her forward so she could reach it. But then the moment she took it in her hand, she looked up at me and told me something that made the blood in my veins turn to ice.

"I am sorry, Ryker, forgive me and, remember, *I will always love you.*"

"Evelyn?" I questioned, but then I felt Van take hold of me from behind. Then the second his hand touched my head and I started to feel a forced darkness take hold of my mind…

I knew what this was…

Betrayal.

CHAPTER 34
THE RIGHT SIDE OF LOVE
EVIE

The second I saw Vander take hold of Ryker, I knew this was it. The moment he could possibly see me for the last time. And the only emotion I saw in those navy-blue depths…

Was betrayal.

Because he knew what was happening a single second before it happened. Before he went limp in Vander's arms, making me scream,

"GET HIM OUT OF HERE! Then I turned with the scepter in my hands and tried to run in the opposite direction to give him the time to escape with Ryker. Because I knew that Hector would follow me and the scepter, over chasing them. And I had been right, because as soon my hair was grabbed in Hector's tight grasp, it halted my escape. One I knew had never been Fated to happen.

"Oh no you don't!" he snarled, dragging me painfully over to the portal.

"Now get the fuck over there and open the fucking portal!" he demanded, tossing me toward the rock and making me land painfully against it, dropping the scepter at my feet.

"I don't know how," I told him, even though this was a lie.

"Pick it up and twist the bird to the left!" I swallowed hard, before doing as I was told, now looking up at the building-size rock and knowing that this was it. This was my only chance. However, the moment I took it back in my hands, I was about to twist it to the right, when I suddenly felt the blade at my neck. I froze, unable to move, as he now stood right behind me. Because I knew if I quickly twisted it and nothing happened, he would just make me twist it back the way I should.

"I said to the left," he snarled close to my ear, making me gulp painfully against the blade. But then I thought on the vision the bird had shown me and when I looked back up at the rock, I knew this wasn't it.

So, hoping I was right, I twisted it to the left, only to feel the blade leave me when the bird clamped down on the Earth at its feet. Then he took hold of my arm and extended it so I could now touch the rock with the tip.

"AAAAHHH!" I screamed as power poured from the center and travelled down to where I was touching it, making blue fire shoot down the staff in my hands. I tried to drop it, but it wouldn't let me, fusing itself to my hand, as if I was its link to the earth it needed. It hurt like the blazes of Hell but at least it wasn't actually burning my flesh.

But then the feeling started to ease enough for me to look up just in time for that same blue fire to erupt, exploding outward. The force of which blew me back into Hector who had been standing at my back. We both hit the ground and after landing half on top of him, I saw my only opportunity, making a grab for it before he noticed.

Then I quickly scrambled to my feet and shifted off to one side, picking up the scepter and taking it with me. As for Hector, he didn't even notice, as his wide eyes took in the sight before us.

It was utterly terrifying.

"Yes... yes... it is really happening... soon, my master, soon you will be free, Baal Zabu!" he said, his malevolent eyes now mirroring the blue fire that had covered the entire rock. The symbols that framed the arch were now glowing white and pulsating with power. It looked as if the flames were being sucked into the center, folding inward like a water flowing into a sinkhole.

But then I could also see the hint of movement from beyond the veil of fire. One that increased just before a Demonic army started to flow through the flames, the power licking at their armor and leaving no lasting mark on the black breast plates. They were horrific to look at, with glowing red eyes, skinless heads, with flesh on show and hammered with metal plates across their mouths. But not all were the same, as this seemed to be only the first wave. Those who followed had rows of spikes in their heads and down their arms. Skeletal bodies that clattered as they moved, with bone helmets dripping in blood.

I looked back at the entrance to the cave, knowing it wouldn't be long before they all spilled out of here and started wreaking chaos on the world. Which meant I only had one chance at this. Hector was already getting his army into ranks as soon as they made their way through. At least fifty Demon soldiers now filled the space quickly.

So, in the seconds I had left, I thought about all the people I had cared for in my life. An image of my mom, standing in the kitchen smiling at me, replaced the one of her dying on that bridge. An image of Arthur the day he picked me up and put me in his truck, telling me only two things I needed to hear,

'You're safe, kid… I am taking you home with me.'

The sight of the cabin I loved and its warm glow from inside. Even the picture of Denise and her quirky coffee shop flashed up.

But then last of all was Ryker. A flicker book of the times we had shared, and all of them possible because of the world he protected against these types of things from happening. The Enforcers, there to fight for mortals when we couldn't possibly hope to win against the Hell they knew was potentially waiting for us. Waiting to burst free just like it did now.

But my mind refused to look back at all my happy memories and see them tainted by what was to come if these things managed to escape this cave. I knew what I needed to do.

So, holding out the scepter as a weapon, I walked toward the portal, thankful to see that the Demons all avoided me. The power of it came out in waves, making it harder to hold the closer to the portal I got. Which made me grit my teeth against the pain, the scepter shaking in my hands and my fingers aching against the strain, I reached up and did what the vision had shown me.

"What are you…!" I vaguely heard Hector calling out, his angry voice only spurring me on. I gripped the body of the bird and with a quick snap of my wrist, I twisted it all the way to the left, forcing it to release its hold on the earth.

"STOP!" Hector roared as he started running. But then I looked back at him and smiled,

"Bye, bye, asshole!" I said before touching the portal, at the same time lifting up the heart stone, one he didn't even realize he had lost, making him look down at his wrist to see it gone. It was no longer wrapped there but instead held in my fist. Then as the portal started to flow a different way, I did what I had done back in the bathroom that day and tossed it inside.

"NOOOOOO!" Hector screamed as the portal erupted into red flames and started to suck everyone back through. So, I closed my eyes, accepting my fate and let myself be dragged through with the rest of them. And all the while doing so with a smile on my face, knowing that now, all that mattered the most to me in life would live on.

But most importantly,

Ryker would survive.

Survive without me… *as I died.*

⚘

"Whoa… there you are… I've got you, Little One," I heard this new voice say the second I felt myself being caught in impossibly strong arms. So, I braved opening my eyes, feeling strangely comforted by the voice, and what I found made my eyes widen in utter shock. But more than anything else, I found myself saying in a breathless way,

"You have his eyes." It was a comment that made the man chuckle as I stared up at him, unable to believe what I

was seeing. Christ, it could have been Ryker's brother! Although considering he hadn't mentioned having one, I knew there was only one other possible explanation to what I was seeing, making me gasp,

"You're Ryker's father!" At this he grinned once more before putting me down back on my feet. Then he took a step back and bowed his head down at me.

"I am King Mammon, ruler of the 4th realm of Hell and you, Little Mortal, are Evelyn Leucosia, my son's Fated Siren," he said with a devilishly handsome smile playing at his lips. Lips that, unlike Ryker, were framed with a trimmed beard as black as his hair. Hair he kept tied back off his face, and it looked long enough to be past his shoulders. He also had a jawline to make most women weep, possessing that natural authoritative air about him, screaming that this guy was the royalty he claimed to be. Of course, being dressed in golden armor, he reminded me of some fairytale knight, ready to save the princess.

"How... how do you know..." At this he smirked, and it was all Ryker when he did because the sight was so similar. This was before tapping on his slim nose, telling me,

"A king has his ways and makes it his business to know them, especially in all matters that concern my son." I released a sigh and told him,

"Yes, well I think your son is going to be furious with me after what I did," I admitted in a deflated tone.

"Yes, for I have no doubt considering the danger you put yourself in... however, I selfishly must thank you for it, as your bravery rewarded my needs greatly." I frowned, now asking,

"How so?" To which he held out a metal plated arm and pointed behind me, making me turn and gasp at the sight.

"You brought the enemy to my gates, brave little Siren." At this I couldn't help but take a frightened step back, finding myself stepping back into him. His metal clad hands came to the tops of my arms, holding me steady.

"Be at ease now, for don't let the sight frighten you," he told me, his voice full of confidence. Of course, in sight of the Hellish battle now going on, I couldn't help but gasp. It was a battle with what was clearly his army fighting the ones that had been sucked back into this realm, and it was clear to see which of those were Mammon's men. Or should I say Demons, because each were dressed the same, in black and gold armor. The gleaming sea of soldiers each wore horned helmets, and were swinging gold tipped swords, they looked like something out of Rivendell from Lord of the Rings. Oh, and they were making short work of killing the bad guys.

As for the land, this was a vast open desert of red sand, with dunes surrounding the space the size of mountains. The sunbaked ground beneath my feet was cracked and a gentle breeze was pushing the red sand along the floor, before disappearing in those crevices.

"Can they... reach us?" I asked fearfully. He scoffed a laugh behind me, before dipping his head to my ear, his tall frame most likely needing to bend quite a bit to reach me because he was even taller than his son.

"They can try, but they would find my blade before I let them reach you." I turned quickly, spinning on my foot and catching the ground as I nearly tripped. Something Mammon prevented when he reached out with lightning-fast reflexes, taking my arm and holding me steady.

"You would protect me?" I asked once he released me and, again, my question seemed to amuse him.

"But of course, for even if you did not mean the weight of the world to my son, you have done me a kindness by bringing me back my scepter, I would be a foolish king indeed if I didn't protect those who are loyal to me enough to do as you have done." I shyly brushed my hair behind my ear and admitted,

"No offence, but I had no idea that this would happen… although, of course I am happy to give you back your scepter… oh, wait, where is it… oh shit, did I lose it?!" At this he boomed with laughter, and it was shocking enough to have me stop looking around the place for it.

"Upon my word, what fun. I can see now why my son is besotted with you, for you are a delight, my dear," he said, making me blush.

"But regardless of what fun I would have with you, I do believe my son would have my head for such thoughts, as well as if I keep you from him much longer… so do not fear for the scepter is where it is meant to be." Of course, if I thought I was blushing before, now I was turning the color of the sand. Jesus, Ryker's dad was flirting with me! But then his other words fully penetrated and I was quickly asking,

"You mean, you can send me back?" At this he grinned down at me, and ran the back of his gauntlet glove down my cheek before telling me,

"Yes, Little One, I can." Then he motioned with two fingers for someone to come forward, making me gasp when a woman wearing very little seemingly appeared from nowhere. She wore a long, hooded robe style jacket, one with slits up the sides and showing her legs, one of which appeared to be made of copper. Her pale skin showed at her belly, and everything below, including the straps of material barely covering her hairless sex. I also tried not to look at the burn marks on one leg, wondering if that was how she got the artificial leg.

As for her face, this was completely covered by the long hood, making me wonder how she saw anything, let alone didn't end up bumping into things all the time.

"Annika, if you would be so kind," he said, making the hooded woman bow, before telling me,

"I will place you back to where you need to be, for there are wounds still left to be healed, and as for mine, I must thank you for returning a piece of my heart." At this she pulled aside her cloak and showed me a healing scar there in between her breasts, letting me know that the heart stone had been named such for that reason. Someone had stolen a piece of her actual heart and cut it right out of her!

"Er... you're welcome," I said, making the King smirk at my obvious nervousness.

"Then I will bid you farewell, Evelyn Leucosia, for if you are ever in need of someone to catch you in Hell, then I will surely be there." Then he winked at me before he turned to walk away, leaving me nearly breathless at the sight of such a powerful man. But none left me quite as breathless as his son...

A man I couldn't wait to get back to!

"Wait, what will happen to Hector? Will he get captured?" I asked the woman the king had called Annika.

She looked back to where the King was walking into the battle, one that looked close to being finished. But then the second his men parted for him, I saw that there, surrounded by Mammon's soldiers, was Hector, tied and beaten on the floor.

"He already has been, and now comes time for his punishment," she said, at the same time Mammon flicked his hand out to the side and produced a long golden blade as he walked closer to Hector. Which gave me first-hand knowledge of just what the King of Greed was capable of. He may have played the handsome flirt toward me, but right now, he was about to play a far more deadly game.

That of this world's…

Executioner.

⚜

A short time later and I found myself outside the last place I ever thought I would be walking into.

A bar.

This was after Annika had told me what I needed to do, for it was like she said, fresh wounds needed to be healed. Something I hadn't fully understood, not until she nodded from the other side of the portal she created and ushered me to walk inside. Clearly, it was a sight that was being masked in front of other mortals because, let's just say, no one started screaming the second they saw it.

So, I mouthed a 'thank you' back at her, making her bow her head respectfully before she spun an arm around making the portal disappear. After that, I faced the bar and walked inside, gasping when I saw a figure I knew sitting at the bar about to drink what looked like a shot of whiskey. Which made me utter his name on a whisper, one he heard as he swung his head my way...

"Vander."

"Evelyn?" he asked, the shock on his face transforming his handsome features from sullen to astonishment. So, I went running to him, just as he turned in time to catch me.

"How... how is this possible?!" he asked, making me step back and reach out to grab his drink. Then I tipped it back and drank it down, because holy hell I needed it,

Then told him with a wink,

"Girl Scout, remember?"

CHAPTER 35
THE HEART OF A THIEF
RYKER

P ain.

Overwhelming, all consuming, crippling pain.

That was all I felt these days. Something that started the moment I awoke and found myself without my Siren. Of course, the second I saw the cause of it all, I found myself nearly killing my second, my bare hands around his neck on the cusp of choking the life out of him!

He barely had the time to tell me that it had been a promise made to Evelyn, but even then, it wasn't enough to save him from his Fate! I swear it had taken everything in me to let go before tearing the fucker's head off! I had been so furious, that it took all of my men to tear me off him. But then I realized where we still were and I had left him to go running back into the cave.

Only to find it...

Painfully empty.

I had fallen in front of the gateway, dropping to my knees and hanging my head as a shaky hand touched the bare rock. Not an ounce of power left upon it, as it was now locked forever. I had scoured the cave for the scepter, in hopes of opening it once more, if only to try and find her but it, like the love of my life…

Was gone.

"She told me she had a plan, Ryker." Vander's voice was one I snarled at, before lifting my head and showing him just what 'their' plan had done to me.

It had fucking broken me.

So as tears flowed freely and for the very first time in my existence, I told him,

"Get out!" He flinched a step back, seeing for himself what he had done to me.

"Ryker, please… I…"

"No! For if you stand here any longer, you will be begging me for your life!" I threatened venomously.

"And what of Evie? Does what she wanted not matter to you?" he asked, making me roar,

"NO, IT DOESN'T!" Then I was on my feet and facing him.

"You don't mean that" he stated foolishly.

"You both betrayed me! You both broke my fucking heart and you stand there now and expect me to what? Fucking forgive you both?! The only reason I don't kill you now is because of the years you were actually fucking loyal to me and nothing more!" I bellowed, feeling the anger building as the realization continued to set in.

"Ryker, come on, I was…" he tried to say more but I growled,

"Get out, and don't ever fucking come back!"

"You… you don't mean that," he stated, hoping it was true, for the pain was easy to see. I fucking relished in it at that moment, despite knowing that it would be nothing compared to my own.

"You are fucking banished, Vander, and if I ever see you again, then the next time... *I will fucking kill you!*" I snarled in such a way, he knew to take the threat seriously. Which was why with pain in his eyes and a heartbreak that mirrored a slither of my own, he let his shoulder slump before doing as I asked. Now walking away, but not before telling me,

"She did it out of love for you, Ryker, I hope that one day you can see that." My reaction to this was one he didn't stay around long enough to witness, as I erupted into my Demonic form and destroyed as much of the cave as I could.

That had been seven days ago.

A whole fucking week. A week of pure torture as I felt like ripping my own heart out just to stop the bleed. The incurable rupture to the very core of me. I had tried to discover what could have happened to her, but it felt like a fucking unachievable task. Which was why, after a week, I had made the decision to leave the mortal realm for good.

I was going home.

Because I couldn't live with this hell any longer. I couldn't live with every fucking reminder that she ever existed. It was torture. I just needed to be somewhere she had never been. That she had no ties to. I just needed to mourn the loss of my Siren in my Demonic form in hopes that I could deal with it better.

I knew this was unlikely, but I had to try. Which was why I was forced back into my office building in downtown Toronto, so as I could inform the King of Kings of my resignation as being one of his Enforcers. Because, in all honesty, now I had lost her, I couldn't have given a fuck if the whole world had burned to the ground.

I just didn't care.

So, I walked through the empty building, after having Faron send all the staff home days ago. His task was simple, to start selling our assets and locking things down. Of course, he had nothing to say on the matter, for my men knew by now that I was no longer the Lord I once was. I was a fucking shell of a man, a walking corpse... *a fucking ghost.*

One that reached for my office door and opened it knowing this would be for the very last time. One phone call and that was it.

I was done.

However, like most things in my life recently, my plans for the future went out of the fucking window, and this was because someone was sitting in my desk chair.

"Have you come about the position?" a female voice from my past said, and I knew then that I must have been fucking dreaming of her again.

"Because I must warn you, it's dangerous being married to me," she said, now spinning the chair around and facing me, making me gasp as I stumbled a step back, my hand needing to go to the doorframe just to keep myself to my feet.

"This... you... by gods please, let you be real this time," I stammered, making her give me soft, tender look, one I had missed more than if someone had taken a fucking limb. Then she stood up and started walking toward me. And fuck me, but I was too afraid to move in case this heavenly moment was ripped from me. The sway of her hips in a tight black dress... she was fucking sin and temptation.

"This has to be another dream," I admitted as she came closer, before suddenly her hand reached up and touched me. Her small feminine hand, one I had taken such pleasure in playing with, it was now cupping my cheek and making me suck in a deep breath.

"Then let us both dream together, for finding you again is the only dream I ever want to wake up to," she said before pulling my face down so as she could kiss me. And the second her lips touched mine, I knew then that this was no dream.

It was my everything.

She was my everything.

Which was why, for the second time in my life, tears filled my eyes and rolled down my cheeks, now merging with her own.

"You're real," I breathed out, making her nod her head, her own emotions overwhelming her enough to rid her of the words. Words I needed to hear.

"Please, tell me you're real, Little Bird, for I fear this is another form of Hell that I cannot survive this time." But then she spoke and said the most beautiful words I could ever have imagined.

"I am real. I am here and I love you, Ryker..."

"...The thief who stole my heart."

EPILOGUE
RYKER

It had taken my men some time, but I had finally tracked down the man I had been hunting. Of course, Evie had no idea, and I would not tell her, not for some time at least. At least not until after the honeymoon, for after dealing with this, that was exactly where I was headed.

Of course, after I finally got my Siren back, it had taken me a while to calm myself enough to even leave the same room as her. I think it had been a whole week where I had locked us both in our room, having only food brought to us, and she was allowed nowhere near the fucking door.

Yes, this may have been as irrational as she accused me of being, but then I would only have to remind her of the pain she put me through and, well... I would get my way. Because I knew she felt guilty for the decision she made that day, but I knew I couldn't blame her forever. Punish her sexually, yes, I did plenty of that in the days that followed. However, she had only one last request...

That I forgive not only her, but also...

Vander.

This, I had an even harder time doing, but in the end, she begged me, and I found that I couldn't deny her any longer. Especially when she told me that she would only marry me if I made Vander my best man. Then pointed out that I would first need to be talking to him once again in order for that to happen.

So, I found my will crumbling and, therefore, he was standing at the end of the aisle wearing a suit next to me at our wedding. A wedding we had overlooking the Grand Canyon. It was beautiful but not as beautiful as my bride, for she simply took my breath away. Her true father, Arthur, walked her down the aisle, looking the proudest man in the world.

It was truly a sight to behold.

Just like the painting he had gifted me with after the reception, the one I had wanted to buy that day I visited him in the cabin. And now one that was hung proudly in our home to remind me of the beauty I saw that day. The same beauty I saw every day when I woke up next to my little bird.

My dove.

My Siren.

Which was why I had one last piece of Evelyn's past I needed to eradicate before getting on a plane and starting the rest of our lives together.

So, I opened the door to the prison cell he was being kept in, and a satisfied smile graced my lips as I saw the man hung by a chain, stripped naked, and beaten enough to know that Vander and the boys had their fun with him. Of course, they all loved Evie, so when they discovered the truth of why she ran as a child, they each wanted a piece of the mortal shit stain.

Hades included.

"Wh-what... are you... going to do... to me?" His fearful voice questioned and, again, I grinned at the sight, before allowing my Demon to take form, knowing his fear was what I truly wanted to see.

Well, not just his fear, a great deal of pain too.

"What do you think? I am here to get the job done properly this time... oh, and my wife, Evelyn, sends her regards." Then I closed the door and cut of the sound of her step-father's screams.

Oh yes...

It was a good day for the Son of Greed.

The End.

ABOUT THE AUTHOR

Stephanie Hudson has dreamed of being a writer ever since her obsession with reading books at an early age. What first became a quest to overcome the boundaries set against her in the form of dyslexia has turned into a life's dream. She first started writing in the form of poetry and soon found a taste for horror and romance. Afterlife is her first book in the series of twelve, with the story of Keira and Draven becoming ever more complicated in a world that sets them miles apart.

When not writing, Stephanie enjoys spending time with her loving family and friends, chatting for hours with her biggest fan, her sister Cathy who is utterly obsessed with one gorgeous Dominic Draven. And of course, spending as much time with her supportive partner and personal muse, Blake who is there for her no matter what.

Author's words.

My love and devotion is to all my wonderful fans that keep me going into the wee hours of the night but foremost to my wonderful daughter Ava...who yes, is named after a cool, kick-ass, Demonic bird and my sons, Jack, who is a little hero and Baby Halen, who yes, keeps me up at night but it's okay because he is named after a Guitar legend!

Keep updated with all new release news & more on my website

www.afterlifesaga.com
Never miss out, sign up to the
mailing list at the website.

Also, please feel free to join myself and other Dravenites on
my Facebook group
Afterlife Saga Official Fan
Interact with me and other fans. Can't wait to see you there!

facebook.com/AfterlifeSaga
x.com/afterlifesaga
instagram.com/theafterlifesaga

Also by Stephanie Hudson

Afterlife Saga

Afterlife

The Two Kings

The Triple Goddess

The Quarter Moon

The Pentagram Child - Part 1

The Pentagram Child - Part 2

The Cult of the Hexad

Sacrifice of the Septimus - Part 1

Sacrifice of the Septimus - Part 2

Blood of the Infinity War

Happy Ever Afterlife - Part 1

Happy Ever Afterlife - Part 2

The Forbidden Chapters

*

Transfusion Saga

Transfusion

Venom of God

Blood of Kings

Rise of Ashes

Map of Sorrows

Tree of Souls

Kingdoms of Hell

Eyes of Crimson

Roots of Rage

Heart of Darkness

Wraith of Fire

Queen of Sins

Knights of Past

Quest of Stone

*

King of Kings

Dravens Afterlife

Dravens Electus

*

Kings of Afterlife

Vincent's Immortal Curse

*

The Hellbeast Series

The Hellbeast King

The Hellbeast's Fight

The Hellbeast's Mistake

The Hellbeast's Claim

The Hellbeast's Prisoner

The Hellbeast's Sacrifice

The Hellbeast's Hate

The Hellbeast's Past

*

The Shadow Imp Series

Imp and the Beast

Beast and the Imp

*

The Lost Siren Series

Ward's Siren

Eden's Enforcer

Wrath's Siren

Emme's Enforcer

Greed's Siren

Evelyn's Enforcer

*

Afterlife Academy: (Young Adult Series)

The Glass Dagger

The Hells Ring

The Reapers

*

Stephanie Hudson and Blake Hudson

The Devil in Me

Other Authors at Hudson Indie Ink

Paranormal Romance/Urban Fantasy

Stephanie Hudson

Xen Randell

Sorcha Dawn

Harper Phoenix

Crime/Action

Blake Hudson

Jack Walker

Contemporary Romance

Gemma Weir

Nikki Ashton

Anna Bloom

Tatum Rayne

Nicky Priest

Milton Keynes UK
Ingram Content Group UK Ltd.
UKHW041304030624
443657UK00033B/194

9 781916 562721